SINFULLY DELICIOUS

SINFULLY DELICIOUS

A Delicious Romance

Denise Swanson

http://www.DeniseSwanson.com

Sinfully Delicious

ISBN-13: 978-0-9861017-4-8

Sinfully Delicious

Take one smoking-hot top chef who thinks food should be a sensual adventure, add a venture capitalist who has struggled with her weight since she was a teenager, and mix well. Is this a recipe that sizzles, or is he just another craving she must resist?

* * *

Deanna Sloan has worked too hard, dieting herself from a chubby teenager to a sleek businesswoman, to give in to her hunger now. Enduring four years as the target of her high school classmates' cruelty taught her that only three things matter—power, money, and looks.

Leaving her small town behind, shedding the excess pounds, and obtaining a job with a six-figure salary are all steps in the right direction. However, in order to keep on target, she needs to outshine the other twenty venture capitalist associates at her new firm, maintain her weight loss, and be prepared to double-cross anyone who gets in her way. Walk in the park, right?

Wrong! Her first assignment is an investment appraisal of one of Chicago's top chefs. Nico Thorne has come to her firm for the seed money to open his own restaurant. He is smoking hot and just a glimpse of his navy blue eyes in a photo clouds Deanna's brain and dampens her panties. Will the flesh-and-blood man make her dissolve into a puddle of mindless lust that will derail her fast track to success?

Like Deanna, Nico's past drives his present choices. He hates his father for using his mother's social status to further his career, then abandoning her. As a teenager, Nico's anger at his father resulted in a hair-trigger temper and a vow never to fall in love. Although Nico may have learned to control his demons, he still avoids women who even hint at wanting anything deeper than a few nights of uncommitted fun.

That is until he sees Deanna. Her cinnamon curls and soft green eyes totally captivate him. As they spend more and more time together, Nico's determination to keep their relationship casual dissolves and he realizes that she might be his amore mio. But will he be able to convince Deanna that he's the one for her?

Deanna fights her attraction to Nico, fearful that giving in will mean the loss of both her figure and her job. Can Nico overcome a lifetime of distrust? Can Deanna embrace life—imperfections and all?

* * *

Publisher's warning: This book contains sensual consummated love scenes.

Series description:

First in Denise Swanson's new Delicious contemporary romance series. All books are complete with no cliffhangers and a guaranteed HEA!

Dangerously Delicious coming in 2017!

For more information, please visit www.DeniseSwanson.com

CHAPTER ONE

Deanna Sloan ignored her growling stomach and focused on the papers in front of her. As per her usual routine, five hours ago she'd had a small container of nonfat Greek yogurt for lunch, and those hundred calories would have to hold her until dinner. The only thing passing her lips between now and then was coffee—black with two fake sugars.

Giving in to her hunger and snacking was not an option. She had worked too hard, for too long, transforming herself from a chubby nobody to a sleek businesswoman. For Deanna, life's lessons had been cruelly taught. But thanks to her miserable high school years, she was well aware that money, looks, and power were the only things that mattered, and she wanted all three.

Shedding seventy pounds and obtaining a job with a six-figure salary were steps in the right direction. However, in order to keep on target, she needed to outshine the other twenty venture capitalist associates at her new firm, maintain her weight loss, and be prepared to double-cross anyone who got in her way. *Walk in the park, right?*

Absolutely. She could have it all, as long as she was willing to check her morals at the door, work twice as hard as everyone else, and starve herself. Was she willing to do whatever it took to get the life she'd always dreamed of having?

Hell yes!

Except once in a while, like right at the moment, she couldn't stop herself from wondering how it would feel to do something reckless. Live a little. Take the weekend off and ravish some sexy boy toy.

Frowning, she shook her head. Hooking up for a night of lust wasn't really her style. Eating a cupcake was definitely more her speed. She brightened. Surely she could handle cheating on her diet.

Deanna's wistful thoughts were interrupted when her boss marched into her office and tossed a packet at her. If a fairy godmother was granting her wishes, there'd been some kind of massive screw-up. Middle-aged Franklin Randolph wasn't a hunk by any stretch of the imagination, and Deanna very much doubted that whatever was in the bulging manila envelope on her desk was frosted in buttercream.

"Here's your first solo assignment. A preliminary investment appraisal." Randolph ran his fingers through the thinning, ginger-colored tufts that perched on top of his head like an orange tumbleweed. "Don't screw it up."

"Yes, sir. I mean, no, sir. I won't." For the hundredth time, Deanna wondered why a man with her boss's money couldn't find someone to give him a decent haircut. Didn't he realize that he looked like an Oompa Loompa?

Randolph gestured to the file. "My admin made you an eight-o'clock reservation at LeBoeuf. If you already have plans, cancel them."

"Not a problem, sir. I'm completely free." Although it was a Friday night, the closest thing she had to a social life was a twice weekly session with her personal trainer. "Is the firm considering investing in LeBoeuf?"

"No. In its head chef. Nico Thorne wants to open his own restaurant. He's who you're checking out."

Deanna flipped open the file and stifled a gasp. Staring up at her from a glossy publicity photo was the hottest man she'd ever seen. His muscular shoulders strained the fabric of his crisp white chef's jacket, and his broad chest tapered to slim hips clad in faded jeans. Flowing jet-black hair and smooth olive skin stretching over high cheekbones reminded her of an outlaw from the Old West, but it was his piercing midnight-blue eyes that

SINFULLY DELICIOUS

were her undoing.

The comment she'd been about to make died on her lips and her mouth went dry. A wave of liquid heat flashed through her body, puckering her nipples and settling between her legs. She squirmed, pressing her thighs together.

Randolph's impatient voice brought her out of her sexual haze. "Any questions?"

Taking a deep breath, Deanna tore her gaze from the picture and shuffled through the rest of the papers. There was a business plan, a financial statement, and a magazine article entitled, "Chicago's Sizzling Chefs."

She swallowed, trying to moisten her throat enough to talk, and finally managed to croak, "I'd love to check him out." *Oops!* That hadn't come out right. "I mean, what did you have in mind?"

"Use your gut."

"Yes, sir." Deanna nodded.

Franklin Randolph might need a good hairstylist and a lesson in manners, but he was still her role model. A brilliant man who had turned a small inheritance into a multibillion-dollar venture capitalist business, Randolph made money whether the economy was on an upswing or about to crash and burn. And unlike Deanna's own father, he encouraged her to go for the brass ring rather than settling for a wedding band. He believed she could and should take care of herself and never suggested she needed a man to watch out for her.

"Are we done?" Randolph snapped his fingers in her face.

"Uh," Deanna hesitated. Her boss was clearly impatient, but she needed more information to complete her assignment successfully. "What kind of things should my gut be looking at?"

"His vibe. Are his employees loyal? Are the customers regulars? His interactions with his staff and his diners. What kind of man is he?" Randolph crossed his arms, scowling. "I

3

shouldn't have to spell this out for you."

"Right, sir." *Damn!* Reading people wasn't her strong point.

"I'll have a report for you first thing Monday."

"On my desk no later than eight a.m." He turned to leave. "Do a good job on this, and you can run with the ball."

"Thank you for the opportunity." Deanna's voice was composed, but her mind raced.

She'd only been with Randolph Ventures six months. It was almost unheard of for someone as new as she was to head a project. This was a golden ticket to impress the boss and get on the fast track to a promotion. On the other hand, if she blew it, Lake Michigan would dry up before she was given another chance.

Randolph paused at the door, looking her up and down. "Wear something sexy. A lone woman in a business suit might make Thorne suspicious. He's aware our firm is investigating him, and he'll be on the lookout for us."

After her boss left, Deanna checked the time. It was already close to seven o'clock. Fifteen minutes to get to her apartment and fifteen minutes from her apartment to LeBoeuf gave her only a half hour to get dressed. What, in heaven's name, was she going to wear?

During the short taxi ride home, she read the magazine profile from Thorne's file. The journalist had dubbed Nico Thorne the Kitchen Casanova and implied he had an unending stream of beautiful women in his bed. The piece also mentioned his famous parents. His father was Ian Thorne, a legendary English chef, and although his mother had lived in America for twenty-five years, she was some kind of Italian aristocrat and hot-shot fashion designer.

Deanna was thinking about the difference between Nico Thorne's sophisticated family and her own rural roots when she got out of the cab and stepped straight into a downpour. She'd been so engrossed in the article about the chef, she hadn't noticed that it was raining.

Drenched, Deanna dashed past the doorman and into the lobby. She lived in one of Chicago's many South Loop apartment buildings. It was modern and featureless, which was exactly what she wanted. There was nothing about the place that would distract her from her goals.

Seeing the metal doors sliding closed, Deanna raced for the elevator. She slipped in just before they shut, and as she was whisked to the twentieth floor, she caught sight of herself in the mirrored wall.

Shit! Just what she needed. Her wet hair had turned into a mass of ringlets. She still hadn't figured out what to wear, and now she had to cope with her out-of-control curls, too.

Deanna stepped into her apartment's tiny foyer, kicked off her shoes as she ran through the living room, and skidded to a stop in front of her closet. *Crap!* She should have gone straight to Sak's.

She loved nice clothes, and having gotten a full scholarship, she didn't have any student loans to repay, which allowed her to spend a part of her huge salary on the expensive labels she craved. So why didn't she have anything to wear?

Deanna shoved hangers back and forth, pulling out the bridesmaid's dress she'd been forced into for a cousin's wedding. *Ick.* She was not wearing purple chiffon and crinolines to one of Chicago's fanciest restaurants. People waited months to get reservations for LeBoeuf, and she wasn't going dressed as Little Bo Peep.

Her second try was better, a black silk sheath with a beaded vee neckline and a lace hem. She'd bought it a year ago for a party, but when her previous boss sent her out of town at the last minute, she'd never had a chance to wear it. The only problem was the back. It was bare to the waist, making it impossible to wear a bra, and she was anything but flat-chested.

Deanna bit her lip. There was no choice. Time had run out. If she was late, LeBoeuf might give away her table, and that definitely would be a career-limiting move.

* * *

Nico Thorne scowled. Tonight had been one crisis after another. His sous-chef had fallen off the wagon and was drinking again. Half his wait staff was out with the flu. And, to top it off, his seafood supplier had delivered frozen—instead of fresh— scallops, as well as second-rate crab, which meant removing several dishes from the menu and dealing with disappointed diners.

As a teenager, Nico'd had a problem with his temper, but he'd learned to control his demons. Even now, as a server slid a barely touched white chocolate raspberry soufflé toward him over the pass, he was able to keep from glaring at the young man.

Instead, his voice unruffled, Nico asked, "What's the problem?"

"It's the woman at number five." The server wrinkled his brow. "She claims everything's fine, but this is the fifth dish that she's only taken a couple of bites from before telling me to take it away."

"Did she say there was something wrong with the taste?" Nico questioned.

Despite the evening's difficulties, he knew he hadn't sent out any bad food. If a plate wasn't right, it didn't leave the kitchen.

"No. She says it's delicious." The server twitched his shoulders. "Marco told me that the reservation was originally for two; maybe her date stood her up, and that's the problem. But why would she stay, order an entire five-course meal, and then not eat?"

Marco was the maître d' at LeBoeuf, as well as Nico's younger brother.

"That's a good question."

"I thought you'd want to know."

"You were right," Nico assured the young man. "I'll go talk to her as soon as I finish up here."

"She ordered an espresso, so she should stay a while longer."

A few minutes later, Nico entered the front of the house. It was ten o'clock and the restaurant was officially closed, but there were still a few guests lingering over their desserts or sipping coffee. He greeted them but kept walking, intent on reaching the woman at number five before she left.

He was several feet from her table when he spotted her. A bolt of electricity zipped through his body, and he jerked to a stop. The hair on his arms stood on end and his dick hardened. Did he know her? He flipped through his mental little black book.

No. He usually dated blue-eyed blondes, and this one had curls the color of cinnamon and eyes that reminded him of fresh mint leaves. Although she seemed familiar, Nico knew he'd have remembered her if they'd ever met before. Actually, it felt as if she should be familiar rather than any real previous acquaintance.

He licked his lips, and a small grin played over his mouth. He believed in trying new flavors to improve his palate, and he wasn't opposed to adding some spice to his sex life. During the past couple of years, it had become increasingly bland, and then ultimately nonexistent. Maybe it was time to rev it back up again. But first, she *did* have to explain why she wasn't eating his food.

When her gaze locked on his, he felt compelled to get closer. It was almost as if she'd cast an invisible lasso that blindly drew him to her. As he walked toward her table, he was aware that something about her called to him at a level he didn't understand.

Suddenly, he heard his mother's voice whisper, "She's *il tuo amore*."

Shit! His breath whooshed out of him. She was not his "love." There was no way he was falling into that trap.

Having witnessed his mother's despair after her divorce, Nico avoided any relationship that even hinted at becoming something deeper than a casual hookup. He should turn around right now, go back to the kitchen, and send Marco to find out why the woman at table five wasn't eating.

A stab of jealousy caught him by surprise. What if his brother felt the same connection he did? What if he asked her out?

He and Marco never competed for women. They had agreed at a young age that there was plenty of fruit on the tree. With so many juicy morsels ripe for the picking, there was no need to fight each other for any particular tidbit.

The roaring in Nico's ears obliterated that rational thought and taunted him with the image of his brother's lips on the woman's creamy throat and his hands on her silky skin. It urged him to hurry, and as he raced an unseen opponent, he wondered what he would say when he reached the finish line.

* * *

The food was amazing. Deanna closed her eyes, remembering the silky crème fraîche and caviar of the lobster blini, and the tangy orange and ginger flavor of the Cornish hen. She hoped that if she ate only a couple of bites of each dish, she could remain within her daily caloric limit. But it was a test of her willpower to stop after the second forkful when what she really wanted was to devour every last scrap. If she hadn't had years of practice in denying herself, she might have licked the plates clean.

As for Randolph's list, she had no idea how to uncover that kind of information. So far, her gut wasn't telling her anything. The servers had been far too hurried for any kind of conversation, and she didn't have a clue as to how to determine if the other diners were repeat customers. It wasn't as if she'd overheard anyone order "the usual."

Deanna had hung around as long as she could, but the restaurant was emptying, and it was plainly time to get the check and leave. Her stomach clenched. She had failed her first assignment. What if Randolph fired her?

Defeated, she turned her head to look for the waiter and nearly stopped breathing. *Sweet Baby Jesus!* Nico Thorne was staring right at her.

In a heartbeat, the sizzling-hot chef, whose mere picture had left her panties wet and her pulse racing, was walking toward her with a determined expression on his extremely handsome face. Had he discovered she was there to spy on him?

No. How could he? And if he didn't know who she was, this was her chance to gather the data she needed to save her job.

Deanna tried to think how to question him without making him suspicious, but as he stopped in front of her, his navy blue eyes seem to laser straight into her soul, and every coherent thought whizzed out of her brain.

His smile was so powerfully erotic that deep inside her soul, a primitive need stirred. It ignited a wild yearning that seeped from her very core.

Deanna tried to breathe normally, but her lungs refused to cooperate. Instead of a smooth inhale and exhale, she gasped for

DENISE SWANSON

air as if she'd just finished running uphill five miles on the treadmill.

What seemed like an eternity went by before the man causing her respiratory distress said, "Hello. I'm Nico Thorne, the head chef here at LeBoeuf."

"Deanna Sloan." She automatically held out her hand. When their palms touched, a wave of heat swept through her, and an image of him naked on top of her flashed in her mind. She quickly let go of his fingers. If she wanted to remain lucid enough to get the facts she needed, touching this guy was obviously off-limits.

"A pleasure to meet you." His voice was deep and sensual, with a hint of an accent she couldn't quite place.

Deanna felt a surge of erotic desire. She was a sucker for a man who sounded as sexy as he looked.

"It's lovely here," she said, barely able to breathe. "I feel as if I'm in a French castle."

"A little formal for my taste." He shrugged. "May I join you for an after-dinner drink?"

"Please do." She moved over and watched as he gracefully slid into the half-circle booth.

At five ten, Deanna rarely felt small next to a man. But Nico had to be at least six foot four, making her feel positively petite.

"Thank you." Nico's husky voice washed over her.

Forcing a casual note into her tone, Deanna said, "I'm fascinated by the restaurant business, and I'd love to hear about it."

"Really?" His lips quirked skeptically.

Deanna studied him as he signaled to the waiter and ordered two Café Nicos. Up close, she could see the faint lines that radiated from the corners of his eyes and the dark stubble shadowing his chin.

Once the server left, Deanna said, "Yes. Really. I've heard

that it's hard to get good staff for a restaurant."

"It can be. However, I've found that if you treat your employees as you'd like to be treated, there's no difficulty hiring and retaining a first-rate team."

"So, have your people been with you long?" Deanna tried to sound nonchalant. Maybe she'd be able to write an acceptable report for Mr. Randolph after all. "Do you think they'd go with you if you went to another restaurant?"

"Probably. They have in the past." He tilted his head. "Are you a job recruiter trying to lure away my workers?"

"Of course not. Just curious." Deanna smiled. "Do you get a lot of repeat business?"

"I'd say at least half our guests have dined here before." Nico's look was appraising. "Are you planning on opening your own restaurant?"

"Don't be silly." She forced herself to giggle—something she hadn't done since she was twelve. "Do you get a chance to come out of the kitchen much and talk with many of your customers?"

"I like to walk through the dining room several times during service, but I wasn't able to tonight because of some issues in the kitchen."

They both were silent as the waiter delivered their drinks to the table.

"Issues?" Deanna prompted, trying not to sound too eager.

"Nothing important." He handed her the glass pedestal mug. "I hope you like it. Café Nico is a house specialty."

"What's in it?"

"Espresso, Godiva liqueur, and a secret ingredient."

Deanna took a cautious sip. The chocolate flavor exploded on her tongue and she sighed. It was heavenly. She licked the whipped cream from her upper lip, then, regretfully, put down the cup. She'd already had too many calories today.

He asked, "Don't you like it?"

"It's great. Just letting it cool off a little."

Nico's smooth forehead creased. "Your server mentioned that you didn't eat much of your dinner. Was anything wrong with it?"

"No. Not at all. It was delicious," she assured him. "The best food I ever tasted."

"Thank you." Nico hesitated. "Do you dislike dining by yourself?"

"Not particularly."

"So, let me get this straight." Nico's jaw tightened. "You enjoyed the food, you aren't upset at having to eat alone, but you sent it all away after barely tasting it?"

Deanna's defenses went up faster than the shields on the starship Enterprise. She didn't owe him any explanations. How much she chose to eat was her business, not his.

"Restaurant servings are too big."

"Perhaps in a neighborhood diner where the motto is, 'It'll fill you up,' but not in LeBoeuf." Nico's nostrils flared. "My portions are perfect."

"Admit it. They're large enough for a family of four to share." She tossed her head. "And I'm not about to stuff myself just to please the chef."

Nico's eyes turned to steel. "Two bites wouldn't fill a hummingbird's stomach."

"I'm far from a hummingbird."

"Now I get it." He gave a short bark of laughter. "You're one of *those* women."

The scorn in his words grated on her. "Those women?"

"A weight-obsessed female who refuses to eat because she might gain a quarter of a pound."

She stiffened as though he had struck her. "You have no idea who I am or why I do anything. Nor does it concern you."

12

She would bet her next paycheck that if she didn't keep to her diet and went back to her chubby past, Mr. Hotshot Chef would have never approached her, let alone asked to join her for a drink.

"You're right. It's none of my business." He stood. "But life is a feast, and if you're not the type of woman who can enjoy it, you might as well stick to eating salad from a bag."

CHAPTER TWO

What the fuck had just happened? Nico slammed through
the double doors to the kitchen. He hadn't lost his temper in ten
years. And to tell off a guest.
Son of a bitch! Had he gone batshit crazy? So she didn't eat
much of her meal. She was right. It wasn't as if he got paid by
the ounce, so why did he care?
Because he'd never met anyone like her before. She'd gone
from appealing to intense to maddening in the blink of an eye,
and he was more turned on with each transformation. There was
something about Deanna Sloan that ignited powerful emotions in
him, and he wasn't happy about it.
Her mouth fascinated him. The way she bit her full bottom
lip when she concentrated, giving him just a glimpse of her
straight white front teeth. Then, when the tip of her tongue
darted out, swiping at the whipped cream clinging to the
succulent raspberry pink of her mouth, it was all he could do not
to rip off her clothes and lick every inch of her smooth vanilla
skin.
It was a good thing he'd never see her again. Just thinking
about it, he felt a swell of heat pooling below his belt, and she
wasn't his type. He didn't like serious women. He liked women
who were as fluffy as milk chocolate mousse, and she was more
like an intense dark truffle.
Even as he tried to convince himself that he was glad she
was gone, he remembered the flood of wanting that had rushed
through him when their hands met. His erection had skyrocketed
from half-mast to full-throttle, pressing painfully against the
zipper of his jeans.
In his mind's eye, he saw her just before he'd marched

away. A pulse had been beating at the base of her throat, and through the thin silk of her dress, he could see her nipples had hardened. Even as angry as he'd been, he'd wanted to taste them.

Before he could stop himself, he spun on his heels and hurried back into the dining room. His gut clenched when he saw that the booth she'd been sitting in was empty. But then he spotted the signed credit card receipt sticking out of the leather holder sitting on the table. If the waiter hadn't picked up the check yet, maybe she was still in the building.

He sprinted to the entrance, speeding up when he looked through the double glass doors and saw her getting into a cab. But he was too late. As he ran across the lobby, she rode out of his life.

* * *

Deanna hit the snooze button on her alarm and stared at the bedroom ceiling. It was four a.m. Monday morning, and she still hadn't written the Thorne investment appraisal. She'd avoided it all weekend, working her usual long hours at the office, then spending extra time at the health club to ensure she was both physically and mentally exhausted.

Now she had no choice. Failing to turn in a report would be career suicide. Deanna still couldn't believe she had managed to have an argument with her first potential client. She could just imagine what Mr. Randolph would have to say about that.

Deanna nibbled on her thumbnail. She needed to do some damage control. If she indicated that the restaurant was a bad investment risk, the firm would turn down the application, and her boss would never find out about her unprofessional behavior.

Could she do that to Nico Thorne?

Deanna'd been unsuccessfully trying to put him out of her mind for the past two days. He'd looked so gorgeous sitting next to her at the restaurant. The candlelight had cast a golden glow on his handsome face, and the starched white cotton of his chef's jacket was the perfect foil for his olive complexion.

But it was his eyes that haunted her. Midnight blue like the Illinois sky before a thunderstorm. She was fascinated by their depth and promise.

Just thinking of him made her itch to run her hands through his silky jet-black hair, down his muscled chest, and past his waistband to...

Stop daydreaming, Deanna ordered herself. *Get your butt out of bed and go write that report.*

Nico Thorne was not part of her five-year plan, and she sensed he wouldn't fit into the life she had worked like hell to build. One look at his picture and a half-hour conversation, and she already felt a tug at her heart. But in the end, like everyone she'd ever cared about, he'd made it clear she wasn't up to his standards.

Growing up dirt poor and having parents who repeatedly told her, "Don't get above your raising," had made it important to Deanna to find a man who loved her for who she was, not who he wanted her to be. Hadn't she learned that lesson yet?

In order to fit into society's expectations, she'd already altered herself so much she sometimes wondered if there was any part of the real Deanna Sloan left. The last thing she needed to do was get involved with someone who wanted her to change herself yet again.

Besides, the magazine article had made it clear Nico was a love-'em-and-leave-'em kind of guy. When she finally reached her goal, and had the time, she wanted a real relationship, not just a few nights of passion. An occasional play date could be fun, but she had a feeling that a fling with Nico would cost her more than she could afford to lose.

Then there was the disturbing little fact that in order to save her dreams of success, she would have to destroy his. She had to write a negative report that would ensure his project was rejected. It was him or her. She couldn't let Mr. Randolph find out about her unprofessional behavior. Venture capitalists did not let their emotions rule their head.

Nico was history, and she vowed to stop thinking about him. Now if only her subconscious would cooperate. As she half dozed off, her body relaxed, and the image of him with his well-muscled chest and thighs pressed against hers appeared almost immediately. She moaned, her palms stroking up and down her hips.

She tried to banish the erotic image, but she couldn't force him out of her head. Slipping farther into the fantasy, Deanna cupped her breasts. At first she skimmed her nipples with her thumbs, but that wasn't enough, and she plucked them until they throbbed with the same beat as her heart. She pictured Nico's dark head bent over her and felt his mouth sucking and licking until she was writhing with need and begging him not to stop.

Her hand moved down and her vision of Nico became more detailed. He was now fully erect and was caressing her. She spread her thighs and slid her fingers between her legs, stroking up and down the center of her sex. She could hear Nico's deep, rich voice whispering in her ear as her fingers found her hot, wet opening.

She pushed them in and out, over and over, envisioning him thrusting into her. Panting, she pulled her fingers out and spread the wetness upward. Then, imagining it was Nico's finger, she started the slow circular sweep guaranteed to bring her to the golden moment she craved.

Deanna's lips parted and her breathing became shallower. Her head rose off the pillow, then sank back down. She rubbed faster, feeling the quivers build to a full-blown ache. She was close, so close, and she pressed harder and more frantically.

As the first luscious spasms overtook her, she tensed, then

as she climaxed, she screamed his name. For several minutes, she lay breathless, keeping her eyes closed, holding on to the picture of him until he faded away along with the last tremors of her orgasm.

Deanna came back to reality with a thud. How could she submit an appraisal that would end the man's dream of his own restaurant after that?

Reluctantly, she crawled out of bed. The clock was ticking, and she had to get to work and write a report that would hurt either her career or his.

Once she was dressed and had hurriedly downed a soy-and-flax-seed smoothie, she headed to her office. After powering up her computer, she began to type. A half hour later, she deleted what she had written, then spent the next several minutes wrestling with her conscience.

Finally, Deanna convinced herself that she had overreacted. She *could* give Nico a favorable evaluation. He wouldn't be any more eager than she would be for Mr. Randolph to know they'd had words.

Hell! Where had her brain been? Nico didn't know she worked for Randolph Ventures. By the time they met again, he'd probably have forgotten her name and wouldn't even recognize her wearing a business suit rather than a slinky dress. Her hair would be in its usual chignon rather than in unruly curls down her back, and her makeup would be subdued. Maybe, just to be safe, she'd get a pair of horn-rimmed glasses.

Feeling better than she had all weekend, she turned to the keyboard and got busy. Thanks to her conversation with Nico, and some time spent searching the Internet, she was able to address all of Randolph's concerns. Her assessment was fair, and Nico had a good chance of getting the money he needed.

Seconds before her deadline, she clicked on the send button. After allowing herself a few moments of satisfaction and a cup of coffee, Deanna straightened her spine and went back to work.

* * *

Nico obsessed over Deanna Sloan all weekend, snapping at his pastry chef, the wait staff, and anyone else who dared cross his path.

Late Monday afternoon as he fumbled with the key to his office, his brother walked up behind him and slapped him on the shoulder. "We need to talk, butthead."

They had worked together in other restaurants, and had always been each other's best friend. Marco was one of the few people Nico cared about and trusted, but even with his brother, he found it hard to share his feelings.

Nico strode inside and said, "That's 'Chef' to you." They maintained a sense of formality at work, but privately, it was no holds barred.

"Okay, Chef Butthead." Marco took a seat and crossed his arms. "What the hell is wrong with you?"

"Nothing." Nico flung himself into the old wooden chair behind his desk. "What's crawled up your ass?"

"Just about everyone who works here. That's who." Marco glared. "You've been acting like you think this is *Hell's Kitchen* and you're Gordon Fucking Ramsay. What happened? You haven't been this short-fused in years.

"So they've all gone running to you?" Nico avoided answering his brother's question. "I hate whiners."

A small smile appeared on Marco's lips. "Now you sound like Dad."

"I wouldn't go there if I were you." Nico felt his blood pressure rocket. Marco knew how much he hated being compared to their father, the man who had broken their mother's heart. "I've wanted to punch someone since Friday night."

"Name the time and place."

"Rocco's Gym, five o'clock."

"You got it." Marco leaned back. "Now can we get this mess straightened out? The staff complaints are bad enough, but two of our best customers told me you were rude to them. If the owner hears about this, you'll be out of a job. And you can't afford to be unemployed with all the money you've sunk into opening your own place. Right?"

"Right," Nico answered grudgingly.

"So tell me what's got you all twisted out of shape."

"Do you remember the woman at table five Friday night?" Nico rubbed his unshaved jaw. "Her date stood her up?"

"Reddish-brown curls, big green eyes, nice rack, but a little skinny?"

"Uh-huh." Nico fought the feeling of irritation his brother's crude description induced. "Her waiter told me she'd ordered a five-course meal, took a couple of bites from each dish, then sent the plates away."

"So you went out to talk to her." Comprehension dawned in Marco's brown eyes. He resembled their mom, while Nico looked like their father. "And?"

"Well, when I saw how hot she was, I asked to join her, and everything was going great. Then I brought up the fact she hadn't eaten much."

Marco leaned forward and demanded, "Tell me you didn't go into your usual tirade about women who eat a single leaf of lettuce and worry about gaining a quarter pound?"

"I might have." Nico shrugged. "But don't try and tell me that doesn't bug you too."

"Yeah. I like women with a little meat. Bones are for dogs." Marco sat back and crossed his arms. "But it's their choice, not mine."

"When did you become all metrosexual on me?" Nico glowered.

This conversation was not improving Nico's mood. Marco was supposed to have his back, not defend a woman who was clearly in the wrong.

"Not all of us still live in a cave." Marco stretched out his long legs. "Besides, what's it to you? She was a hot babe, but you two obviously don't click. Forget her."

Nico slumped in his chair. "I tried."

The image of her licking her lips had refused to leave his mind and had occupied his dreams. He'd woken up with more than his usual morning wood every day since he'd met her.

"Then call her," Marco interrupted his thoughts. "You did get her digits, didn't you?"

"No," Nico mumbled.

"Well, shit. What happened to the smooth Nico Thorne who never walked away without a phone number?"

"She got under my skin and I stormed off."

"But now you want to see her?" Marco needled.

"Just to show her how wrong she was about food."

Nico would certainly not admit that he was consumed with lust. If a girl said no, Nico moved on. Marco would never let him live it down if he admitted that thoughts of Deanna were driving him crazy.

"Why bother?" Marco wasn't convinced. "What happened to your philosophy that there are millions of cream puffs in the bakery, why worry about a particular pastry?"

Nico kept his expression bland. "She just needs to admit I was right."

Marco narrowed his eyes but didn't pursue the matter. Instead he asked, "Did she pay by credit card?"

"Yeah."

"Then I got you covered, bro." Marco got up. "What's her name?"

"Deanna Sloan."

"I'll be right back."

Nico read the same inventory page over and over until his brother returned twenty minutes later.

Marco frowned as he dropped into the visitor's chair.

"Aren't you trying to get money from Randolph Ventures for your restaurant?"

"Yeah. Why?"

"'Cause that's who she works for."

Nico went rigid. "Son of a bitch!"

This was bad. This was beyond bad. Randolph Ventures was his last chance. Restaurants were too risky for standard bank loans, and the other venture capitalist that he'd approached had said his project was too small. If Randolph Ventures refused to invest in his business, he'd lose everything—his life savings, the downstate riverfront building, and his one chance to outshine his father.

Marco's voice was grim. "Do you think it was a setup to see how you handled problems or just bad luck?"

Nico shrugged. What did it matter? Either way he was screwed.

The brothers sat in silence for a while, until Marco looked at his watch and said, "I've got an appointment, but I can cancel if you want."

"Nah. Go ahead." Nico shook his head. "I'm fine."

"I don't suppose you want this." Marco held out a piece of paper. "Even though it was a corporate credit card, I was able to get her home address."

Nico grabbed the Post-It note. An idea was forming. If Deanna Sloan had deliberately used her sex appeal to trip him up, then he would use his to regain his balance. And even if it had been just bad luck that he'd lost his temper, he had to fix things.

Fortunately, there had been a definite attraction between

them. Maybe that chemistry would be enough to save him. After all, they didn't call him the Kitchen Casanova for nothing.

CHAPTER THREE

For Deanna, Monday passed as slowly as if she were stuck in the middle seat of a plane flying to Australia. Not only had she checked her watch every few minutes as she waited to hear from Randolph about her report on Nico Thorne, she'd even eaten lunch at her desk so she wouldn't miss his call.

By six, when there still hadn't been any word from her boss, Deanna gave up. Her concentration was shot, and there was no way she was getting any work done. She might as well go home.

Her logical side knew that it was entirely possible Randolph hadn't seen her evaluation yet. Business often kept him out of the office for entire weeks, and her report probably wasn't on the top of his to-do list.

However, the panicky part of her brain insisted he had read her appraisal and tossed it in the trash. Along with her career.

Even her session with the trainer didn't calm Deanna's restless feelings. What was wrong with her? It wasn't as if she'd never had to wait for results before.

Was it because she had so much riding on the outcome of this report? Or was she on edge for an entirely different reason? One with heartbreakingly blue eyes and a butt to die for.

* * *

After meeting Marco at the gym and working out his aggressions in the boxing ring, Nico showered and went shopping. LeBoeuf was dark on Monday and Tuesday nights, and when Deanna got home, he planned to be on her doorstep with a hot meal and his hot self.

While keeping a tight rein on his own emotions, he would woo her over to his side. Deanna Sloan was *not* his *amore mio*.

She was merely a means to an end. His reaction to her was just a sign that he'd been celibate too long, nothing more. A problem he planned to fix tonight. He'd secure a good report and get laid at the same time.

Except for a few promotional appearances arranged by his publicist, Nico had stopped dating last winter. The women he'd been seeing bored him, and it was an effort to work up enough interest even to take them to bed. Then with all his attention and energy focused on opening his own restaurant, he hadn't noticed the months slipping by. Now that he was aware of the problem, he'd fix it.

Nico's only true love was cooking, and he couldn't let anything, or anybody, come between him and opening his own restaurant. Certainly not a beautiful, if possibly devious, venture capitalist.

He would regain control using the weapons he knew best— incredible food and amazing sex. Deanna Sloan was about to learn why no one ate only a few bites of Nico Thorne's dishes, and why women begged him to be their dessert.

*   *   *

It was much earlier than usual when Deanna got home, seven thirty versus her customary nine o'clock, and she stood in her foyer wondering what she would do with herself until bedtime. There was no one she could call to go out for a drink or a bite to eat. After years of putting her career first, of continually making excuses and canceling plans, most of Deanna's friends from college had faded away.

Sage, her BFF, was halfway across the country working at a big cat sanctuary in Nevada. And of her other two closest pals, one had moved to California to pursue her career as a corporate attorney and the other had joined a psychological practice in the western suburbs. Granted, Naperville was only thirty miles away, but with Deanna's schedule, it might as well be a thousand.

She was too wound up to read or watch TV. Maybe a bath would relax her, then afterwards she'd call Sage and see how the wild beasts of Las Vegas were treating her. Once they'd talked about the men, Deanna wanted to hear about the four-legged animals, too.

As she waited for the tub to fill, Deanna gazed at her reflection in the mirror. It was hard to see herself naked. Difficult not to dwell on the imperfections. But once in a while, she forced herself to take a long look.

For the most part, her body was okay. Her arms and legs were firm and she had nice breasts, but her less-than-completely-flat stomach was a constant frustration. No matter how much she dieted or exercised, there always seemed to be a little pooch under her belly button. Her personal trainer claimed that if she lost ten more pounds, it would go away, but that would mean cutting another two hundred calories from her diet, and she hadn't been able to do that. As it was, she was already always hungry.

The ringing of the doorbell snapped her out of her reverie, and she hurriedly shrugged on her robe. It was probably someone who had come to the wrong apartment. She hardly ever had any visitors of her own.

Putting her eye to the peephole, Deanna froze. Nico Thorne, looking hotter than ever, was standing outside her apartment. And he appeared to be leading a parade.

* * *

Nico rang the bell again. He knew Deanna was in there. He'd bribed her doorman with a gift card for two dinners at LeBoeuf to get the guy to call him as soon as she got home.

"Yes?" an uncertain voice answered his second ring.

Damn! What was he going to say?

"Uh, it's Nico Thorne." He should have realized she wouldn't just fling open the door. "I've come to apologize for my behavior Friday night."

Yeah. That's good. In his experience, women liked men who could admit they were wrong.

"Thanks, but you shouldn't have bothered."

Okay. He'd known she would be more challenging than the airheads he usually dated, but he was up to the job.

"Could you open the door?" Nico kept his tone light. "To show you how sorry I am, I've brought you a gift."

Women never turned downed presents.

"No. Really, that's not necessary. I forgive you."

Hell! Nico swore silently. *Now what?*

"I'd feel better if you'd look me in the eye and accept my apology." Nico knew he had to get inside. Even *he* couldn't charm a woman through two inches of steel.

"I'm not dressed for company."

Frustrated, he brought out the big gun. The one word he'd never had had to use on a woman before. "Please." *Fuck!* He hated begging. "It's important to me."

"Well..."

"Please." It tasted just as bitter the second time around. After what seemed like forever, Nico heard the lock click, and then he was drowning in her soft green eyes. He tore his gaze from hers and asked, "May I come in?"

Deanna nodded hesitantly.

As Nico stepped over the threshold, he said, "Do you have any plans for this evening?"

Deanna shook her head. "Just a bath."

Immediately he realized that she was naked under the silk kimono she was wearing, and his dick instantly pushed hard against his zipper.

"Good." His voice was husky when he asked, "Where's your kitchen?"

"On the left." She pointed down a short hall. "Why?"

Ignoring her question, he motioned with his chin to the people waiting in the corridor and said, "This way."

Transferring the grocery sacks he'd been carrying to one hand, he took Deanna's elbow with the other and tugged her along with him. His army of workers trailed after them.

Nico deposited his bags on the counter and glanced around. As he suspected, the stove was pristine, as if it had never been used. In fact, from what he'd seen of the apartment, the whole place looked as if she'd just moved in a couple of days ago.

The lone item of furniture in the foyer had been a table holding only a purse. His glimpse of the living room had revealed a tan sofa, cream chair, and glass coffee table. The flat-screen television hanging on the wall was the only decoration. There weren't any pictures or knickknacks or color of any kind. How could she live in such a cold, sterile environment?

A waiter rolling a serving cart cleared his throat, bringing Nico's attention back to his mission. The server was followed by a woman carrying flowers and a young kid with a sound system. A tuxedoed man holding two bottles of wine in one hand and an ice-filled bucket in the other brought up the rear.

Once everyone had assembled, Nico said, "In there, please."

He gestured to the attached dining area. A glass table and four white chairs continued the colorless decorating theme.

When he'd organized the dinner, Nico had thoroughly briefed everyone on how he wanted things set up, and they all worked with high-speed efficiency. Nico watched in satisfaction as the waiter spread a white linen cloth over Deanna's table, lined up a pair of silver candlesticks, then arranged two place settings of delicate china, sparkling crystal, and gleaming flatware. As soon as he was finished, the florist placed a cut-glass vase of flowers in the exact center.

Meanwhile the sommelier set up the wine bucket, and the kid plugged in the sound equipment. The teenager hit play, and soft jazz filled the room, entwining with the sweet scent of roses and the faint waxy odor of the candles.

Nico tipped everyone generously, thanked them for their help, and showed them out. After returning from the foyer, he found Deanna standing as still as an ice sculpture, clutching her robe, and staring at the scene with her mouth slightly ajar. She hadn't moved or said a word since they had gotten into the kitchen.

When he touched her shoulder, she straightened her spine and raised one perfectly arched eyebrow. "This is some apology."

* * *

From the bedroom, Deanna could hear Nico moving around in the kitchen. It had finally dawned on her that this wouldn't be a quick visit. The man didn't intend just to hand her a gift and leave. And when she'd realized that the touch of his hand on her elbow had hardened her nipples, making them clearly visible through her thin robe, she knew that she needed to put on some clothes.

Why was Nico here? How had he found her? Did he know she worked for Randolph Ventures? And more importantly, why in the world had she let him in?

When she'd seen him through the peephole, she'd had every intention of sending him away without ever opening her door. So, how had he ended up making her dinner? It was almost as if he had cast a spell over her.

Deanna blew out a disgusted breath of air. She was being ridiculous. She had never been the fanciful type, and she wasn't

29

about to start now. It was simple. She was hungry. Hungry for a good meal, and, if she were honest with herself, hungry for a good... *No.* She wasn't going there. Whatever he was cooking smelled like heaven, but she knew he was the devil in disguise.

She'd eat his peace offering, assure him there were no hard feelings, and send him home. She was definitely not letting him into her bed. If Randolph green-lighted the restaurant, she and Nico would have to work together. And boinking a man for whom she had a financial responsibility was a bad idea.

In fact, even if her job wasn't a factor, getting involved with Nico Thorne would be a bad idea. He wasn't her type. He was too smooth, too hot, and he made her feel too out of control.

With that in mind, Deanna put on sweat pants and a T-shirt. She deliberately didn't use any makeup, then, rather than fix her hair, she scraped it back with a headband. And in case he didn't get the hint by her appearance, she intended to tell him she wasn't interested in him.

Entering the kitchen, she opened her mouth, but before she could outline the ground rules, he moved toward her.

Heaven help me! He was looking at her as if she were the last piece of candy in the Godiva box. She felt her heart stutter. What had she been about to say?

He wanted her. Wasn't that a kick in the pants? Why would someone like Nico Thorne be attracted to her?

"You are so beautiful," he murmured, winding his finger through one of her curls. "Your hair reminds me of the cinnamon swirled though crème brûlée."

The brush of his hand against her collarbone made her whimper, and she fought to keep from leaning forward and pressing her mouth to his. Where was the resistance that she'd marshalled while she'd been dressing?

Although she would never admit it to herself, she wanted him to touch her. He was gorgeous and fascinating, but what could he possibly see in her?

"Do you taste as good as you look?" He caressed her cheek with his knuckle.

Deanna's breath came faster. He took another step forward, and she felt the heat of his body. Raw need rushed through her with a primal intensity, all of her senses went on red alert, and the urge to wrap her arms around him was nearly uncontrollable.

Drawing on every bit of willpower she possessed, Deanna backed away and said in a disdainful voice, "Do you get all your lines from romance novels?"

He doesn't have to know that I love reading romances.

Nico gave her a grin that sent her pulse racing. "No one's complained before."

"At least not to your face." She shrugged one shoulder. "You have no idea what women say about men to their friends."

His eyes darkened, and he opened his mouth but then snapped it shut. A heartbeat later, his tight expression relaxed into a smile.

He turned away from her and said, "You're right. I'll try to be more original in the future. But for now, let me pour you some champagne. Then I'll finish making you a dinner you'll never forget."

Deanna trailed him to the dining area and watched as he retrieved a bottle with a pink label from the wine bucket. Nico dried it with the towel he had tucked into the waistband of his black jeans, expertly popped the cork, and filled two glasses.

"Veuve Clicquot Rosé." He handed her a flute. "One of my favorites." Raising his glass, he toasted, "To forgiveness and fresh starts."

Deanna clicked her rim to his. "I'll drink to that." As she sipped, enjoying the hint of fresh berry, she noticed that Nico had been busy while she was changing out of her robe. The table held a crystal bowl that was heaped with caviar and surrounded by toast points and shucked raw oysters.

Following her gaze, Nico spooned a mound of the tiny black pearls on an oyster and held it out to her.

She tried to take it from him, but he murmured, "Allow me."

She opened her mouth and he tipped the delicacy between her lips. The firm spheres popped on the roof of her mouth, and she savored the sweet, buttery flavor. She'd had no idea fish eggs could taste so good.

A tiny drizzle of caviar ran down her chin, and Deanna caught the errant beads with her finger. Embarrassed at dribbling, she glanced upward and found her gaze locked with Nico's.

Before she could lick away the mess, he leaned forward and closed his lips around her fingertip. When his tongue lapped her skin, a bolt of desire shot straight to her center and she gasped. What was it about this man that made her want him so much? Was she willing to risk everything for one night of pleasure?

The thought shocked her, and she yanked her hand away, forcing a cynical laugh. "Just remember, I'm not on the menu."

* * *

Nico scowled as he plated the lamb chops and dressed them with horseradish-mint sauce. They were one of his specialties, and clearly he needed the zesty kick of the horseradish to add more heat to his seduction. Because, so far, Deanna had resisted all his attempts to charm her.

She had taken a seat at the head of the table and was studying him with a cool expression on her face, almost as if she were watching a cooking show on the Food Channel. When he had sucked the caviar from her finger, his erection had gone from wood to steel, while she had appeared unmoved. Had, in fact, made fun of him. That mocking laugh should have killed his desire but, strangely, had aroused him even more.

Nico placed one dish in front of her and the other to her right. After bringing over the asparagus spears, he poured them both more champagne, then sat down.

When she remained motionless, he raised his glass and said, "Bon appétit."

Remembering her reaction to large portions, he had chosen the smallest lamb chops he could find and put them over half the amount of couscous he would normally serve.

"Thank you." Deanna finally picked up her fork. "It looks wonderful."

"The chops taste better if you eat them with your fingers." Nico reached over to her dish, intent on feeding her. He wanted to feel her soft lips and tongue on his fingers, but before he could pick up the lamb, she snatched it from the plate and took a quick bite.

As she chewed, she closed her eyes, her expression nearly orgasmic. Watching her eat was a sensual experience. She obviously loved food, which made it all the more frustrating that she had sent every course back barely touched on Friday.

Before he could broach the subject, Deanna said, "So, is this your customary apology when you're rude to a diner?"

Nico shook his head, offering her a contrite smile. "You may not believe this, but I've never snapped at a guest before."

She dipped an asparagus spear into the hollandaise sauce, shook most of it off before lifting it to her mouth. "Then, why me?"

He shrugged, finding it hard to concentrate as he watched her tongue circle the slender stalk. "Bad day, I guess."

Deanna nodded. "I can understand that." Finishing the vegetable, she picked up the lamb chop and took another bite. "How did you find me?"

Another difficult question. Nico forced his fascinated gaze from the creamy yellow sauce on her lips. "Uh...well." He was slipping. Normally, a slick answer would effortlessly occur to him. "My brother's a whiz on the computer. Since I knew your name, he was able to get me your address."

True, but not the whole truth. That was better. The old Nico was making a comeback.

"I'd better see if I can get my personal info off the Internet." A concerned crease marred the smooth skin of her forehead.

"Definitely." Nico nodded and teased, "You don't want some crazy stalker showing up at your door."

She'd accepted his explanation and he could relax. Apparently good food put her in a less combative mood.

"I know a lot of people love doing research online, but I like hard copy better," Deanna commented.

"Me, too." Nico was unsure where she was going with that line of thought, but he smiled because they were finally having a normal first-date kind of conversation.

"In fact, I read an article about you in a magazine just the other day."

"Oh?" He stiffened. *Hell!* It had to be the one *Today's Chicago* had done. "Stuff like that is exaggerated. I don't really date a different woman every night."

"Sure." Deanna mouth curved in a mischievous smile. "I believe you. But your mother *is* some kind of royalty, right?"

"Not really. Somewhere, way, way back, one of our ancestors had an affair with a Borghese duke and had his child."

Her expression was wistful and he wondered what she was thinking. Surely she wasn't one of those women who dreamed of marrying Prince Harry or whichever heir to the throne it was who was still single.

"Oh." Deanna looked disappointed. "Still, your mom must be amazing."

"She is."

"The article said she's lived in the United States for twenty-five years."

"Yes. I was three and my brother had just had his first birthday." Nico's smile was tender. "A clothing designer offered her a job, and she couldn't pass up the opportunity to work with him."

"And your father's a famous chef."

"I guess." Nico didn't allow what he was thinking to show on his face.

Ian Thorne had been nothing more than a photograph on his mother's bedside table until Nico was a teenager. Then, when he turned sixteen, Mariella had discovered her son's talent in the kitchen and sent him to his father to be trained.

Once Nico was in England, Ian's new wife, Clarissa, hadn't waited even twenty-four hours to inform him how his father had exploited his mother's social status to further his career. The awful woman had said that once Ian hadn't needed Mariella's influence any longer, he'd divorced Nico's mom and made Clarissa, who had been his longtime mistress, his wife.

Nico'd already hated his father for making his mother so miserable. Mariella had always claimed the reason she hadn't remarried was that Ian was the only one for her. That there could be no else.

With Clarissa's revelation, even the slim chance of a better father-son relationship had been ruined. Nico would never forgive Ian for discarding his mother as if she were a soiled napkin.

"So both your parents are talented." Deanna finished her lamb chop and absently licked her fingers. "I can't even imagine how cool that would be."

Her words brought Nico back to the present. Watching Deanna's pink tongue flick in and out of her mouth took away his breath. He had to shove his hands into his pockets in order to stop himself from reaching over and pulling her into his lap.

His out-of-control reaction to her scared him. He had learned the hard way that lack of self-discipline was never a good thing. Why did he lose his ability to reason when she was around? He studied her, trying to see what made her so different from the rest of the women who paraded week in and week out through his restaurant.

Even though she wasn't his type, something he needed to keep reminding himself, the soft green of her eyes called to him. If he was honest with himself, the women he usually dated had nothing more on their minds than a good time and lunching with their girlfriends.

Deanna was too smart, too ambitious, and too complicated. She shouldn't interest him at all—so why did she? When had getting her naked and underneath him become an obsession?

"Nico. Nico. Are you all right?"

Her voice made him realize he had been staring at her. She really did bring out the idiot in him.

"Sorry." Nico forced a smile. "I must have zoned out for a minute. I'm fine." Trying to regain command of the situation, he asked, "What do your father and mother do?"

"Dad works in a factory and Mom cleans houses." Deanna's tone was casual, but her cheeks turned pink.

He could see that she was embarrassed by her blue-collar roots, and since her working-class background obviously bothered her, he was impressed that she told him the truth when it would have been easy for her to lie. Her honesty and vulnerability touched something inside of him—was it affection?

No. He never got emotionally involved.

Mentally regrouping, he pushed back his chair and got up. "Are you finished?"

"Yes. It was scrumptious." She beamed at him. "I can't

remember the last time I had a meal like that. Probably never."

"Are you ready for dessert?" The idea of feeding her the strawberries he had stuffed with a combination of mascarpone cheese and grated dark chocolate made his voice husky.

"No. Sorry. I'm way past my limit." Deanna leaned forward and blew out the candles, then stood and stuck out her hand. "Thank you for a wonderful dinner. It more than made up for our little run-in."

He knew the sensible thing to do would be to leave. She had obviously forgiven him and wouldn't sabotage his chances with her boss, but her dismissal caused a searing pain in his gut. He reached out, but instead of shaking her hand, he pulled her into his arms.

Nico's mind kept insisting that he was making a big mistake. Ignoring his heart's whisper that he already felt too much for her to walk away from her, he vowed that once his application for the investment had been approved, he'd let her down gently and go on with his life.

Then, feeling as if he had no choice, he closed the gap between them, slid his leg between her hers, and cupped her head with both hands. "Just one taste," he whispered.

As his mouth touched hers, all thoughts of how wrong, how crazy this was vanished. He licked the seam of her lips. They were as sweet as one of his delicious creations. The glide of her mouth against his was luscious, and pleasure coursed through him.

At this moment, it didn't matter that she held his fate in her hands, or even that she stirred up emotions he didn't want to feel. Nothing mattered except his hunger for her. He wasn't aware he had moved them into her bedroom until he felt the mattress against the backs of his legs.

He pulled her down on the bed, and the heat from her body engulfed him. His thumb caressed her jaw, then dipped lower to

37

touch the base of her throat. He felt her pulse surge, beating frantically, and she made an urgent yearning sound. Cradling her cheek, he lowered his head once again to cover her mouth with his.

In the moment before their lips met, he saw an answering flame in her eyes, then as they touched, a shockwave soared through his body. He felt an explosive rush that reminded him of when he used to drag race—the split-second when he pushed the gas pedal to the floor and passed the pack of cars ahead of him. Except, instead of the satisfaction that usually followed that sensation, this one left an unrelenting need in its wake.

Heat rocketed through him when she swept her tongue across his bottom lip. It was all the invitation he needed, and he plunged his tongue into her mouth allowing no shyness, no hesitation, and no second thoughts. He ran his hands down her body, reveling in the small noises she made as he rubbed his thumb over her nipple. Her shuddering and sighing signaled her growing desire.

Deanna's skin was softer and sweeter than whipped cream, and he wanted to feel and taste every inch of it. Her body was lush and supple, and all he could think of was how much he wanted it writhing beneath him.

Nico felt her hands pull off his T-shirt and caress the muscles at the base of his spine. His resolve not to get involved with any woman went up in the flames of his passion for her.

He pushed Deanna's sweat pants off. She reached for his zipper. As she slid the metal tab down the length of his erection, he shivered with the sensation. His hands gripped her hips, and he settled into the cradle of her thighs. All that separated them were his knit boxer briefs and her silk bikinis.

Intent on removing those last barriers, he slipped a finger under the elastic of her underwear. But before he could remove them, he heard the first few bars of "Hail to the Chief," and

Deanna stiffened. In a flash, she leapt from the bed, pulled on her sweat pants, grabbed the cell phone from her nightstand, and disappeared into the bathroom.

Nico frowned as he heard the lock click. Was she involved with another man? And why did he care?

CHAPTER FOUR

"I'm sorry it took me so long to answer, Mr. Randolph," Deanna said softly.

She was huddled in the bathtub to prevent Nico from overhearing her conversation. The tiled wall was as far from the bathroom door as she could get, but the occasional drip from the showerhead kept her squirming to find a dry location.

"That better not be all you're sorry about," Randolph thundered. "Your report on Thorne sucked the big one."

Deanna nearly dropped the phone as his voice ricocheted through her head. She managed to catch the cell at the last minute and clutched it to her ear.

Breathlessly, she asked, "In what way, sir?"

A wave of dizziness swept through her. She'd blown her chance. Randolph was probably seconds away from firing her. Was there any way to save her job?

"What you turned in read like a goddamn book report!" Randolph's enraged roar echoed in her brain. "I need to know if Thorne's a good manager. Will his restaurant have a competitive edge over the others in the area? What's the size of his market? Where will he get his customers? He's chosen to go downstate, rather than stick to Chicago or the suburbs, and city people sure as hell aren't going to drive to Bumfuck, Illinois."

"Sir," Deanna's mind raced, searching for an excuse, "what I turned in to you was a preliminary summary. Just my first impressions. I'd planned a much more thorough assessment once I had the answers to those questions." She crossed her fingers and bluffed, "As I'm sure you're well aware, in order to get the kind of information you mentioned, I'll have to thoroughly research both Chef Thorne and the location he's selected."

"And how do you plan to get the inside scoop on Thorne?" Randolph paused. "That is, without him discovering that we're investigating him."

"Uh...I..." Deanna glanced guiltily at the bathroom door.

Could she do that to someone? Pretend to be interested in a romantic relationship and spy on him?

Chewing her lip, she rationalized what she was about to propose. She wouldn't have to fake her attraction to Nico. He was the hottest guy she'd ever seen. And even before her boss had interrupted them, she'd been about to have sex with him.

Granted, sex with the yummy chef was probably a bad idea on a lot of levels, but his kiss had aroused her more than all her previous boyfriends' lovemaking combined. Not that there had been that many guys in her life, but still.

However, no matter how she justified it, she couldn't sleep with Nico just to further her career. There was a name for women who did that, and it wasn't CEO.

Could they go out on a few casual dates and not end up in bed? Would he even be interested in that? Considering his Kitchen Casanova reputation, he wouldn't want any type of real relationship, but he probably did expect sack time from his women.

Then again, she was pretty good at diverting men from those types of encounters. And she only had to distract him a few times. Just until she got the needed info and saved her job.

It was a good idea. So why was she hesitating?

Before she could understand her reluctance, Randolph yelled, "Uh, what? Did you fall asleep on me, Sloan? How are you going to get the goods on Thorne?"

"As it happens," Deanna said slowly, "Chef Thorne seemed interested in me. If I went out with him, I could probably pump him for information."

"Hmm." Randolph blew out a thoughtful breath—either that

41

or he was smoking one of his contraband Cuban cigars. "That might work. He certainly likes to play the field and you're a good-looking woman. Take your hair out of that bun, wear something with a little cleavage, and you shouldn't have any problem getting the dirt on him." Randolph smacked his lips. "I'll give you a week, but you better have something for me by next Monday morning or don't bother to come into the office."

"Yes, sir." Deanna sighed in relief. "Thank you for giving me another chance."

"Yeah. I'm just an old softy." Randolph snorted. "But remember, you're pumping him for information, so don't get carried away pumping him any other way. Make sure he has a good time, but don't get emotionally involved, because you're mine."

"Excuse me?" Deanna was alarmed at the thought that her boss might be interested in her romantically.

"As long as you work for me, I own your ass," Randolph bellowed. "Use it to get the info you need. Promise, but don't deliver. Got it?"

"Yes, sir." Biting her tongue in order to keep from screaming at her boss's crudeness, Deanna ended the call. Suddenly, all the rich food Nico had fed her threatened a reappearance.

What had she agreed to do?

She shook her head. Had she really spent four years in college and two more years getting her MBA for this? To be at the beck and call of someone like Randolph? To be reduced to using a man's attraction to get what she wanted?

Evidently she had sunk to the same level as the girls she'd sneered at in school and at the office. The ones who had used their looks instead of their brains to get ahead. About to do just that, she sent them all a mental apology.

Stepping over to the mirror, Deanna stared at herself. She

looked worse than awful. Her curls were matted, her complexion was pasty, and she was dressed more for the gym than for seduction.

Straightening her shoulders, she gritted her teeth. If she was going to do this, she needed to do it right.

Fifteen minutes later, Deanna stepped from the bathroom. Her hair was combed and bronzer alleviated her pallor. She wore the clothes that she'd been air-drying over the shower rod—a pair of black skinny jeans with a red V-neck sweater.

The bedroom was empty. Where the hell was Nico?

Just as she began to panic, thinking that he'd left while she was putting herself together, she heard whistling from the kitchen. *Phew!* She wasn't sure what she'd have done if he had ducked out. Would she have had to get another reservation at LeBoeuf to talk to him again?

Nico had washed the counters, packed his equipment, and relit the candles on the table. What he hadn't done was get dressed. Yeah. He'd pulled on his jeans, but he hadn't zipped them, and his chest was bare.

Deanna gulped. Her no-sex rule might be harder to enforce than she'd thought.

When Nico caught sight of her by the table, he frowned and said, "Why did you change clothes?"

"It seemed like a good idea," Deanna murmured, asking herself the same question. "I see you've been busy."

"Yeah." Nico shrugged. "Mama taught me to always clean up after myself, and I can't stand a messy kitchen."

Deanna warmed at his affectionate reference to his mother. She wished she had that kind of relationship with her parents, but they couldn't understand why she wanted a life that was different from the one they led. They were angry that she'd gone to college and accused her of thinking she was better than the rest of the family.

Forcing away the hurtful memory of their rejection, Deanna gestured to the table and asked, "Why did you light the candles again?"

"I thought since you'd had some time to digest dinner, we could have dessert."

"No, I—" Deanna cut off her refusal.

If she wasn't going to sleep with him, she'd have to let him feed her. He seemed almost as intent on cooking for her as seducing her. Maybe he'd be satisfied watching her eat.

Although it meant doubling her workout time, she smiled and said, "That sounds great."

Nico beamed, opened the second bottle of champagne, poured them each a glass, and then took a tray from the fridge. After setting it on the table, he seated her and pulled his chair close to hers.

Sparks danced up Deanna's skin as his arm touched hers, and she jerked away. His smile flickered, but he leaned forward and plucked a stuffed strawberry from the platter.

Holding it to her lips, Nico whispered, "Open for me."

His voice was whiskery rough, and Deanna had to fight a flash of desire to open her thighs rather than her mouth. Parting her lips, she allowed him to place the fruit between her teeth. As she bit into the juicy berry, she groaned. The silky mascarpone and decadent chocolate were pure bliss.

Nico's gaze intensified, blazing a path from her breasts downward. Without him ever touching her, she felt his scorching heat.

Deanna finished the hulled strawberry, and when Nico reached for another, she rushed to grab one before he could. Winning the race, she held the fruit to his lips. His white teeth gleamed as he grinned, then he sucked both the berry and her fingers into his mouth.

Paralyzed, her blood pulsed with every sweep of his tongue.

She stared into his blue, blue eyes and forgot where she was and what she needed to do. Deanna shuddered. She'd never had such an intense experience. Certainly not fully dressed and outside the bedroom.

They continued to feed each other until the tray was empty. When she realized that they'd finished the dessert, she sighed. For once, her mind didn't immediately begin totaling the calories. Instead, she scooped the last bit of mascarpone from the platter and popped it into her mouth. She'd pay for her indulgence tomorrow, but tonight she was determined to enjoy every morsel.

Nico brushed a curl behind her ear and said, "In some cultures, sharing food is the greatest intimacy that can be offered."

Deanna swallowed, unable to respond. As he gently stroked from her cheek down her throat to her collarbone, his touch stole all of her words.

"Food should be a delight to the senses." Nico continued his caress. "It should awake dormant eroticism." His fingertip dipped into the vee of her sweater and paused over her rapidly beating heart. "When I prepare food, it is my love letter to the diner. I want everyone to delight in the meal and embrace the flavors."

There was something too compelling, too enticing about this man. Deanna knew that he could make her forget about all her rules and leave her shattered beyond repair.

Needing to break the spell he was weaving, she said, more sharply than she intended, "That's because you've never had to worry about calories."

"And you do?" His tone was challenging.

"Yes." Deanna held on to her patience. "And unfortunately, that means watching what I eat."

"I can understand that, but an occasional treat won't hurt

you." He stood and drew her into his arms.

She stiffened, but he waited patiently. Slowly, his warmth softened her, and she rested her cheek against his chest, wishing he'd just drop the subject of food.

Nico stroked her back until she'd fully relaxed, then said, "I don't want to fight with you."

Deanna murmured her agreement.

"You're a beautiful, desirable woman." His fingers tunneled between the waistband of her jeans and the bottom of her sweater. "A pound or two won't change how gorgeous you are. No one will see you any differently."

Deanna wanted to scream at Nico. How dare he make such a ridiculous claim? Mr. Perfect-Face-and-Body had probably never had to suffer the scorn of being the fat kid.

Using the willpower that had allowed her to transform her life, she eased herself from his embrace and said, in a deceptively mild tone, "Perhaps."

She stepped away from Nico, blew out the candles, and walked out of the dining area. He had no choice but to follow her. When she stopped in the foyer and put her hand on the doorknob, he wrinkled his brow, clearly confused at the abrupt end to their evening.

Smiling tightly, Deanna said, "Thank you again for dinner. The meal was delicious. It was far too much for an apology."

"It was my pleasure." He moved closer to her. Taking hold of her chin, he tilted her face up and said, "I'd like to see you again."

"That would be nice." Deanna tried to ignore his thumb caressing her jawline. She'd wanted his interest in order to gather information about him, but she needed to concentrate to make it work. "I imagine you're busy most evenings."

"LeBoeuf is dark Mondays and Tuesdays." Nico's lips skimmed the sensitive skin beneath her ear. His breath tickled her neck. She shivered as his mouth moved to her cleavage. The sensation stuttered down through her stomach and pooled between her legs. His eyes were dilated when he raised his head and asked, "What are you doing tomorrow night?"

"Nothing." Deanna's pulse was pounding so hard she could barely speak. "I have a session with my trainer after work, but that's it."

"Which health club do you go to?" Nico nibbled on her earlobe.

"Rocco's." Deanna gasped as he gently bit down.

"Small world. Me, too." Nico looked at her and grinned. "How about I meet you there? We can work out, then grab a bite to eat."

"Sounds like fun." Deanna tried to step back, but Nico tightened his arms around her. "Is six okay for you?"

"Perfect."

Nico lowered his head, and when his lips closed over hers, every lucid thought fled. She moaned and his tongue swept inside her mouth. Stroking and sucking until there was nothing but their kiss.

As he edged her toward the bedroom, indecision chewed at her. Despite what had nearly happened between them earlier, Deanna didn't do one-night stands. Casual sex hadn't ever appealed to her. She'd always guarded both her heart and her body, never sharing the former and rarely the latter.

Summoning up all her hard-won self-discipline, she moved out of his embrace and said, "It's getting late." Stepping over to the door, she opened it and forced a cool smile. "I'll see you at the gym."

"Fine." His eyes narrowed, but he walked to where she stood and pressed his lips to her cheek. His mouth curled at one corner as if he knew she needed to get him out of her apartment before they ended up in bed.

He stared at her for a moment, and she felt as if he were seeing through all the walls she'd so carefully built to keep her heart safe.

Finally, he smiled and said, "I'll pick up my equipment tomorrow night."

Before she could object or tell him to take the stuff now, he walked away.

Great! Now she'd have to let him come back home with her. She had a feeling keeping him out of her bed a second time would be even more difficult than it had been tonight.

* * *

Alone in the elevator, Nico adjusted himself. He was so hard he'd probably have an imprint of the zipper's teeth on his dick by the time he regained control.

Why had Deanna stopped their kiss and sent him away? Unless he'd completely misread her, she'd been as turned on as him. Did it have something to do with the phone call that interrupted them the first time? Who was on the other end of that ringtone?

Hmm. Would she assign a boyfriend a song like "Hail to the Chief"? Maybe it had been her boss. When Nico had met with Randolph to talk about getting seed money for his restaurant, the guy had certainly acted as if he thought he occupied the Oval Office.

As Nico steered his SUV through the Chicago traffic, he considered what he was doing. Deanna had accepted his apology, and he'd swear she wasn't the type of woman who allowed her personal feelings to interfere with her professional judgment, so there was no reason to see her again.

Why was he meeting her at Rocco's tomorrow night? Why did his heart race at the thought of her in tight workout clothes?

And why was he pursuing a woman who obviously wanted to keep him at arm's length?

Nico Thorne didn't do relationships. He didn't go on platonic dates. And he certainly didn't have to beg a woman to enjoy his bed.

* * *

Shit! Shit! Shit! Deanna impatiently stabbed the blender button. She was running late and it was all Nico Thorne's fault. Apparently she'd forgotten to set her alarm and she'd overslept.

Bad enough that she'd been tormented by erotic images of the sexy chef half the night. But the nightmares that had been regular visitors while she was in high school had returned with a vengeance.

It had to be her idiotic conscience. She'd worked hard to suppress her middle-class sense of right and wrong. Evidently she felt uneasy about what she was doing to Nico. Spying on him while pretending to date him must have pushed her guilt button. That would have to stop. She had no choice. It was him or her. In the world of venture capitalism, scruples were a hindrance she couldn't afford.

Wrinkling her nose, she drank the soy-and-flax-seed smoothie. It was one of her usual breakfasts, and although she hated the taste, it would satiate her hunger until noon. Today it was even less palatable because she'd used unsweetened soy milk to make up for last night's dinner binge.

With one last glance at her watch, she chugged the rest of the foul-tasting drink, grabbed her purse, and headed into the office. If she wanted to coax information out of Nico, she needed to be prepared before she saw him again. Which meant she had a lot of research to do.

CHAPTER FIVE

Tuesday night, Nico arrived at the gym early and tucked himself into a partially hidden corner where he could observe Deanna as she worked out. He wasn't sure why he wanted to watch her without her knowledge, but his instincts were rarely wrong.

He saw her emerge from the women's locker room wearing tight calf-length knit pants and a white tank top. Compared to most of the women in Rocco's, she was overdressed, but he couldn't take his gaze off her curvy little bottom as she turned to walk toward a hulking guy with a shaved head at the far side of the room. Her trajectory was perfect for Nico's viewing pleasure, and with every step she took, he stared at her cute heart-shaped butt.

Baldy must be her trainer. The man only took on female clients and had a reputation as quite a player. Nico searched his mind for the guy's name but came up blank. Fighting the urge to drop the barbells and go claim Deanna as his, he kept an eye on Romeo.

The trainer started Deanna with a light aerobic warm-up, then stretches. Once that was over, he had her lift weights. Twenty minutes later, Cue Ball helped her to her feet, then, sliding his hand up and down her arm, led her to an elliptical. The machine was in use, but the woman exercising on it held up one finger indicating she was nearly finished.

Nico's head pounded when he saw Lover Boy lean in to whisper into Deanna's ear. That had to stop right now. He tapped his chin, then hurriedly slipped into the men's locker room.

Emerging a few seconds later, Nico carried a pair of boxing gloves. Since he'd been too busy watching Deanna to work up a sweat, he was able to pretend that he'd just arrived at the gym. Striding over to Deanna and Mr. Touchy-Feely, Nico said, "Hey. Looks like you're just about to start your cardio. How about I teach you a little boxing instead? It's even better for your vascular system than the elliptical."

"Really?" Deanna's tone was mild. "And you'd be willing to show me all your moves?"

Nico nearly missed the quick look she exchanged with her trainer. A flicker of unease shot off his spine. Why was the guy smiling?

"Sure." Nico's voice wasn't as confident as usual. "I promise to go easy."

Chrome Dome's grin broadened, but Deanna's expression was bland as she said, "Sounds like fun."

After they got on all their equipment and climbed into the ring, Nico said, "Let's start with the basics. Stand with your feet one in front of the other, knees bent." He demonstrated. "Put your fists up and keep your elbows close to your body. Punch in front of you at shoulder level, fully extending your arm."

"Like this?" Deanna asked.

"Exactly." Nico was surprised at how well she followed his instructions. Her movements were smooth, with none of the hesitation a first timer usually exhibited.

Next, he took her through jabs, uppercuts, lunges, and squats. He was impressed at her near-perfect execution of all the moves. She was a natural.

After they ran through everything several times, Deanna asked, "When do we actually box?"

"Well." Nico hesitated. He didn't want her to get hurt. "We could do a little sparring, I guess. But aren't you getting tired? You must have already done a good portion of your workout before I even got here."

"Nope." Deanna grinned. "I'm fine."

They donned their head gear and mouth guards and squared off. Nico danced around. He intended to let Deanna land a few blows to get the feel of the sport, then end things without throwing a punch.

His attention had wandered to the cute frown of concentration between Deanna's brows when suddenly a powerful uppercut clipped his jaw, and he saw stars.

* * *

When Nico staggered back, Deanna grinned. She'd started boxing when she'd been a sophomore in college. She'd been told that it would tighten up her midriff and arms, which were saggy from all the weight she'd dropped in the previous twelve months.

She had hoped that fitting into single-digit-size jeans would lessen her insecurities, but no matter how small she got on the outside, on the inside she still felt like everyone saw her as the fat girl.

Eventually, she'd joined the university's boxing club. Twenty minutes of jumping rope, followed by an hour and a half of calisthenics, along with practicing the various punches sculpted her muscles. And being part of a team helped her learn to socialize without fear of rejection.

By the time Deanna was a senior, her competitive nature had kicked in and she went from non-contact to sparring. She kept up the sport after she graduated and had always resented the assumption of the male boxers that the women didn't stand a chance in the ring with them.

Still, as Nico rubbed his jaw and winced, Deanna felt a tad bit guilty. She shouldn't have pretended to be a novice. That hadn't been fair. Why did the man seem to bring out all her baser instincts?

Cristiano, her trainer, was chuckling. She shot him a dirty

look, spit out her mouthpiece, and said, "I'll see you on Thursday."

Before leaving, he helped her out of her gloves and murmured in her ear, "You need to get back in the ring more. That punch used to make your opponents hit the mat."

Deanna scowled at Cristiano until he shrugged and walked back to the exercise machines. He was right, she *was* out of practice. But sparring with the few other women boxers who frequented Rocco's was boring. None of them were much of a challenge.

Once her trainer was gone, she turned to Nico and said, "Sorry about that. Are you okay?"

"Yeah. I'm fine." Nico moved his jaw back and forth. "You sure catch on fast, and for a little thing, you pack quite a wallop."

Deanna's cheeks warmed. She was by no means small, but in comparison to Nico, she felt positively tiny. She was also impressed that he didn't claim she'd landed a lucky punch. His chin might be bruised, but she hadn't damaged his ego.

"Well," Deanna smiled and said, "did I mention that I belonged to a boxing club in college?"

"Sneaky." Nico flashed a heart-stopping grin. "Next time we get into the ring, I'll bring my A game."

"You want a chance at me now?" Deanna offered. It hadn't been right to trick him.

"Nah." Nico put an arm around her shoulders. "Let's clean up and get something to eat. You've had a long workout. You must be starved."

"Not really." Deanna shook her head in denial at the exact same time her stomach chose to let out a loud growl.

Nico's grin widened, but instead of calling her on her blatant lie, he said, "Well, I'm ravenous. I'll take you to my favorite burger joint."

"I'd rather..." Deanna started, then corrected herself, "Sure.

Sounds great."

She nearly swooned at the thought of biting into a juicy cheeseburger, but mentally smacked herself. She'd order a turkey or veggie burger without the bun and a salad. No greasy French fries for her.

As they parted at the locker room entrances, Nico said, "I'll meet you by the front door." He leaned down and pressed his lips to her temple. "Bring your appetite."

Deanna showered and dressed in record speed. It would take too long to wash and style her thick, curly hair, so she left it in the French braid she'd worn for her exercise session. After stuffing her office and workout clothes into her duffle bag, she pulled on jeans and a sweater. A quick dusting of bronzer and some mascara, and she was ready.

As Deanna hurried into the lobby, she saw Nico staring out the front window while he talked on his cell.

There was a firm note in his voice as he said, "Lorenzo, of course I'm mad you didn't show up for work Sunday. You need to give me notice if you're not coming in." Nico listened, then said, "I understand that you couldn't miss your daughter's recital, but if you were really planning to go to Annamarie's performance, you could have arranged to take the night off a month ago." Nico's tone changed. "You're a great sous-chef, but this isn't about a family obligation, this is about the booze."

Deanna stepped behind a pillar and listened intently. This was her chance to evaluate Nico's management style. When he continued to speak, she leaned in, not wanting to miss a word.

"No." Nico shook his head. "I'm not firing you. Go to an AA meeting tonight, and I'll put you back on the schedule for next week." Nico paused, then added, "But if I smell alcohol on you, you're out the door." He nodded at the phone and said, "You're welcome. Just don't let me down. I'm only giving you one second chance."

Deanna nodded to herself. That had been impressive. Nico had handled his errant employee perfectly. He'd given him instructions on how to correct the situation, an opportunity to make things right, and a consequence if he didn't do so.

Smiling, Deanna walked over to Nico and said, "I'm ready if you are."

Reassured she'd made the correct decision in dating Nico to gather intel about him, Deanna allowed him to push open the glass door for her and preceded him out of the gym. If this was any indication, she should be able to wrap up her evaluation of Nico by the end of the week and meet Randolph's deadline without a problem.

Her giddy relief was interrupted when Nico took her hand and electricity zipped up her arm. They had way too much chemistry for Deanna's peace of mind. If she was going to make it to Monday without sleeping with him, she had to keep their skin-to-skin contact at a minimum.

Dropping his fingers, she snatched her phone from her purse and said, "Sorry. I need to make sure my boss isn't trying to reach me."

Nico raised a questioning brow but didn't comment as she checked her cell. Interesting that he'd never asked any details about her job. She'd said she was in finance. He probably thought she was one of the many businesswomen hustling to make a dime in the city and didn't care about the specifics.

Which was good. *Right?* She wouldn't have to lie. Still, her chest tightened that he cared so little about her. Obviously, he was just intent on a meaningless fling and nothing else.

Deanna sighed at her own foolishness, shifted her duffle to her left hand, and kept her purse in her right.

With all ten of her fingers occupied, Nico had nothing to hold, but he rested his palm against her back as he said, "Nell's is at the end of this block."

They were silent as they strolled, and Deanna was just beginning to relax when he guided her into the brightly lit diner. A delicious aroma of frying meat and cooked onions tickled her nostrils, and she licked her lips. It would be harder to resist the food here than she'd thought.

Most of the tables and booths were occupied, but when a middle-aged woman came out from behind the counter and hugged Nico, he said, "I hope you saved my usual spot, Nell."

The woman nodded and led them to a booth in the back. Nico waited for Deanna to take a seat, then instead of sitting on the opposite bench, he slid in next to her. His thigh pressed against hers and she frowned.

The skin over his cheekbones tightened in a predatory smile, and there was no mistaking the blaze in his eyes that told her precisely what he wanted from her. Staring, he moved a fraction closer.

Her voice breathy from her racing pulse, Deanna said, "Where are the menus?"

"You don't need one." Nico glanced at the owner and said, "We'll have the Nell burgers with fries and chocolate milkshakes."

Deanna poked him and said, "I'd prefer—"

Nell ignored her and hurried away.

"I can't eat all that." Deanna frowned. What was it with this man and feeding her?

"I bet you could if you tried." His eyes twinkled.

"You're right." She arched a brow. "Which is why I said I can't, not that I'm unable to eat it."

"Loosen up." Nico ran a finger from just below her ear, down her throat, and paused at the vee of her thin sweater.

The touch of his calloused fingertip on her skin sent desire hurling through Deanna. Her breath caught and she swallowed hard. The temptation to do whatever it would take to make him happy nibbled at her usual self-restraint. Would a burger and fries really hurt?

Realizing how close she was to giving in, Deanna stiffened. This would never work. She couldn't sleep with Nico, and she couldn't allow him to stuff her with fattening foods, either.

What else could she offer to keep him interested long enough for her to gather the information she needed? Maybe she should just reveal the name of her employer and ask him for the information she needed.

Yes. That was what she'd do. She'd put things between them on a professional level, and he'd quit trying to seduce her with tasty treats.

Opening her mouth to admit her true identity, Deanna hesitated. Was this a good idea? Her boss had specifically told her not to disclose her identity.

While she was still mulling over her choices, Nell came back with their order. The heavenly aroma of the burger and perfectly golden French fries made her mouth water. Before she could stop herself, she snatched a fry and popped it into her mouth. The salty goodness exploded on her tongue and she sighed.

Nico thanked Nell, assured her they didn't need anything else, and watched Deanna chew. His satisfied gaze made her self-conscious. When she didn't reach for another fry, he raised a brow but remained silent.

Picking up his own burger, he bit into it. With his attention off of her, Deanna cut her sandwich into quarters. She separated one portion and nine fries from the rest of the platter.

Before Nico could comment, Deanna said, "How long have you been at LeBoeuf?"

"Five years." Nico sucked down half his shake, then said, "But I'll be leaving soon."

"Oh?" Deanna nibbled her second fry slowly, savoring the

taste of her forbidden treat. "Has another restaurant lured you away?"

"In a matter of speaking." Nico's smile held a hint of something she couldn't pinpoint. "I'm opening my own place."

"Nearby?" Deanna took a tiny bite of the burger. The seasonings were exquisite.

"Downstate."

"Why's that?" Deanna forced herself to pause between bites. "Wouldn't you have a better chance at success if people who already enjoy your cooking had easy access to your new location?"

"Maybe." Nico toyed with his straw, not meeting her gaze. "But my gut tells me there's less competition where I'm going and more likelihood to really stand out. It's close enough to St. Louis to draw from that crowd, and I was able to get an amazing riverfront property for a fraction of what I'd pay for a tiny spot in Chicago or even one of the popular suburbs like Naperville."

"Sounds like some good reasons." Deanna paused to enjoy her third fry. "Did you do any market analysis of the area?"

"Nothing scientific." Nico shot her a sharp glance.

As Deanna finished her quarter burger, she debated. Should she tell him she represented Randolph or not? She was getting some good information this way. Would he clam up if she revealed she was writing a report on his investment potential?

She couldn't risk telling him and upsetting her boss. She'd have to keep deceiving him. Her appetite gone, she pushed away her plate and rolled her neck.

It felt as if someone had laid a barbell across her shoulders. She really needed to book a massage soon or her migraines would return.

Deanna was so intent on her own thoughts, she was shocked when Nico threaded his hands through her hair, began to release it from her French braid, and murmured, "This looks so tight and uncomfortable. Let's undo it so you can relax."

She tried to bat him away, but the pull of arousal from the slight tug of his fingers through her curls weakened her resolve. She was acutely aware of the weight of her breasts and the throb between her thighs. But more disturbing was her brain's refusal to allow her to move out of his reach.

The hard beating of her heart pounded at her resistance to his charm, and she snapped, "I can take care of myself. I don't need a man telling me what's good for me."

A muscle ticked in his jaw, and Deanna noticed a faint bruise there from when she'd punched him. She winced inwardly but refused to allow him to see her concern. She had to stay strong.

"Everyone needs help once in a while." Nico's tone was mild, but Deanna could see the irritation in his eyes. "I was only trying to make you more comfortable."

"Maybe broken wings are more your type," Deanna countered, keeping her defenses firmly in place. "You can't handle it that I can take care of myself."

"Oh, I can handle it." Nico's shoulders were rigid. "I think you're the one who can't stand the idea of giving up even an ounce of control."

CHAPTER SIX

Nico stared at Deanna, daring her to deny the truth. *Hell!* Forget letting her hair down, both figuratively and literally, she hadn't even admitted she worked for Franklin Randolph.

Of course, he hadn't pressed her about her employer, either. A twinge of guilt skittered across his conscience. He was using her. Or at least he had started out intending to use her to make sure Randolph invested in his restaurant.

But that had been before last night. Before he'd kissed her. Before they'd come damn close to making love.

Seeing her tonight had nothing to do with business and everything to do with pleasure. Clearly, she didn't feel the same way. Or if she did, she was resisting their attraction with every ounce of the same impressive willpower she used to push away the food that she obviously craved.

Maybe he should just let her go. Opening a restaurant was hard enough. He didn't have time to tear down her defenses. And with those barricades in place, they didn't have a chance at a relationship.

Nico recoiled. Where had that word come from? He wasn't interested in anything serious. All he wanted from the women he dated were a few laughs and some mutually enjoyable sex.

Glancing at Deanna's stiff posture and seething expression, Nico rolled his eyes. It didn't look as if she'd be willing to fulfill either of those requirements.

Time to end this farce as gracefully as possible. He couldn't afford to make her any angrier. He didn't think she was spiteful enough to ruin his chances with her boss. However, that saying about a women scorned had been around for hundreds of years for a reason.

Nico was still trying to come up with a neutral way to extricate himself from the situation when Deanna said, "Let me out of the booth." When he didn't move, she pushed at his biceps. "I need to get going."

"Sure." He automatically began to slide over.

"Here." She tried to hand him a twenty. "This should take care of my share."

Still blocking her exit, he took a second to tamp down his furious reaction to the money she was waving in his face. The anger that had been brewing since she sucker-punched him in the boxing ring threatened to erupt.

Seriously? She couldn't even allow him the control of paying for her burger? A burger she barely tasted?

Gritting his teeth, he said, "Put that back." When she hesitated, he ordered, "I asked you here. I'm footing the bill."

"But...I... You don't..." Deanna stuttered.

"I don't what?" Nico snapped.

"This isn't a real date." She clicked her wallet open and closed. "It's clear I'm not the kind of woman you enjoy seeing."

Although he'd been thinking the same thing, he looked at her and frowned. Her lashes were lowered, but there was a vulnerability in the quick peeks she kept giving him.

"What kind of woman would that be?" he asked, curious where she was heading with this conversation.

"Like in the magazines." Deanna shrugged, and a shadow blinked across her face so fast he wasn't sure he hadn't imagined it. "Sexy." Her shoulders hunched and she whispered, "Beautiful."

Hell no! Nico's intention of ending the evening evaporated. There was no way on earth that he was allowing her to believe that she wasn't as desirable and as gorgeous as any of those surgically enhanced bimbos she thought she should look like.

"You're wrong." Nico's voice was implacable and her gaze

jerked to his face. Once he had her complete attention, he softened his tone. "Most of the girls that I've been photographed with are dates that LeBoeuf's publicist set up to enhance my image and draw in customers."

"Okay." Deanna pursed her lips, obviously wavering, then shook her head. "But I'm sure you don't object to dating some of Chicago's most stunning women."

"No. Can't say that I do." He watched Deanna's eyes shutter, then put his lips to her ear and whispered, "Which is why I asked you out."

"You seriously think I'll believe that I can compete with actresses and models?" Deanna snorted.

"It's all an illusion." Nico smiled. When she raised a questioning brow, he said, "Plastic surgery, special bras, hair extensions, and makeup."

"Really?" Deanna smiled gleefully.

"Yep." Nico stretched his arm behind Deanna and toyed with a curl she'd missed when she'd tucked the rest of her hair back into her braid. "It's like going to bed with one person and waking up with a completely different one."

"And it bothers you that they aren't pretty in the morning?" Deanna pulled away from his touch, frowning.

"That's not the problem." Nico struggled to keep his tone patient.

She was as prickly as a spiny lobster. Would she be as delicious if he cracked open her shell?

"So what's your objection?"

"I don't like liars and fakes." Nico saw an image of his father's cheating face.

"Oh." Deanna nodded; splashes of red appeared on her cheeks. "Sometimes it's not so much lying as being discreet. Confidentiality is an important part of many professions."

Nico held back a smile. So, Ms. Hard-hearted

Businesswoman felt guilty about keeping her corporate identity hush-hush. Why did that please him?

"Secrets aren't the same as lying," Nico conceded. "As long as they aren't meant to hurt someone."

He leaned down, slowly bringing his head level with hers. Her eyes were locked to his and her lips parted.

"Maybe even help them," Deanna murmured.

Nico watched as her lips parted and she took a stuttering breath. Then, before she could exhale, he sealed his mouth to hers. As she clung to him, her warmth began to soak into the frozen places in his heart.

He tightened his arms around her. Her breasts rubbed against his chest and he groaned. Did she have any idea how much he wanted her? Surrendering to his need, he lost himself in her heat.

* * *

What am I doing? Deanna asked the seductive little voice in her head that was encouraging her to forget where she was and take the pleasure Nico offered her. A few more sweeps of his tongue and she might just strip him right there in the booth and ravish him in front of everyone.

She drew a shuddering breath and moved out of his arms. What was wrong with her? First she'd indulged in a cheeseburger and fries, now all her careful plans to avoid having sex with the smoking-hot chef were about to be destroyed.

Her insides were a quivering jumble of need. She and Nico were an explosion waiting to happen. She had to get away from him before the detonation because once that bomb went off, the aftershocks would be impossible to control.

Seemingly unaware of her panic, Nico lifted her hand to his lips, nibbled on her fingers, and murmured, "Let's get out of here."

Although Deanna suspected her reason for wanting to leave and his were diametrically opposed, she nodded her agreement. Allowing him to help her to her feet, she forced herself to step away from the warmth of his hand on her back. As he stopped at the register to pay the check, she waited for him at the exit.

If she was as smart as her IQ score indicated, she'd walk through the door, grab a cab, and be gone before he was finished settling the tab. As she placed her palm on the metal plate, ready to push her way to freedom, that plan's flaw popped into her lust-addled mind.

Running away would stop her from having sex with him, but it wouldn't get her the information she needed to write a thorough report. And although she'd gathered a lot of good data tonight, she needed to know more about his choice of downstate location. Surely he hadn't really chosen it using only his gut reaction. One or two more dates should do it, but she had to end this one platonically first.

When Nico joined her, he escorted her outside and asked, "Did you drive here?"

"Yes." Deanna's stomach churned at the lie, but she didn't want to share a cab or be alone with him in his car.

"Okay." Nico cupped her elbow. "I'll walk you to your car, then follow you back to your place."

"Actually"—Deanna eased away from his grip—"I forgot something at Rocco's, so why don't we call it a night."

"I don't mind waiting." Nico's tone was even, but a line appeared between his brows.

"Where did you park?" Deanna asked, scrambling for an excuse to get away.

"The garage on Halstead."

"I'm in the opposite direction, so I guess this is good-bye." The lie came out smoothly, and before Nico could respond, Deanna said, "I'll pack up all your equipment from last night's dinner and leave it with the doorman so you can pick it up whenever you're in the neighborhood, or even send someone else to get it if that's more convenient."

"If that's what you want." Nico's expression darkened.

"But I'd love to see you again whenever you're free," Deanna added.

"Really?" Nico raised an eyebrow. When she nodded, he shrugged and said, "I have to work tomorrow, then I'm taking a couple of days off and heading down to Alton to talk to my contractor about the restaurant remodel." He shoved his fingers through his hair. "And I have to be at LeBoeuf over the weekend, so how about Monday?"

"You know," Deanna said, gazing at him flirtatiously from under her lashes, "I enjoy a good road trip, and it would be interesting to see the location of your new restaurant."

Nico's expression showed his confusion at her abrupt about-face, but he shrugged and said, "I'd love to have you come along. You can help me scope out the competition. Can you get off of work?"

Deanna studied Nico. Was there something predatory in his eyes? Did it matter? She had to go with him. Between the long ride and the opportunity to hear him discuss the remodel with the contractor, even if he was the Big Bad Wolf and considered her Little Red Riding Hood, she really had no choice.

Summoning up her composure, she said casually, "I have some flex time coming."

"Terrific." Nico wrapped his hands around her arms. "Better not plan on getting back until Friday. I usually stay over."

"Okay." Deanna gulped.

The slow slide of his calloused palms from her elbow to her wrist sent flutters of sensation to her core. *Oh. My. Gosh.* His simple caress felt better than the orgasms she'd had with other men. How in the world would she resist him during their trip?

65

CHAPTER SEVEN

Wonder of wonders, when Deanna talked to Randolph, he didn't have a problem with her taking the time off to go to Alton. Despite the fact it was for a project that he'd given her, she'd been sure her boss would snipe at her for being away from the office. But he didn't.

Of course, he *did* inform her that his munificence didn't include any extended deadlines for her other assignments, which meant she'd be working into the wee hours for the next two days.

Thursday morning, Deanna slid into the passenger seat of Nico's SUV and gazed at the handsome man next to her. He wore low-riding army cargo pants and a tight black T-shirt. His concentration was on the heavy morning traffic, which gave her a chance to study him.

His big hands gripped the steering wheel, and she could see faint scars on his knuckles. Recalling the sensation of those hands on her body sent a shiver down Deanna's spine.

Nico glanced at her and asked, "Is the air conditioning too high?" He grinned. "Being in a hot kitchen so much, I probably like it colder than most folks."

"I'm fine," Deanna assured him. His deep, sexy voice plucked at every nerve in her body, and she shivered again. "A goose must be walking over my grave."

"My mom always says that." Nico's brow wrinkled, then he added slowly, "You remind me a little of her."

Taken aback, Deanna blinked. He thought she was maternal? Maybe Nico wasn't as sexually attracted to her as it seemed.

When he didn't continue, she asked, "Do I look like your

mother?"

"Not at all." Nico kept his eyes on the road as he eased the big SUV onto the I-90/I-94 ramp. "But she's smart and strong and never backs down."

"I like her already."

Deanna had figured any woman who managed to create a design empire while raising two sons on her own had to be amazing. And hearing the affection in Nico's voice for traits that many men wouldn't admire, but that she shared, was a balm to her soul.

A desire as sweet and rich as a gooey chocolate brownie swept through Deanna. She gripped the armrest to stop herself from flinging herself at Nico.

Was it possible that she could have a real relationship with him? If things went well today and she was able to complete her evaluation of his restaurant's return-on-investment potential, she'd admit who she worked for at dinner. And if Nico didn't hate her for her deception, maybe they could start over. Was there any chance for them as a couple?

* * *

Nico felt the tension drain from his shoulders. They were finally out of the heavy Chicago traffic and he could relax.

When he'd pulled up to Deanna's apartment building at nine a.m., he'd planned on having a cup of coffee with her before hitting the road. But Deanna had been waiting for him at the curb and hopped into his SUV before he could even get the vehicle into park. It was now nearly ten thirty, and he craved caffeine and sustenance.

Deanna was gazing out her window and seemed lost in thought, so Nico cleared his throat before he said, "I need a shot of java. Okay with you if we go through a drive-up?"

"Sure." Deanna nodded. "That'd be fine."

67

"I'll take the Route 30 exit coming up." Nico put on his turn signal. "Since there's a mall here, there should be someplace to grab a cup."

Once they'd gotten their drinks and were back on the highway, Nico watched as Deanna doctored her coffee. She'd asked for it black, but after digging in her purse, she pulled out two pink packets and added the fake sugar. Evidently realizing she should have requested a spoon, she rooted through her bag again and came out with a pencil, which she used as a stirrer.

Nico felt as if a hand had wrapped around his heart. Deanna really was like his mother. Too independent for her own good. Mariella had never been one to ask for help, and he doubted that Deanna ever did, either. Both were awesome women but tough to love.

Wait! Who had said anything about love? He and Deanna had mad chemistry, but once that craving had been sated, they'd both go their separate ways. She clearly had no desire for any kind of relationship, and he certainly didn't want one.

As he forcefully pushed aside the thought of getting involved with Deanna, a little voice echoed through his head, "She's *il tuo amore*. Don't blow this."

Attempting to block out any more unwanted messages from the great beyond, he turned on the radio, and Frank Sinatra singing "Something" oozed out of the speakers. Slamming his palm against the button, Nico shot an apologetic look to Deanna.

Damn! His brother always messed with his stations when he borrowed the SUV. And Marco's taste for Vegas Rat Pack music sucked.

Still, it had almost seemed like that song had been a sign. Pounding his forehead with his fist, Nico grabbed his cup. If he was starting to believe in omens, he was obviously more in need of caffeine than he'd realized.

Taking a cautious sip of the hot beverage, Nico refocused

on his plan. Bloomington was the next city of any size, and they would be there around noon. He intended to stop there for lunch. And because food was such a touchy subject with Deanna, he'd searched the Internet and found a place that was known for its healthy menu.

Which reminded him of the treat he'd baked for her. Reaching into the backseat, he retrieved a plastic container and handed it to Deanna. She raised a questioning brow as she pried off the top.

"I made these muffins this morning." Nico saw Deanna start to close the lid and hurriedly added, "I swapped out the butter for nonfat Greek yogurt and reduced the sugar."

"For me?" Deanna's expression was full of wonder. "That was really sweet of you."

"It was sort of fun to figure out a way to lighten the recipe." Nico winked. "I like a challenge."

"So I noticed." She laughed, then peeled the paper off and took a bite, moaning as she chewed.

The dazed look in her eyes and the sexy groans she made as she devoured the muffin hardened him instantly. Hoping she didn't notice, Nico reached down to adjust himself.

"Thank you." Deanna licked her fingers. "That was delicious."

"Glad you enjoyed it."

They both sipped their coffee in companionable silence, until Nico asked, "What do you like to do besides work out and lure unsuspecting men into the boxing ring with you?"

"I don't have a lot of free time," Deanna said absently, her gaze locked on the passing countryside.

"How about before you got so busy?" Nico persisted. "What did you do for fun then?"

"Once a week, my sorority used to have a night where we'd play old board games and eat popcorn and talk about our dreams." Deanna's voice was soft and Nico could hear the warm memories as she spoke.

"Somehow I can't picture you as a sorority girl," Nico teased, then frowned when he caught Deanna's hurt expression. What had he said wrong now?

"Because I'm not beautiful?" Deanna lifted her chin. "You don't think I have the looks to get a bid from a sorority?"

"That wasn't what I meant." Nico exhaled loudly. "I meant because you seem too serious. I assumed you wouldn't be interested in them, not the other way around."

"Really?" Disbelief glimmered in Deanna's eyes.

"Really," Nico assured her. "The sorority girls I've met are pretty shallow. Not interested in much beyond the next party or the next guy."

"There are sororities like that," Deanna admitted. "But they're in the minority, and Alpha Sigma Alpha isn't one of them. We're all about lifelong friendships and seeking to be the best we can be."

"Are friendships important to you?" Nico asked.

He frowned. Why had he asked that? Did he really want to know her that well? *No. Yes.* He was getting confused and that never happened. He was always sure what he wanted and marched toward that goal without any detours. But Deanna's apparent inconsistencies intrigued him. And that couldn't be good.

* * *

Nico's question had slammed into Deanna's chest as if the SUV's airbag had gone off. Friendship *had* been important to her, but she'd somehow pushed that need aside in her drive to be successful. All those phone calls and texts she didn't take the time to return. The invitations she'd turned down. The relationships she'd so carefully nurtured in college that she'd thrown away without a single thought.

Sage was the only one of her sorority sisters who hadn't given up on her. How pathetic was it that her only remaining friend lived seventeen hundred miles away?

Deanna sank back in her seat. Was it time for a change? Would having a high-powered job with a huge salary make her happy? Did anything she'd accomplished in the last several years have a positive impact on anyone's life?

Yes. She'd made a lot of money. She'd been poached from her previous position and been given a golden opportunity at Randolph Ventures. And she was sure she could beat out the other associates at the firm and eventually move into the number two spot in the company.

But at what cost? Was a friendless, loveless, soulless life what she really wanted?

The sound of Nico tossing the empty muffin container onto the backseat made Deanna realize she'd never answered his question. She looked at his profile. His eyes were on the road, but he continued to sneak peeks at her as he waited patiently for her response.

"Friendships are important," Deanna hedged. Considering her behavior, she wasn't sure she could honestly claim that they were important to her. "Do you have a lot of friends?"

"Define friends," Nico countered.

"People with whom you feel comfortable sharing your innermost thoughts." Deanna squirmed, realizing how much she missed having that kind of support.

"Then no." Nico shrugged. "I guess I have a lot of friendly acquaintances. My brother Marco's the only one I really trust."

"Oh." Deanna nodded slowly. "I guess you and I have something in common."

"Probably more than you realize." Nico blew out a breath as

if he wasn't entirely happy about that conclusion.

Deanna's throat tightened. Both at his obvious reluctance to see them as anything but two people sexually attracted to each other and at the aura of sadness that surrounded him.

Deciding it was time to change the subject and get to work, Deanna said, "Tell me what to expect once we get to Alton."

"We'll go straight to the property." Nico seemed relieved at her impersonal question. "My contractor is meeting us at four, and I figure we'll burn about an hour in Bloomington for lunch."

"Is the restaurant you bought in pretty good shape?" Deanna asked.

"I had it inspected before I closed on the deal, and the structure's solid." Nico's eyes glowed with enthusiasm. "But the inside is a complete gut. I want the place to reflect my style and my food."

"Won't that be expensive?"

"It won't be cheap." Nico's glance was speculative when he said, "I hope to get some cash from a venture capitalist."

Deanna held her breath. Did he know who she was? Maybe she should just admit that she worked for Randolph.

Before she could decide, Nico said, "I'll do whatever I have to in order to make my restaurant succeed."

Deanna snapped her mouth closed. *Nope.* This was not the time to reveal her occupation. The last thing she wanted was Nico seducing her to get his money.

Feeling a strange disappointment, Deanna heaved a sigh and said, "Tell me more about how your place will be different from all the competing restaurants."

"It'll not only be the destination for special occasions, but the menu will continually change, so people will come back to see what's new." Nico's enthusiasm was obvious. "I've been in contact with local farmers, foragers, and fisherman. I want to source the best ingredients possible and make them shine."

"That sounds intriguing."

"And I'm planning to have my own garden with no herbicides and no pesticides, just a lot of TLC and compost."

"That will definitely attract the trendier diners."

"I'm not looking for those types of people." Nico sounded insulted. "I want diners to feel nurtured and cared for as if they're coming home."

"Okay." Deanna wished she could take notes. She should have set up her cell phone to record the conversation. Evidently, she needed to brush up her undercover skills. "What kind of décor are you planning?"

"Simple." Nico shrugged. "Plain but not rustic. Definitely an open kitchen and big screened-in back porch."

Deanna's pulse jumped. Nico's vision sounded fresh and new. Exactly the kind of place people would be interested in trying. The only question in her mind was the location. Would being outside a large metropolitan area be the kiss of death?

CHAPTER EIGHT

Deanna held her breath when Nico pulled into a gravel parking lot and cut the engine. She really wanted the property to be as wonderful as Nico described.

He swept his arm toward the large building clinging to the edge of the bluff and said, "What do you think?"

"It looks as if it could hold a lot of diners," Deanna answered, not ready to give a more in-depth opinion. "Can we walk around and look at the rest of it?"

"Sure." Nico got out of the SUV, walked to the passenger side, and opened Deanna's door. "I'd love to show you where I'm putting the garden."

Deanna examined the enormous structure. She didn't know much about architecture, but it reminded her a little of the pole barns that were popular in her rural hometown. Only this one had weathered wooden siding instead of metal. It was a simple rectangle with floor-to-ceiling triple windows across the front and a massive porch. As Nico had said, the outside appeared to be in good shape.

Crossing the gravel lot, Deanna asked, "Do you plan to pave this?"

"I'll lay asphalt once the remodel is done." Nico slid an arm around her waist, his fingers brushing the skin between her T-shirt and jeans.

It was only the barest touch, but her breathing stuttered. He must have felt her sudden inhale and he pulled her closer. He stared down at her, and his heated gaze made her girly bits snap to attention.

Ignoring her hormones, Deanna stepped away from his embrace and said, "How about landscaping?"

The entrance lacked the lush perfection she'd expect of a high-end restaurant. There was an untended lawn studded with dandelions and sorely in need of mowing. The bushes and flowers looked equally neglected.

"This is pretty much it." Nico narrowed his eyes, clearly unhappy that she'd distanced herself from him. "I'm going for a natural feeling."

"Does that mean you aren't painting, either?" Deanna marched over to the building and examined the uneven siding.

"It does." Nico joined her, took her hand, and tugged her around the corner. "Isn't this terrace amazing? Picture it with comfortable chairs and some tables. It will be perfect for folks to enjoy drinks."

"Very nice." Deanna could see the after-work crowd congregating to mix and mingle. "How do you plan on attracting people?"

"I've spoken with several of the singles clubs and local online dating sites about advertising in their newsletters." Nico's thumb brushed over Deanna's knuckles and sparks shot up her arm. "I plan on venting the kitchen out here."

"Why's that?" Deanna shivered. It was difficult to concentrate when his slight caress ignited a lust she tried to ignore.

"Studies show that the aroma of food arouses a passionate response." Nico's fingers stroked up her arm. "Great chefs are inspired by both the kitchen and the bedroom. Food needs to appeal on all levels—sight, flavor, smell, and touch."

"Smart." Deanna pretended to see something, freed her hand, and strode toward the back of the building.

Nico followed, obviously not fooled. "I'll offer a special happy hour with a free tasting buffet."

"How much will that cost you?"

"We'll at least break even." Nico hurried to catch up with

her. "Even at half price, booze is a moneymaker."

As they stepped around the structure, Deanna gasped. The view was spectacular. From where they were on top of the bluff, the mighty Mississippi flowed lazily in the sun. There was a graceful cable-stayed bridge in the distance, and a paddleboat was churning its way down the river.

Tearing her eyes from the stunning panorama, Deanna turned and saw a large deck spanning the entire length of the restaurant's rear wall. A good half of the space was enclosed by screens.

Nico followed her gaze and said, "I plan to use that for private events."

"What's the capacity?"

"Fifty-five seated. More than twice that for a cocktail party," Nico answered. "There are also several interior spaces that can accommodate guests."

Nico moved behind Deanna, pulling her back against him. Immediately, his earthy scent elicited a primitive urge in her. The sudden buzz of adrenaline scared her, and once again she wiggled out of his arms.

He frowned, then his face smoothed and he said, "Ready to go inside?"

"Sure." Deanna glanced at her watch. "It's nearly four. Your contractor should be here any minute. Is he usually on time?"

"Yep." Nico guided her to the front entrance, fished a key from his pocket, and unlocked the door. "Walker's the best."

"How did you find him?" Deanna stepped over the threshold. The floor was uneven, and broken furniture littered the main area. Her nose wrinkled. The odor of rancid grease hung in the air. Nico was right. This would be a total gut job.

"Culinary school."

"He's a chef?"

"Nope," Nico laughed. "Walker was there because of a girl. When she dumped him, he quit cooking and went back to his first love, building things."

His deep, sexy chuckle sent a surge of awareness through Deanna, and she fought to control her reaction. Evidently she failed to conceal her response, because Nico grinned and looped an arm around her shoulders.

Deanna wrinkled her brow. He watched her so closely, half the time it was almost as if he could read her mind. Before she could decide what to do about Nico's seemingly clairvoyant abilities, a big red pickup roared into the parking lot. A huge man extracted himself from the truck and hurried toward the restaurant juggling several cartons.

After the boxes were deposited on the floor, the two guys exchanged manly hugs, then Nico said, "Deanna Sloan, this is Walker Deacon."

Walker drawled, "So nice of you to bring a gorgeous decoration to brighten up this dump."

"Seriously?" Deanna raised a brow. "Did you just call me an inanimate object?"

"No points for the gorgeous part?" Walker took her fingers and brushed his thumb over her knuckles.

"None whatsoever." Deanna frowned at the handsome man. "I prefer to be judged for my intelligence and personality, not my exterior. I prefer that strangers keep their hands to themselves."

"Got it." Walker grinned. "Sorry. Thorne here usually hangs with the dumb but beautiful chicks. I, on the other hand, like my women smart and sassy. I apologize for being a sexist pig."

"Accepted." Deanna's tone was brisk.

Swallowing the pang of jealousy that shot through her chest, Deanna closed her eyes. She knew Nico was the Kitchen Casanova. He'd probably introduced his friend to dozens of women, maybe hundreds. So why did the idea of him with Suzy

77

Cheerleader make her stomach ache?

* * *

While Nico made his way through the interior discussing the renovation with Walker, he kept an eye on Deanna. All the life had drained from her face, and she leaned against a wall with her arms wrapped around her middle. Was she sick?

He started to go over to check on Deanna but saw her straighten and head toward them. Clearly she'd put whatever had been bothering her aside. But what had caused her such distress?

Interrupting Nico's thoughts, Walker said, "You sure you want the kitchen completely open to the diners' scrutiny?"

"Absolutely." Nico crossed his arms and glanced at Deanna. She had physically joined the men but seemed to hold herself a bit apart from them. "With all the celebrity chefs cooking on TV, guests are now fascinated by what goes on in restaurant kitchens. They like to see the creative ways fresh ingredients can be used to make wonderful dishes. People consider a view of the chef and cooks as part of the experience of dining out."

"What would you think about using frosted glass?" Walker asked. "It would allow your diners a peek but let you decrease your equipment costs and give you a buffer from the guests' constant inspection."

"I don't mind interacting with the diners," Nico said, then paused. "But some of my kitchen staff might feel more comfortable with some distance."

"How about a rain wall?" Deanna asked. "When I was rese…reading, I saw that a chef in Seattle put in a floor-to-ceiling clear wall that had water flowing down the glass. He put in several portholes for an unclouded view. Patrons get a fascinating glimpse of the kitchen action, but no more than a peek."

"That's brilliant." Walker beamed at Deanna. "We can put in under-counter refrigeration and replace the stainless-steel kitchen tables with granite." He draped his arm across Deanna's shoulders. "To keep the kitchen clean and clutter free, we can customize the granite with holes cut for garbage cans to sit underneath, and install under-counter shelving."

Nico stared at his friend's hand on Deanna's bare shoulder and barely stifled a growl. She'd said she didn't like strangers touching her, and Walker was ignoring her wishes. Nico had never experienced such a violent surge of protectiveness and, if he was being honest, possessiveness. He couldn't deny how much the sight of another man's fingers on her skin infuriated him.

When Deanna pointedly removed Walker's arm and moved out of his reach, Nico let out the breath he hadn't realized that he'd been holding. Walker was too damn good-looking. He should never have allowed Deanna to meet him.

Deanna studied Nico for a second, then asked, "What do you think of the rain wall?"

"I like it." Nico managed to keep the irritation from his voice. "A rain wall would allow the sounds and smells that can really help work up an appetite, but permit some privacy as well."

It was hard to talk around the lump of rage in his throat. Walker needed to keep his fucking hands to himself. If he touched Deanna again, Nico might have to punch him.

Sliding his arm around Deanna's waist, Nico shot a warning glare at his friend. When she tried to step out of his embrace, he anchored her to his side and looked down at Deanna, refusing to allow her to glance away. Their gazes locked. The craving he felt for her swelled inside of him, escalating his need to make her happy. To bury himself in her warmth and make her scream his name. To make her his.

Deanna's lips were parted, and her chest rose and fell rapidly as if she were feeling the same desires. Like she couldn't get enough air in her lungs. The same lack of oxygen he seemed to experience whenever he was near her.

Nico drew in a deep breath, and Deanna's sweet fragrance enveloped him. He hardened as hunger raced through him with a fiery need only she stirred.

She enthralled him and he struggled to rein in his lust. Clenching his jaw, he summoned all his self-control.

Abruptly, Deanna jerked out of his grasp. A few seconds later she cocked her head, concentrated for a moment, then shot him a dismissive glance.

Nico narrowed his eyes. When he made love to her, he'd make her lose that aloof, disdainful look. And that was happening tonight.

While Nico fantasized about their evening together, Deanna turned to Walker and asked, "How much would a rain wall add to the renovation costs?"

"My best guess would be two to four hundred a square foot, plus a couple thousand for the operating system."

"Hmm. That sounds expensive." Deanna frowned. "I'm not sure it's worth the outlay."

"You sound like you're financing the place," Walker snickered.

"Right." Deanna's laughter seemed forced.

"But it would be something unusual to draw people to the place." Nico quickly stepped in. The last thing he wanted was to corner her into admitting she worked for Randolph. "Walker, can you get me an estimate ASAP?"

"Sure." The contractor nodded, then glanced at his watch. "Let me go over a couple more things with you, and I'll work up a price by tomorrow morning."

Deanna stayed with Nico and Walker as they discussed the

bar going against the rear wall and the bathrooms, but she didn't offer any more suggestions or opinions. Her presence caused a constant thrum inside of Nico, and he was relieved when Walker left.

While he had been saying good-bye to Walker, Deanna had stepped over to the old hostess stand. Now Nico watched her as she stared at her cell, chuckling over a text she was reading. The honeyed sound of her laughter rippled over his flesh like a caress, and he realized that it wasn't just her physical appearance that appealed to him, it was her genuineness. There was nothing fake about her.

Striding toward her, he closed the distance between them. He needed to touch her soft skin before he went insane. Without doing a damn thing other than be herself, Deanna was sheer sensuality from the top of her head to the pretty pink toenails peeking out from her sandals. She looked up as he approached, shoved her phone in her pocket, and gazed at him as if mesmerized.

Silently, Nico stroked a single fingertip along her collarbone, and his name was an uncertain plea on her lips. Deanna's wide-eyed vulnerability pounded a fist into his gut.

"We shouldn't." Deanna's husky voice was damn irresistible.

Nico's body went into sensory overload. He cupped the back of her head and demanded, "Tell me you don't want this."

"I try not to lie."

Nico saw that Deanna was fighting to control the desires that were bubbling inside of her, and he slid his fingers through her silky hair, tugging at her curls until her face was at the perfect angle for his lips.

She made an encouraging sound, and Nico's erection hardened to the point that he was in real danger of keeling over from the shortage of blood to his brain.

Leaning in until his lips barely brushed hers, a sudden question overwhelmed him. Was it possible that he wanted to do more than just seduce her? More than just claim her body? What if he wanted all of her?

At that thought, something seized in his chest. Had his heart just stopped beating?

CHAPTER NINE

When Nico's mouth met Deanna's, everything changed. She'd intended to stop him after the first touch of his fingers on her collarbone. Certainly when he'd wound her hair around his hand and tugged her toward him. But then he barely kissed her and all bets were off.

In a daze, she leaned into Nico as he held her, gliding the tip of his tongue over her lower lip, stopping only to lightly suck on it. He teased her that way until she panted for air. At her heated gasp, he sealed his mouth to hers, and every coherent thought fled her mind.

Deanna's tongue met his, stroke for greedy stroke. She'd never been kissed by a man who was able to interpret her every reaction. To capture her response and give it back to her.

Suddenly it was too much. Deanna had never been a woman who was able to go from zero to sixty in ten seconds. What was this man doing to her? She ripped herself from his arms and backed away from him.

Nico's blue eyes were almost black as they met hers in a scorching stare. Mini bursts of need exploded up her arms, and before she could stop him, he massaged the tiny bumps that had appeared.

"This is a bad idea," Deanna murmured, unable to pull away from his touch.

"Why?" Nico continued to caress her arms, moving upward until his fingers skimmed her shoulders in hypnotizing circles. "We're both single and over the age of consent."

Fueled by the need for more of his touch, more of his kisses, Deanna was struck with the almost ravenous impulse to drag him to the floor and have him take her hard and fast right here in the middle of the derelict restaurant.

Swallowing the urge, she said, "We hardly know each other and we have nothing in common."

Nico glided the tips of his fingers into her top's V-neckline and brushed against her puckered nipple. Immediately, a bolt of electricity zipped through her, and she almost missed his words when he said, "I'm guessing that we have more in common than you might want to admit."

Shit! Was he testing her? Did he know that she worked for Randolph Ventures? *No!* She was freaking herself out. But she needed to come clean with Nico about her employer before going to bed with him.

Nico continued to skim his fingers across her nipples as he said, "Making love is a great way of becoming better acquainted."

His raspy voice whiskered down her spine, and Deanna's sex clenched with need as full-scale arousal rocketed through her core. Involuntarily, she leaned into his caresses, needing more, harder, something.

With a slight grin, Nico withdrew his fingers from her breast and slipped his big hands over her bottom. He cupped both cheeks and squeezed. Pulling her up onto her tiptoes, he aligned their bodies until she could feel his erection straining against the vee of her legs.

Nico's rapid breathing shuddered against her mouth. Not quite kissing her but sensitizing her lips and making her want more.

His heart pounded in the same erratic rhythm as hers, and pure need detonated low in her belly. It felt as if she were on fire. As if she were burning from the inside out, ready to burst into flame.

Only the barest caress of his lips on hers, his erection separated from her by layers of clothing, and Deanna was already a stroke away from shattering in his arms. How did he do it?

Obviously reading her mind again, arousal flared in Nico's eyes, and he pulled her closer, grinding his hardness against her sex.

Moment to moment, the pleasure of being with him continued to shock her, and she met him thrust for thrust. They were both panting, and although she knew she should stop, she couldn't focus long enough to force herself away from the pleasure.

What was there about this man that pushed aside her common sense, turned off her brain, and made her feel instead of think? She hadn't experienced this with any of her previous lovers. What was so different about Nico?

An unfamiliar woman's voice whispered, *"Il tuo amore."* *Great!* Now she was having auditory hallucinations. *No!* She was overwrought and imagining things. The stress of her job and this situation with Nico was getting to her. He was not someone special. He was not her *amore.* And why was the voice in her head speaking Italian?

Taking a shuddering breath, Deanna wrenched herself out of his arms, moved halfway across the room, and stood with her hands on her knees, panting.

Nico stalked her like the panther he resembled. As he neared, she held up her palm and said, "Please. Stop. I need a second."

"Do I scare you, sweetheart?" His eyes gleamed with predatory satisfaction.

"You don't frighten me." Deanna inhaled sharply. "I frighten me."

"Let yourself go." Nico had somehow moved from where he had been a second ago to right next to her, and he brushed the back of his hand over her cheek. "I promise we'll be good together."

Nico was a man who usually got his way, especially where women were concerned, and that wasn't a trait she normally found attractive. But somehow, with him, she did. His confidence was intoxicating, and when he took the control out of her hands, it felt good.

However, she needed to think over the situation, and she definitely needed to tell him the truth before she had sex with him. Which meant they needed to get out of here, clean up, and go to dinner.

Feeling like the worst kind of tease, Deanna said, "Let's take a break and see how we feel later. You mentioned you had seven-thirty reservations at a restaurant you wanted to scope out, and it's nearly six now. We need to check in to the hotel and change."

"Just so you know, you aren't fooling me." Nico scowled. "And once we eat, I'll have the rest of the night to convince you to sleep with me."

"Uh-huh," Deanna murmured noncommittally.

Growling, he scooped up a carton of samples and escorted Deanna outside. He turned to lock the front door, and as he balanced the box, Deanna stared at the way the strong muscles in his arms flexed and bunched.

Who was she kidding? Blowing out a frustrated breath, Deanna admitted to herself that there wasn't a chance in hell that she wouldn't end up in Nico's bed before the evening ended.

* * *

Driving toward the hotel, Nico watched Deanna as she toyed with the silver bracelets on her wrist. She was deep in thought, a tiny line etched between her feathery brows. Something was bothering her. Was she deciding whether to admit she worked for Randolph Ventures?

From their time together, Nico was sure that the subterfuge was killing Deanna. She had a directness about her that would find misleading him difficult to tolerate. Maybe he should just admit he knew who she was. Tell her he was attracted to her, not her job.

But would she believe him? He'd allowed the deception to go on too long. Conned himself into believing that he was only seeing her to charm her into approving the investment in his restaurant. He'd waited way past the time he should have confessed his knowledge.

It was a good bet that no matter how he put it, she would feel used. Still. He couldn't make love to her with that secret between them. So after dinner, he would have to tell her the truth.

Nico pulled into the hotel lot, parked, walked around the SUV, and opened the passenger door. When Deanna didn't budge, he asked, "Ready?"

Deanna looked up as if she hadn't noticed they'd arrived. Blinking, she nodded.

"This hotel has a conference center," Nico blurted out, to fill the silence. He helped her from the SUV, grabbed their suitcases from the back, and persisted, "I've arranged to have my restaurant included in the local information folder they place in each guest room."

"Uh-huh."

Deanna's continued silence revved up Nico's nerves, and as they entered the lobby, Nico babbled, "I've made similar arrangements with hotels near the St. Louis airport."

"How far is it from the airport to here?"

"About twenty-five miles," Nico answered, relieved she was finally talking. He followed her as she marched up to the check-in counter and said, "Eventually, I'd like to get a van and provide round-trip transit, but that'll have to wait."

"You'd need to crunch the numbers to see if there would be an adequate return on investment." Deanna tilted her head.

"Of course," Nico agreed. Was this his opening? Should he bring up her employer? "I—"

"May I help you?" The clerk glanced between Nico and Deanna.

"Reservation for Thorne," Nico answered, a little relieved. It would be better to have that conversation with Deanna in private.

"Yes, sir." The woman smiled and typed on her keyboard. "Here we are. Two adjoining rooms."

"Right." Nico nodded to the clerk. Catching the surprised look on Deanna's face, he grinned and said, "What, did you think I was going to trick you into staying with me? Pretend the hotel was fully booked and there was only one room left that we would have to share? Like in the movies?"

"Maybe," Deanna murmured, her cheeks a pretty pink.

"I'm not that kind of guy." Nico traced a finger down the inside of her arm and smiled when she shivered. "I'd never force a woman to be with me."

Nico turned his attention back to the clerk, completed the check-in, and gave Deanna her key. They didn't speak on the elevator ride, and when they got to their rooms, Nico waited for Deanna to open her door, then put her suitcase on the luggage rack for her.

As he walked out, he said, "Knock on the connecting door when you're ready to go. The restaurant's only a couple blocks away, so we don't need to leave until seven twenty."

"Okay." Deanna nodded, then asked, "Should I dress up?"

"It wouldn't be a bad idea," Nico answered, then headed to his own room.

After throwing his suitcase on the bed, Nico stripped and

got into the shower. Just being around Deanna kept him semi-hard, and after almost taking her on the restaurant's floor, he needed to cool down. He had a strategy for tonight—dinner, frank discussion, and sex—none of which would happen as planned if he didn't get himself under control.

An hour later, Nico heard a timid tap and flung open the connecting door. Deanna stood on the other side looking so gorgeous she took his breath away. In a blink, his erection was at full mast.

The soft material of her dress molded her curves and although the plunging V-neckline was covered in some sort of sheer mesh, her creamy white skin played peekaboo and screamed for his caress. Then when she entered his room and he saw the dress's plunging back, he thought he'd explode without even touching her.

Realizing that he'd been staring at her, Nico cleared his throat and said, "You look beautiful."

"Thank you. I bought this yesterday on my lunch hour." Deanna's pretty green eyes sparkled. "You look great, too. I love a man in an oxford shirt."

"How about out of it?" Nico teased as he guided her into the hallway.

"That, too." She winked.

Deanna seemed different. More confident. More willing to flirt. What had happened in the forty minutes or so that they'd been apart?

Nico kept the conversation light on the short ride to the restaurant. He was determined to tamp down his lust and be a perfect gentleman.

Ushering Deanna inside, he saw that she was studying every detail of the place, and he whispered in her ear, "This will be my main competition. It's the only other fine-dining establishment in the area, but the atmosphere is a lot more formal than what I want to create."

"Which is good." Deanna pursed her soft pink lips, and Nico couldn't stop himself from pressing a brief kiss on them. She quirked a brow at him and continued her thought, "Distinctive is better. If you were opening a similar venue, this restaurant's diners would likely stay loyal and not try your place."

Nico nodded, then turned to the hostess and gave his name. Once they were seated at a window table and the hostess left, he said, "Although I've looked into this restaurant, I haven't eaten here." He cocked his head. "Even if you aren't able to finish it all, I'd like to order a full four-course meal so we can taste everything."

"Definitely." Deanna wrinkled her nose. "Let's just hope the chef doesn't come storming out because I left food on my plate."

"I'll defend you," Nico laughed. "Will you trust me to order for us?"

"Absolutely." Deanna wrinkled her nose. "As you may have gathered, I'm not a foodie."

"I'm determined to change that," Nico said. Ignoring her dismissive snort, he added, "Just you wait and see."

When their server appeared, Nico ordered a bottle of Taittinger Brut La Française, then examined the menu.

Once their waitress returned and had poured the sparkling wine, he looked at her and said, "We're going to start with the crab cakes and blue cheese kabobs. Next we'd like the baby greens with apple and the goat cheese salads. For our entrées we'll have the duck and the scallops. And for dessert, the butterscotch and walnut bread pudding and the gooey butter cake."

After the server left to turn in their order, they chatted until their appetizers were served. Up until that point, Nico had been having fun, but as the courses progressed and each dish tasted better than the previous one, his mood darkened.

Finally, after sampling both desserts, Nico said, "This place is damn impressive. Opening a restaurant so close by might be a problem."

Deanna picked up her champagne flute and sipped before she said, "I still think you'll be okay. People who come here are looking for a different experience than what you're offering."

She paused, drank again, then continued, "From what you told me, you're going for more of a wholesome, fresh milieu. Family friendly and fun rather than formal and stiff."

"True." Nico took her hand. "I want to enjoy cooking again. Apart from sex, cooking is among the most sensual experiences on the planet." He stared into Deanna's eyes until her pupils dilated and both their breathing became shallow. "I want my guests to enjoy eating without all the heaviness that so many fine-dining establishments bring to the table. I want it to be a pure pleasure."

"I have every confidence that's precisely what you'll be able to do." Deanna straightened, squeezed his fingers, then said, "And because I believe in your vision, I have something I need to tell you."

Holy hell! Nico struggled to keep his expression blank. This was it. The big reveal. He only hoped that Deanna would still want to be with him after she found out that he'd known her secret all along.

CHAPTER TEN

Deanna's mouth was suddenly so dry she couldn't swallow. Maybe she should have waited until they were in private to tell Nico about her employer. That had been her original plan, but when he'd given her the perfect opening, the words just popped out of her mouth.

Having made up her mind during the restaurant inspection to recommend that Randolph Ventures invest in Nico's business, the minute she was alone in her hotel room, Deanna had fired up her laptop. She'd done a little more research, then completed her report. Once she'd saved it, she'd taken a quick shower and dressed. And then, after a thorough reread, she'd clicked send.

Now that there was no longer any need to keep her job a secret, Deanna had intended to tell Nico everything the minute they returned to the hotel room. Wishing that she had stuck to the original plan, she gathered her thoughts.

While she'd been holding the lengthy internal conversation with herself, Nico had been silently staring at her.

Pushing her glass of water toward her, he said, "Take your time."

His voice was soothing and his expressive blue eyes soft. He was being so sweet. How long would that last after she told him the truth?

After taking a sip of water, Deanna held the cool glass to her cheek. She was burning up. Was she having a hot flash? Maybe she was going into early menopause.

Finally, she put the glass down and said, "Do you remember me telling you that I worked in finance?"

"Yes. I remember everything you've ever said to me." Nico captured her restless fingers, held her hand, and teased, "Are you going to tell me that you're really a jet-setting socialite?"

"No." Deanna's pulse raced. He needed to stop being so nice to her. Ignoring the trickle of fear sliding through her, she said, "I'm a venture capitalist. I work for Randolph Ventures."

"I kn—"

Nico was interrupted when the hostess and a man dressed in a double-breasted white chef's jacket appeared at their table and said, "Chef Thorne. My wife told me you were our guest tonight."

"Thank you for a wonderful meal. Your food was delicious." Nico let go of Deanna's fingers, stood, and shook hands. "Please call me Nico and this is Deanna."

"I'm Bryan Caulker and this is my wife, Serita." Bryan slid his arm around his wife's waist and winked. "She's a big fan of yours."

"Have you eaten at LeBoeuf?"

"We have." Serita smiled shyly. "After I read the magazine article about you, I insisted we dine there on our last trip into Chicago."

"I hope my cooking lived up to your expectations," Nico said.

Deanna watched as Nico charmed the woman. It was clear that although Serita loved her husband, she was a bit dazzled by Nico.

"It certainly did." Bryan hugged his wife to his side. "What brings you to Alton?"

Deanna shot a look at Nico, who shrugged. No use trying to hide his intentions.

"I bought the old Riverside Restaurant." Nico shoved his hands in the pockets of his dress slacks. "I'm renovating it and am going to open my own place." He glanced at Deanna. "I'm just waiting for the final bit of financing to come through before I make any announcements."

Deanna held her breath. Would the other chef be angry that Nico was invading his territory?

A long second ticked by, then Bryan clapped Nico on the back and said, "Welcome to town. Let me know next time you're going to be here, and we'll have a little party to introduce you to some of the other chefs in the area."

"Thanks, man." Nico beamed. "As soon as the money comes through, I'll be moving down here permanently. It'd be great to meet folks."

"Awesome." Bryan flicked a glance at Deanna and said, "If you're around, we'd love to have you join us, as well."

"Thanks." Deanna smiled, but her heart was heavy.

The chance of her and Nico still dating by then was slim to none. Even if he didn't hate her for hiding her real job, according to the magazine article, the Kitchen Casanova's romances rarely lasted more than a couple of weeks. Her time was already nearly over.

When a large group of people appeared at the hostess stand, Serita excused herself, and after a few more minutes of conversation, Bryan said, "I've got to get back to the kitchen." He shook Nico's hand and added, "Great meeting you both. Don't be strangers."

Deanna's soul basked in being treated as Nico's girlfriend. But her brain sneered at her for believing any kind of real relationship was possible. She feared that Nico was like candy. A moment on the lips and forever a burden on her heart.

Once the Caulkers were gone and the server dropped off their check, Deanna said, "I'm a bit surprised at how friendly Bryan and Serita were toward you."

"You were expecting an asshole chef like the ones you see on those television cooking competitions?" Nico raised a teasing brow.

"Or at least some resentment." Deanna tipped her head.

"Are all chefs so nice?"

"Like any profession, we have our jerks, but for the most part, it's a small enough world that the vast majority of chefs believe what goes around comes around." Nico shrugged. "Being angry at the competition is a waste of energy. A part of having a successful restaurant is luck, but mostly it's the food, the service, and the atmosphere that makes or breaks a place."

"And I believe you'll have all three, so here's to your restaurant." Deanna picked up her champagne flute and toasted him.

After Nico clinked his glass to hers and drank, he asked, "Where were we before the Caulkers showed up?"

"I was confessing that I work for the venture capital firm that you're hoping will finance your business." Deanna, needing some liquid courage, took another gulp of the Taittinger. "And I was about to admit that I was the one assigned to assess your restaurant's potential."

Nico opened his mouth, but Deanna rushed to add, "That's why I was at LeBoeuf the night we met. But my boss wasn't satisfied with my report. He wanted a more comprehensive analysis, and he didn't want me to reveal that I was the associate investigating you."

When Nico was silent, Deanna added, "I'm so sorry to have deceived you, but it really was better for both of us this way. I was able to get a much more in-depth picture, and you were able to tell me about your plans without feeling you had to sell yourself."

"Well," Nico started, "that all may be true, but the problem is—"

Deanna interrupted him again, "This afternoon at the hotel, I finished my report and recommended that we invest in your restaurant."

"That's fantastic." Nico grinned for a moment, then his

smile faded. "Now I have to tell you something."

"Oh?" Deanna gritted her teeth. A statement like that rarely ended with good news.

"I…" Nico cleared his throat, drained his champagne glass, and said, "I've known who you were from the beginning."

"When you joined me at LeBoeuf?" Deanna frowned. He sure hadn't acted like he knew she was evaluating him that night.

"Not then, no." Nico grabbed her hand and held fast when she tried to free her fingers. "But I couldn't get you out of my mind. Then when I told my brother I wanted to find you, Marco located your credit card slip, and since you used your corporate Visa…"

"You figured out why I was at the restaurant." Deanna's heart clenched and she jerked her hand out of his grasp. "That's why you've been pursuing me ever since." She pushed her chair back and sprinted out of the dining room.

* * *

Fuck! Nico shot to his feet. Deanna had jumped to the exact conclusion that he'd been afraid she'd reach. He rushed after her but stopped and trotted back to the table. Digging out his wallet, he shoved his AmEx into the check folder, then went in search of his runaway date.

When he reached the entrance, Serita was behind the hostess stand. She glanced at him, tilted her head as if considering her options, then shrugged and pointed toward a short corridor. Nodding his thanks, Nico hurried into the hallway.

Faced with the door to the ladies' room, Nico lurched to a halt and swore. *Now what?*

Folding his arms, he leaned against the wall and prepared to wait. He might not be able to go in, but Deanna had to come out sometime.

Minutes ticked by. Was Deanna really in there? What if she'd left the building, but in some sort of female solidarity, Serita had misdirected him?

He glanced back toward the hostess stand. If Serita had led him astray, would she admit it?

No women had gone in or out of the restroom since he'd been watching. If Deanna was in there, she was alone. Time to find out.

Grabbing his cell from his pocket, he dialed Deanna's number. When he heard the *Hell's Kitchen* theme song "Fire," he smiled. She'd given him his own ringtone. That had to be a good sign.

Nico knocked on the door and called, "Deanna, let me explain."

Nothing.

He hated the silent treatment. Nico ground his teeth in frustration. He'd have to go inside.

Nico eased the door open a couple of inches and shouted, "Warning! Man entering."

When there were no screams of indignation, he stepped over the threshold and looked around. The sink and mirror area was classy with lots of dark wood and a nice quartz countertop. Unfortunately, it was also empty. And all the full-length oak stall doors were shut.

Nico tried dialing Deanna's number again, but this time there was no song. Evidently, she'd figured out his strategy and muted her phone.

He clenched his jaw to keep his irritation from bubbling to the surface. *Yes.* She had a right to be angry, but she was being ridiculous.

Raising his voice, Nico said, "I'm sorry for not telling you I knew who you were, but you owe me a chance to explain."

When there was no response, he added, "You're just as guilty as I am."

Seconds dragged by, and Nico was contemplating the difficulty of picking the locks on the bathroom stalls, when the door at the far end swung open.

His gut felt as if he'd been hit with a cast-iron frying pan. Deanna's eyes were red and it was clear she'd been crying. It was painful seeing such a strong woman upset. Especially knowing that he was the cause of her tears. He'd hurt her at a level so deep she couldn't maintain her customary mask of indifference. The façade that she used to defend herself from assholes like him had been breached.

He hurried to her and took her in his arms. She stiffened, but he held tight and murmured into her hair, "We were both wrong. When I came to your apartment to apologize for my behavior, I should have admitted that I knew you worked for Randolph Ventures."

"And that same night, I should have told you why I had been at LeBoeuf." Deanna's voice was so low that Nico could barely make out her words.

"Why didn't you?" Nico leaned back so he could see her face.

"When you first showed up, I was so shocked it didn't even occur to me to say anything." Deanna's brows drew together. "Then when I had time to think, I intended to just eat and get rid of you."

"But that wasn't how it went down." Nico tucked a curl behind her ear.

"No." Her face reddened. "I wasn't... When you kissed me..."

"Everything changed," Nico completed her thought and cupped her cheeks. "For me, too."

"You swept into my calm, orderly life." Deanna leaned into

his palms. "And I kept doing things I knew I shouldn't."

"But then we were interrupted by a phone call," Nico encouraged.

He wanted to forget all about playing true confession, just kiss the hell out of her and get back to the hotel ASAP. But the small part of his brain not connected to his dick knew they needed to talk this out. Then he'd kiss the hell out of her, take her back to the hotel, and make love to her all night long.

"As you probably guessed, it was my boss calling." Deanna rolled her eyes. "Randolph was not pleased with my initial report on you, and I had to tell him that it was just a preliminary summary and that I planned on doing a more in-depth analysis."

"Which meant you needed to get the inside scoop on me and my plans."

"Yep." Deanna sighed. "Without you discovering that I was investigating you."

"So you pretended to be interested in a romantic relationship and spied on me?"

Nico's chest tightened. Was the attraction he felt for her one-sided?

"I was spying on you." Deanna chewed her bottom lip and Nico's pulse raced. "But I never had to pretend to want to be with you. It was all I could do not to let our relationship become sexual."

"You were pretty damn good at wiggling away and distracting me." Nico recalled how she'd kept him at arm's length up until now.

"It wasn't easy." Deanna's tiny smile sent a flicker straight to Nico's crotch.

"And sex was a bad idea because...?" Nico asked, enjoying how pink the conversation turned her fair skin.

"Because sleeping with you while I was investigating you felt too much like women who screw their bosses to further their careers."

"And now?" Nico pressed his mouth to her temple. "How do you feel about sharing my bed now?"

"Well." She gazed up at him, and the tip of her tongue swept her bottom lip. "Now, I'm wondering how fast you can get us back to your room."

CHAPTER ELEVEN

Deanna clung to the SUV's panic strap as Nico took a turn so fast she could have sworn only two wheels were on the pavement. They were silent as Nico drove them to the hotel. He was obviously concentrating on breaking the speed of light barrier, and she was focused on not throwing up. Maybe she should have mentioned that she had a tendency to get motion sick.

Once they reached the parking lot and found an empty spot, Nico turned off the ignition, leaped out, and ran around the hood to open Deanna's door. He gripped her elbow and hurried her toward the hotel entrance. As they stood waiting for the elevator, Nico curved an arm around her and nestled her to his side.

Deanna tensed.

"What?" Nico looked down at her, concern wrinkling his forehead.

"I'm not comfortable with public displays of affection."

"No one's watching us."

Deanna looked around. He was right.

"Mmm." Melting against him, she allowed her lust-addled brain to take over and burrowed her fingers between his shirt and pants. His back was hard and smooth and so hot she almost ignited.

Inside the mercifully empty elevator, Nico pulled her closer and took her mouth. His kiss was deeper than she thought possible. It consumed her, stealing her breath away. He seemed determined to take everything she had, and she feared her heart was on that list.

When they reached their floor, Nico lifted his lips from hers and asked, "Yours or mine?"

Deanna barely recognized his guttural voice or her own hoarse reply, "Yours. It's closer."

"I like the way you think, baby." Nico's grin was infectious. He kept her plastered against him as they walked down the long hallway. After using his key card to unlock the door, he ushered her inside. As soon as they'd both crossed the threshold, he flicked on the light, backed her against the smooth steel panel, and turned the deadbolt. He pressed his hard length into her soft curves until there wasn't an inch of her body left untouched.

Framing her face with his hands, he leaned his forehead against hers and sighed. Deanna's heart sank. Was he having second thoughts?

An instant later, Nico's hungry mouth came down on hers. As he devoured her, Deanna wound her arms around his neck, opened her lips, and shamelessly begged for whatever he could give her.

Nico's tongue stroked deeply, and the blast of pure desire that rocketed up Deanna's spine pushed away all her remaining qualms. She quivered as an acetylene torch of blistering desire ignited her insides. A fiery spike of need blazed all the way from her nipples to between her thighs.

How long had she been suppressing her wants? It had started when she eliminated everything that tasted good from her diet. Then she'd sacrificed friendship. And finally, she'd forfeited love. Well, for this one night, these few hours, she would open herself up and take it all back.

Deanna gasped for air when Nico's lips left hers and wandered down her throat. As he pressed openmouthed kisses along her collarbone and into her neckline, she panted, trying to catch her breath.

"Off," she gasped, yanking at his sleeve. Although she was far from cold, her hands trembled as she fumbled open the buttons, then stripped the shirt from his body. She was desperate to get him naked, to touch his bare skin.

Running her palms over his chest, she felt his muscles tense beneath her fingertips. Arousal buzzed low in her stomach, and she pushed him slightly away so she could run her lips from the hollow of his throat to the tiny dip of his belly button.

The peppery smell of his aftershave was tantalizing, and need prickled through Deanna's core. As she reached for Nico's belt, goose bumps rose on her arms. Fumbling with the cold metal buckle, she stabbed herself with the prong. But before she could release the clasp, he grasped her shoulders, halting her progress.

Deanna's eyes shot to his, her brow furrowed in confusion. Why was he stopping her?

"It's your turn." Nico's voice had a gravelly quality that liquefied Deanna's legs.

"M-my turn?" she stuttered.

"My shirt is off," Nico explained, a crease appearing in his tanned cheek. "It's your turn to lose some, no, make that all, of your clothes."

"Oh." Deanna moved away from him. "Of course. Sure. How about we turn off the light?"

She was astonished at her reluctance. As turned on as she was, why did removing her dress cause a lump to form in her throat? She frowned. Was it because she wanted Nico to find her attractive? Needed him to like the far-from-perfect body he was about to see?

Although she'd dieted and exercised, her stomach still wasn't perfectly flat. Plus her thighs were too big, muscled from her workouts. And those were just the most obvious imperfections.

Glancing at Nico, she saw his perplexed expression. Then he shrugged and flicked off the overhead bulb. Deanna scowled. The moon shined too brightly through the sheer curtains. It illuminated the room like a spotlight.

Nico stepped toward her and ran his thumb from the plunging vee back of her dress to the bottom of the full skirt.

Arching an inquiring brow, he asked, "Zipper?"

Deanna took a deep breath and said, "On the side."

Wanting more than anything to please him, she turned slightly and raised her arm. He guided the tab slowly downward and she straightened her spine. Why was this so hard? She hadn't minded her previous boyfriends seeing her naked. Was that because she hadn't cared as much about their opinion as she did about Nico's?

He slid the straps off of her shoulders, and her dress pooled at her ankles, leaving her with only a pale pink bra and lacy panties. She kept her gaze down. The fear that she'd see disappointment on his handsome face paralyzed her breathing. Hearing Nico's sharp inhale, the sensation of being vulnerable and exposed made her raise her arms to cover herself.

"No." Nico's voice was firm. He gripped her fingers in one large hand and held them over her head. "Let me see you."

She glanced at him through her lashes, and the desire on his face made her feel beautiful for the first time in her life. In the dim light, his eyes smoldered with passion. She wanted to be with him, even if it was only this one time. She'd take these precious moments and engrave them into her memory to replay again and again when he was gone.

Nico grasped her chin and tilted it upwards. The worshipful look he gave her was profoundly intimate. When she flushed, he pulled her close, his arms folding around her until she couldn't remember how to be any way separate from him.

"You are so gorgeous." Nico's reverent whisper washed over her soul, soothing her fears and calming her anxieties.

His breath in her ear spiked her nipples and made her throb lower down. Feelings she'd tried to ignore wound their way to a spot she'd sworn to keep safe from a man like Nico. A spot suspiciously near her heart.

As he reached for the clasp of her bra, an incessant craving overcame any thoughts Deanna had of resistance. She'd take this one night and enjoy every moment of his touch. And if, in the morning, this single evening was all she had, she'd deal with the hurt then. But in the meantime, she would indulge her desires.

* * *

Nico allowed Deanna to tug him out of the moonlight. He knew she was feeling self-conscious, and if, this first time, she needed the darkness, he wouldn't deny her the shadows. Although he would have to fix that pretty damn quickly because very, very soon, he was going look his fill at her beautiful body.

But for now, he'd give in to her modesty. Because unlike the women he'd been with in the past, it wasn't just her body that called to him. It was her. Before Deanna, he'd always grown bored after a few dates and stopped calling.

But Deanna fascinated him. Her contrasting personalities intrigued him. He'd seen her smoothly sophisticated in a designer dress and heels at LeBoeuf. As a fierce competitor in the boxing ring. And sweetly enthusiastic when they'd explored his new restaurant.

Her sharp mind and even sharper wit were as erotic as her soft curves and gorgeous face. Nico had never met anyone like her.

He loved the shine of intelligence in her big green eyes. And when her emotions took over, when she lowered her thick dark lashes to shield her thoughts, his sense of deprivation was crushing. He wouldn't let her hide from him tonight. He needed to see the sparkle when she was happy and the heat when he entered her.

Nico hid a smile. She had maneuvered them into the

DENISE SWANSON

dimmest corner of the room between an armchair and the bed and was yanking off his pants, taking his socks and shoes at the same time. Once he was in nothing but his boxer briefs, she paused as if unsure what to do next.

Realizing that she needed to regroup before they took the next step, Nico made no attempt to remove her panties. Instead he stroked her back and murmured into her hair, "No need to rush. We have all night."

Several long seconds later, her breathing slowed. When she burrowed against his chest and wrapped her arms around his waist, he put a finger under her chin to raise her lips to his. *Interesting.* Although sensual as hell, there was a naïveté in Deanna's kiss. Why did that please him so much?

From what she'd told him, she had to be in her late twenties or early thirties, so he would have sworn she'd have had a fair amount of sexual experience. Instead, she seemed almost innocent. A trait so rare in Nico's life it made something awaken deep inside his soul.

The fact that she hadn't shared this kind of intimacy with dozens of others sent a stab of possessive need through him. Made him want to ensure that no man except him ever touched her again.

As he deepened his kiss, Nico's hands stroked the curve of her hips. Tunneling inside her lacy underwear to palm the supple flesh of her generous bottom, he molded her against his hardness. The feeling of her pressed against his rock-hard erection was indescribable.

Deanna's soft gasp warmed Nico's lips, and the cloud of emotion swirling in her mint-colored eyes heated him to his core, but he continued to move slowly. If he pushed her too fast, he risked her running away. And if she distanced herself from him this time, it might be for good.

Before tonight, she was able to rationalize continuing to see him. She could justify her actions as a necessary business arrangement. But now, if he let her withdraw, she would have no excuse for allowing him into her well-ordered life. No defense for her lack of self-control.

As he continued to tangle his tongue with hers, he removed one hand from her bottom and skimmed it down her front, pausing when he reached the top of her panties. She stiffened and her eyes popped open, uncertainty flickering in the depths.

Nico met her gaze and said softly, "Trust me."

She gave a brief nod and he resumed kissing her, caressing her bottom as he coaxed her to let him continue. To let him give her more.

After a second, she relaxed, but gasped when Nico slid a finger beneath the elastic and into her slick folds. He was already beyond hard, beyond aching for her, but forced himself to delay his own satisfaction. He wanted their foreplay to be all about her arousal. Her pleasure.

Against her mouth, he whispered, "Hearing you breathe like that is the ultimate turn-on. Knowing that I've excited you, I can't explain what that does for me. It's like you've given me a gift. The gift of your desire."

Deanna's eyes darkened, and she delved under the band of his boxer briefs, engulfing his erection in a determined grip. The slight smile playing along her lips made Nico realize that despite her lack of experience, she wouldn't be a passive participant.

Her silky palm caressed his length, and Nico instinctively thrust into her hand. His head told him that he had to stop soon or it would be over before they really got started. But his body refused to listen.

As Deanna stroked him, Nico continued to tease her damp folds, sliding from the apex down to her wet opening. The eager sounds she made drove him wild, and her eyes, heavy-lidded with longing, pushed him even higher.

Making himself pull away from her heavenly touch, he swept the covers from the bed, hastily removed her panties, and laid her on the mattress. Her deep green eyes scoured his face, but he was relieved that she didn't shrink from him or tell him to stop.

Ridding himself of his underwear, Nico climbed next to Deanna and stretched out by her side. He rested his head on his hand, gazing at her creamy hills and valleys. When she frowned and tried to sit up, to cover herself, he placed a palm on her stomach. She settled back, but Nico wasn't risking her having second thoughts.

Pressing kisses from the hollow of her shoulder to just below her belly button, he rubbed her mound, trailing downward until he was at her glistening entrance. He slid a finger inside of her, slowly pushing in and out.

When she moved her hips trying to increase the speed of his rhythm, he murmured, "Tell me when what I do makes you feel good."

Her needy response was all the encouragement Nico required, and he sheathed a finger inside of her creamy tunnel. He felt her internal muscles ripple around his finger and added a second, accelerating his thrusts.

Deanna's eyes drifted closed, and incoherent sounds of hunger and craving tumbled from her parted lips. Her head whipped back and forth on the pillow, and her nails scraped the sheet, nearly shredding it.

Nico curled his fingers, searching for the slightly rough, puffy patch inside of her that would bring her the most pleasure. Once he found her sweet spot, he used his thumb to swipe her tight pulsing bud until she screamed his name and shuddered her release.

CHAPTER TWELVE

Previous boyfriends had never been able to get Deanna off with their fingers or, for that matter, any other way. It had always felt too awkward. Too much loss of control. She'd worried too much about how she looked naked, if she was moving enough or too much, what she should say. She'd never been able to relax enough to orgasm.

So she'd been astonished at the first quiver that washed through her. The next had been a surprise. But it was the final blast of pleasure that shot her into an upward spiral of bliss. Afterwards, all she could do was lay stunned, riding the tidal wave of delight.

Deanna's body felt alien, as if it belonged to someone else and she was occupying it but had no control over it. And her mind seemed unable to form a single lucid thought. Both sensations were confusing, like she'd stepped through a wormhole to another dimension—one filled with warmth and brightness and pleasure.

Before she could recover, Nico's talented fingers began to move again. His strokes were faster, harder, and even more persistent than the first time. Sooner than she dreamed possible, the sensations reignited. Tremors burst like fireworks, one sparking the other until she gave a soundless cry and broke into a million pieces of light.

A few seconds, or maybe a few years later, Deanna's mind revved up and she frowned. She never let her body take over. Never stopped thinking. Never allowed herself just to feel. Could losing her heart to Nico be far behind?

No! She couldn't allow that. It was time to regain some control over the situation. When she tried to sit up, Nico caught her wrists in one large hand and gently held her arms above her head. Before she could struggle, he used his legs to pin hers to the mattress.

Deanna started to protest, but then her gaze snagged on the handsome man looming over her. She had seen his chest more times in her fantasies than she'd ever admit, but the reality was unbelievably better.

Nico was more impressively built than even the trainers at her gym. He was so big, so perfect, so...intimidating was the only word that came to mind.

Warm olive skin attesting to his Italian heritage covered his firm pecs and hard abs. Flat, brown nipples were barely visible in the tangle of dark hair tapering downward toward his narrow waist. His bronze body was like a flawless sculpture against the white sheet.

Forcing herself to look away, she glanced at Nico's face. His flowing black hair covered a perfectly shaped head. And as she met his blue, blue eyes, their sensual shimmer sent heat sizzling down her spine.

"I've dreamed of seeing you this way," he said, staring at her as his thumb stroked the wrists he held.

Tearing her gaze from his, Deanna heaved a sigh of regret. Nico was too perfect for her. His aristocratic background, his body, his...she gulped...his gorgeous erection. His arousal was more than breathtaking, it was overwhelming. And as she looked at it, jutting out from the thatch of dark curls, it grew thicker and longer.

Pushing aside her reservations, Deanna resolved to enjoy the moment. She lifted her head and pressed her mouth to Nico's, kissing him with a passion she hadn't known she possessed. He tasted as if it were the last cupcake on earth, and she was ready to devour him.

When their lips parted, Nico's eyes were dilated until there was only a thin rim of blue. Freeing her wrists, he used both hands to caress her breasts. He stroked and squeezed nearer and nearer, tormenting her with his touch but never going quite far enough.

Deanna was unable to take the torturous need building up inside of her, and her lashes fluttered to her cheeks. At that moment, Nico grasped her nipples, rolling them between his thumb and index finger until the near pain turned to exquisite pleasure.

Demanding little licks of fire ignited along her skin. Then Nico took her nipple in his mouth, and when he sucked it, she arched off the mattress.

"Too much. Too good." Deanna fisted his hair, but he overrode her objections and switched his attention to her other breast.

Continuing to tongue her nipple, Nico guided Deanna's right hand to his erection. The smooth skin covering his hard length was like heated velvet, and she rubbed her fingers in the same rhythm as Nico's mouth worked her breast.

He groaned and settled into the intimate vee of her body, allowing the movement of her palm to stimulate them both. As she twisted and turned, hunger built in her core and arousal overwhelmed her thoughts.

Seeming to sense her growing need, Nico reached over to the bedside table and snatched a foil packet. Breathlessly, Deanna watched him roll the thin latex down his shaft.

As he knelt above her, he paused and asked, "Are you all right with this?"

When she nodded, Nico entered her slowly, inch by inch, until he was fully seated. With a gasp of elation, she felt the stretch and the fullness of him completely inside of her. And when her tunnel slickened, he began to move.

Speechless with the depth of her emotion, she caressed the

deep valley of his spine, trying to convey what she felt for him through her touch.

As the sensations increased, she whispered disjointed words. Unable to articulate what she wanted, needed, she made incoherent sounds urging him deeper and harder until sparks of pure bliss splintered through her soul.

The tension built, and every fragment of her body melted in a fiercely liquefying thrill that unlocked her release. A couple of thrusts later, Nico followed her into paradise.

They lay unmoving for several minutes, then Nico shifted off of her. Deanna frowned until she realized he was getting rid of the condom. A few seconds later, the bed dipped as he climbed onto the mattress and pulled her against him.

He cupped her head and nestled it into the hollow of his shoulder. His right arm held her close to his side as his other hand caressed her hair, her cheek, her throat. Nico's tenderness overwhelmed her and she blinked back tears. Her heart swelled. No one had ever taken such care with her, as if she were someone important to them.

Deanna snuggled, intent on remembering every single moment of this night. She wanted to tuck away all the touches and pleasures. That way, later, when Nico was gone and she was alone again, she could take them out and replay the experience frame by frame. Enjoying in her imagination what she no longer had in her life.

* * *

After they both took separate trips to the bathroom to clean up, they must have dozed off for a while, because when Nico felt Deanna's palm slide over his chest, his eyes popped open. Pulling her closer to his side, he ran his thumb gently over her ribs.

Was she aware of how her body instinctively sought his, not only in bed but anytime they were near each other? How could she miss the way that her curves fit against his hollows as if they'd been one loaf of bread that had been cut into two? Did she feel the same sense of completeness that he did when they were together?

He gazed into her half-closed eyes and savored the softness he found there.

"I..." Deanna stammered, her cheeks an adorable pink. "I don't usually... I mean, it's never been like that for me before..."

"Baby, I'd wager it's never been like that for anyone before."

Nico brushed his lips over her temple, then, powerless to resist, he kissed down the side of her face and sought her mouth. His tongue licked against the seam, and when she opened, he swept inside. Unable to keep his hands off of her, he teased her nipples until they once again resembled his favorite cinnamon jelly beans.

Deanna broke their kiss. "So you haven't...?"

"Uh-uh." Nico knew she needed to hear the words. "This is totally unique."

He'd never joined with a woman so completely. When he'd seated himself so deeply inside her body, he'd felt a surge of fundamental rightness. Thinking about it, pressure swelled in his chest. He'd long ago locked away his heart, but suddenly, it felt as if it was trying to break free. Unwilling to allow it to escape, he reclaimed her mouth.

Instantly, the kiss became intense, scorching, enthralling. Deanna's silken lips and velvet tongue seduced away his reason. And when she pushed him flat on his back and straddled him, all he could do was moan, surprised that he was already hard again.

The insides of her soft knees rested against his hips, and she held her beautiful body poised over his. After reaching for a condom from the nightstand, she quickly tore open the packet and sheathed him. Then, lowering herself slowly over his straining erection, she took him in inch by inch until her slick tunnel fully surrounded him.

The sudden wave of wet heat nearly liquefied his spine. The sensation was so forceful Nico was stunned, and for an instant, the world seemed to stop spinning on its axis. On one hand, it felt as if he and Deanna had been making love for years; on the other, it felt as if this was the first time he'd ever been with a woman.

As their bodies slid together then apart, the fusing electrified his nerve endings and enhanced all his senses. The air around them seemed to change. With each breath he took, it became heavier and heavier, until his lungs felt as if they would burst with each inhalation.

Unadulterated desire shot through his veins and he wanted more of her. More of her snug channel squeezing him with a silken grip. More of her moans begging for release. More of her heart.

Looking up at the magnificent woman bringing him so much pleasure, Nico knew he couldn't bear to lose her. Could never let her go.

As she tightened around him, he leaned up, resting on his elbows. Finding her lips, he caught her scream of bliss in his mouth and savored every last sound as she reached her climax. The whimpers of her pleasure tasted like the finest French champagne, and he didn't want to waste a drop.

Without breaking their connection, Nico effortlessly flipped Deanna onto her back. When her inner muscles clenched his shaft, refusing to allow it to leave her body, his eyes locked on hers and his heart slammed against his chest.

The connection was more than just physical. The words *amore mio* echoed inside his head, and a fierce possessiveness flooded through him. He'd known from the very beginning that she was different. Now, he finally admitted it to himself.

As he plunged into her liquid heat again and again, a long, honeyed surge of ecstasy ran from his belly up to his chest and into his heart. It was the purest joy he'd ever known.

Wanting them to experience the bliss together, Nico reached between them. At his first stroke, he felt Deanna's breath hitch. At the second, her pulse started to race. Then her channel rippled around his erection, and it only took one more thrust before a white-hot burn hurtled him over the edge.

As he held her tightly, together they rode the waves of pleasure until the exquisite sensations of their lovemaking faded away. Nico reluctantly withdrew from her enclosing warmth, dealt with the condom, and then eased her back into his arms.

After Deanna's breathing evened out and her eyes drifted closed, Nico struggled to understand what had just happened between them. This was supposed to have been just another fun interlude with a woman he found attractive. When had his feelings changed, become so intense he felt like they might suffocate him?

Nico knew that there was no way Deanna was ready to hear what he was thinking. *Hell!* Even if she was, he wasn't ready to say it out loud.

They both needed some time to process the experience. It was entirely possible that in the morning things would look different. His emotions would be back under control, and his heart would have retreated behind the brick wall that he'd built for it the day his father deserted his mother.

Slowly moving away from Deanna's soft, sweet curves, he fled to the bathroom. He needed to put some distance between them. Was there any nice way of suggesting that Deanna sleep in her own room?

CHAPTER THIRTEEN

Deanna resisted coming fully awake. If this was a dream, it was the best one that she'd ever had, and she didn't want it to end. Cradled in Nico's arms, her whole world had narrowed down to him, the moment, and a sense of contentment she'd never before experienced.

For several long minutes, she lay perfectly still, her eyes clenched shut. But she couldn't shut off her brain forever, and her mind slowly switched back on. It whirred noisily like an annoying exhaust fan, reminding her that for the first time since she'd become an adult, she'd done something spontaneous, irrational, and quite possibly life altering.

Under Nico's hands, his mouth, his body, every single one of her protective walls had crumbled. He had seen her at her most vulnerable and taken care of her. Was that why she felt closer to him than she ever had to any other man?

With the truth staring starkly at her through her closed eyelids, Deanna was powerless to deny that making love with Nico had been shattering. It wasn't the fun diversion or the little treat she'd expected. It was more, a lot more than she could handle.

He had looked at her like no one else ever had. Like she was beautiful and desirable, and like he couldn't get enough of her. He hadn't noticed her flaws. Or told her that if she just worked a little harder, changed one more thing about herself, then she might finally be good enough for his love.

Evidently, all of his easy charm and love-'em-and-leave-'em reputation hid the true man inside of Nico. And that guy was devastating.

If the Kitchen Casanova grew tired of her, she would've

been unhappy for a few weeks. But if this other Nico, the one he'd just shown her, threw her aside and moved on, she wasn't sure she'd be able to survive the loss.

She couldn't fall for him. She had to get away before he came back from the bathroom. She jumped up and grabbed her dress from the floor. Where was her underwear? She heard the toilet flush. He'd be out any second now.

There was no time to search for her panties and bra. It was a shame that they were her favorite set, but she'd have to sacrifice the lingerie in order to make her escape. Maybe she could retrieve it in the morning.

Deanna was nearly to the connecting door when Nico walked into the bedroom. She froze. His gaze met hers and he frowned. Before she could move, he crossed the short distance to her, wrapping his arms around her waist and pulling her against him.

"Where are you going?" He nibbled at her earlobe until her resolve thawed and her dress slipped from her grasp.

"My room?" Deanna heard the question in her voice and swore at herself. But she couldn't stir up any enthusiasm to end his embrace.

"Why?" Nico's mouth brushed a burning trail down her throat.

"To sleep?" Again, instead of a statement, Deanna's tone was uncertain.

"Stay." Nico took her hand and drew her toward the inviting bed.

"But—"

"Let's see. How can I convince you?" Nico gently lifted her onto the mattress and lay beside her. "I promise that I don't snore."

"Maybe I do." Deanna felt her resistance melt away. "I bet you're a cover hog."

"Not when I have you to cuddle." Nico tucked her against him and curled an arm protectively around her shoulder.

The tender gesture was almost too much. Why was he being so sweet? So loving? She had to leave before he stole another piece of her heart.

"I'm a restless sleeper," Deanna protested, but only moved millimeters away from him.

"No problem." He grinned. "I sleep like the dead, so you won't bother me."

"I need a shower." Deanna grimaced. She must reek of sweat and sex.

"Later." Nico buried his nose in her neck and inhaled. "I love the way you smell." He winked. "Like a well-satisfied woman."

"Well..." Deanna trailed off, running out of both excuses and willpower.

She sighed. His skin was so toasty warm it was almost as if he were a supernatural creature that burned brighter than the rest of the mere mortals in the world.

"You can even pick the side you want." Nico stroked down her arm, then moved his hands to her stomach and teased her belly button.

As his fingers ventured southward past her rapidly dampening curls, the fire that had banked in the afterglow of their lovemaking flared up again. She moaned as flames licked along her nerves and arousal heated her core.

He caressed her slick folds, and Deanna felt the last of her self-control turn to ash and blow away in the wind of her desire. A siren voice whispered that one more time wouldn't hurt. That she could be strong once she got home. That she'd never have to see him again.

By next week, Nico would have another woman on his arm and in his bed. Deanna would turn the page of a magazine and see him gazing down at someone new. Someone truly beautiful. Someone in his league.

A primal urge to hunt down his future girlfriend and tear her apart surged through Deanna's chest. She jerked, eliciting a protesting murmur from Nico, who glanced up, then went back to caressing her.

Deanna's pulse hammered. She had never been the jealous type, believing that if a man could be lured away, he wasn't someone she wanted. So why did the thought of Nico with another woman bring out a possessiveness she'd never before felt?

Maybe it was because she'd been involved with so few men. Or it could be because the guys she'd dated weren't the type to attract other women.

In contrast, Nico would always be like a chocolate cupcake, and all the hungry females would line up to take a great big bite. The thought of those hordes of women waiting for their piece of Nico twisted like a knife in Deanna's stomach. She berated herself. She was acting crazy. The pain she was feeling was ridiculously disproportional to the amount of time they'd been together.

Like the few other treats she allowed herself, she'd enjoy this taste of Nico. Then she'd go back to her sensible diet of bland food and even blander men.

* * *

What the fuck! the voice in Nico's head screamed at him. One minute he was trying to figure out how to get Deanna into her own room, and the next, he was pulling out every bit of charm he possessed to keep her in his bed.

When he'd come out of the bathroom and seen Deanna slinking toward the connecting door with her dress clutched to her breasts, instead of the relief he should have felt, misery washed over him. Why was she sneaking away without a single word? Why was she leaving him?

His heart racing, he'd rushed across the carpet and pulled her into his arms. His only thought was to make her stay the night.

How pathetic was that?

Nico had tried to remind himself that less than a minute ago, he'd been scheming to get Deanna out of his bed. That he didn't actually like having a woman sleep next to him. That he avoided that morning-after kind of intimacy at all costs.

Hell! He never brought his dates home because he didn't want to wake up with them. He didn't want to see the hurt in their eyes when they realized that he'd been telling them the truth. His only interest really *was* just a quick roll in the hay and nothing more.

Damn! Deanna had a hold on him that he didn't understand and certainly didn't like.

But even as he'd been telling himself to let her leave, he'd been persuading her to stay. Before he knew it, they were back in bed. As she continued to object to sleeping with him, her husky, sensual voice reminded him of how she sounded after she'd screamed his name.

Her cheeks had still been a pretty pink and her cinnamon curls in an adorable tangle. A single drop of sweat had trickled between her breasts, and he'd dipped his head to lick it from her creamy skin.

At her little shiver, he'd trailed his fingers downward, and his inner beast had roared its pleasure when he found her slick and hot and ready for him again.

When she'd finally relaxed, enjoying his caresses, Nico had watched, enthralled, as her expression changed from cool and reserved to hot and passionate. This was a peek at the Deanna hidden beneath her controlled, detached, venture capitalist public persona.

Nico's chest puffed when he realized that he was being allowed a glimpse at her that he suspected not many other men had ever seen. But then she'd tensed and scowled, and now he wondered if he should let her go back to her room. Could she really want to be alone?

Telling himself to let her go, he ignored his good advice and tightened his arms around her. Despite her obvious withdrawal, he needed to comfort her. To remove the frown from her lips.

A long-dormant desire to protect someone other than a family member surfaced, and Nico rubbed his hands down Deanna's back. He massaged the muscles on either side of her spine until he felt them loosen. And he sighed in satisfaction when she cuddled into his chest.

Like his mother, Deanna wasn't the type of person who would ever ask for support. And like Mariella, Deanna undoubtedly didn't even think she needed it. But something inside of Nico was certain that despite what his better judgment was shouting at him, he had to look after the woman he was holding. Had to shield her from all the arrows the cruel world would fling at her.

The unfamiliar emotion felt strange. So as he continued to stroke her soft skin, he forced himself to concentrate on the sensual pull between them rather than the urge to ask what had caused her sudden unhappiness. If he asked, that would mean he cared too much. And Nico Thorne didn't worry about anyone except his mother, brother, and himself. Certainly not about a woman. Even if being with this particular woman felt completely different than any others he'd dated.

Sex stripped away defenses, and Deanna had more of those than the US Army, Navy, Air Force, and Marines combined. She'd probably had an unaccustomed bout of vulnerability, and feelings that she normally repressed had broken through her fortifications.

Nico convinced himself that Deanna wouldn't thank him if he tried to talk about her reaction. So instead, he cupped her bottom and pressed her against his erection. Another round of sex would help them both sleep better.

CHAPTER FOURTEEN

Deanna woke early. Only a few feeble rays of sunshine pierced the dark room. Despite having had a shower before going to sleep the night before, she needed another one this morning. Nico had slept wrapped around her, and she had to wash off his scent if she hoped to have any chance at behaving rationally on the ride home.

Gingerly, Deanna lifted Nico's arm and slid free of his entwining legs. Immediately she missed his warmth. Easing off the bed, she hunted for her clothing, spotting the lace of her panties buried beneath Nico's boxer briefs and her bra hiding under the desk.

After plucking her dress from where she'd dropped it when Nico had lured her back into his arms, she collected her underwear and headed for the connecting door between their rooms. Thank goodness the walk of shame was only a few private feet instead of a public cab ride to her apartment.

As she grasped the knob, she glanced back. Nico was still dead to the world. His claim to be a deep sleeper hadn't been a lie. Mesmerized by his handsome face, she hesitated for a second. Drinking in his thick lashes, high cheekbones, and tousled ebony tresses.

These final moments of sweet intimacy might very well be the last time she saw him like this. Her only future sightings would probably be during a business meeting where his suit and hair would be perfectly styled.

Deanna's heart gave a painful thud. Nico could have any woman he wanted. It was amazing that he'd wanted her even for this one time. There certainly wouldn't be any happily ever after with him.

Sighing, she crossed the threshold into her room and closed the door behind her. She'd known going into last night that any kind of relationship with Nico had an expiration date. He was a hot-blooded man who enjoyed life to the fullest, and that included sampling women the same way he tasted the tempting goodies in a farmers' market.

But with nothing other than lust in his heart for her, his interest would soon spoil like milk left too long in the refrigerator. And Deanna didn't want to wait until she was only a sour taste in his mouth. It would be better to end it now, on her terms, rather than to wait for the hurt when Nico's attention wandered elsewhere.

* * *

The click of the door closing woke Nico and he reached for Deanna. The spot where she'd been cuddled next to him was still warm, but she was gone. Disappointment flooded over him, but he ruthlessly flung it off.

It was better this way. They both could go through their morning routines without worrying about imposing on the other person.

Nico glanced at the alarm clock on the nightstand. Not even six a.m. If he hurried, they could be home by early afternoon, and he'd have time to relax before going to LeBoeuf for dinner service.

Jumping out of bed, he headed for the bathroom. As he waited for the water to get hot, he tried not to think about last night's shower. Deanna dry was beautiful. Deanna glistening wet with soapsuds decorating her breasts and bottom was breathtaking.

Shaking his head, he stepped inside the stall and closed the door. If he didn't stop picturing her, palms flat on the tile as he pounded into her warm center from behind, he would have to take matters into his own hands. And that would be about as satisfying as drinking a light beer after enjoying a full-flavored microbrew. Sex with Deanna might have ruined him for anyone or anything else.

As he washed, dressed, and packed up, Nico considered his next move. Deanna was skittish. He couldn't risk letting her cool off or she'd never agree to go out with him. And despite his own reservations, as well as the emerging unfamiliar emotions he didn't exactly enjoy, he did want to see her again. Although his need to be with her wasn't something he'd expected, he recognized the futility of fighting the urge to have her in his life.

He wouldn't have a free evening until Monday, and she'd mentioned that she spent her weekend days in the office, but he suspected that giving her even forty-eight hours to build her walls against him wouldn't be a good idea.

Which meant, before he dropped her off at her apartment, he needed a plan. But his mind was blank. He couldn't remember ever having to work this hard to keep a woman in his life. Or actually, having to make any effort at all. He was usually the one avoiding anything long term and hiding from the females who didn't get the message that his interest had waned.

*　*　*

Deanna was thankful when Nico kept the conversation light on their ride back to Chicago. Although she couldn't forget for one second the man sitting in the driver's seat, the conversation had been surprisingly pleasant. And she was relieved that he didn't mention their lovemaking.

At least she should have been relieved. In reality, it made her antsy. She waited for the other shoe to drop and kept wondering why he was being so impersonal.

Then as they'd exited the highway and entered the city

streets, Deanna became more and more depressed. She'd been right. Nico had satisfied his itch and was ready to move on to his next conquest.

Intellectually, she knew she was being irrational. She'd fully intended not to see him again once he dropped her at her apartment. But now that it seemed as if he was completely unaffected by what they'd shared together, her chest hurt. She rubbed the spot over her breastbone, trying to ease the ache.

Nico glanced at her and said, "I hope that fast-food taco didn't give you heartburn." He turned onto her street and added, "I'm sorry I was in such a rush to get back. Maybe we should have stopped somewhere nicer."

"I'm fine." Deanna waved off his concern. "The grilled chicken was good."

Nico pulled the SUV in front of Deanna's building and asked, "Are you heading into the office for the rest of the day?"

"Uh-huh." She checked her watch. "It's only two, so I have time to catch up on work from yesterday." She opened her door, but instead of getting out, she said, "I suppose you have to get to LeBoeuf."

"Yep." Nico draped his arms over the steering wheel. "I hope the guy who filled in for me didn't leave too much of a mess, but I'm not counting on it. He's a good chef, but disorganized."

"Well..." Deanna took a breath and forced herself to step onto the sidewalk. This was it. Her time with Nico was officially over. "Thanks for the, ah..." Seriously, was she really going to thank him for the sex? After he'd gone to such lengths to avoid the subject? "For the getaway. It was great to see your restaurant."

"I enjoyed the company." Nico grinned. "And your insights were very helpful."

Nico exited the SUV, retrieved her bag from the back, and

joined her. Seeming unconcerned that he was parked in a loading zone, he took her elbow and started toward the building's entrance.

"You don't have to walk me up." Deanna tried to snatch the handle of her suitcase, but Nico held tight. "I don't want you to get a ticket."

"It'll be okay for a couple of minutes." Nico continued walking toward the elevator.

"Really." When it arrived, Deanna tried again to grab her bag. "Go ahead. I'll be fine from here. It's only a few steps to my apartment."

Nico ignored her and got inside the car, waited until she followed, then pushed the button for her floor. She frowned. What was he up to? She knew he had terrific manners, but this was more than that.

The short ride was silent, but a few seconds later, as Deanna fumbled with her keys, she noticed a thoughtful look on Nico's face. He opened his mouth, but as they crossed the threshold, "He Ain't Heavy, He's My Brother" began to play from his pocket.

"Sorry." He scowled, dug out his cell, and said, "I have to take this."

"Sure."

Giving him some privacy, Deanna took her suitcase into the bedroom and unpacked. When she was finished, she could still hear Nico talking, so she changed from her travel clothes into a business suit, fixed her makeup, and put her hair into a chignon.

Once she was dressed for work, she checked to see that she had what she needed in her briefcase, grabbed it and her laptop, then went to find Nico. He was seated at her kitchen counter still talking, but when he saw her, he quickly finished his call.

Standing, he slid his phone in his pocket, faced Deanna, and said, "Since you're ready, how about I give you a ride to your office?"

"It's out of your way," Deanna protested. "Didn't you tell me that your place is in the opposite direction from Randolph Ventures?"

"Spending more time with you is worth it." Nico took the briefcase and laptop from her and steered her toward the door. "As you probably guessed from the ringtone, that was my brother calling. Marco said that the kitchen is in good shape for tonight's dinner service, so I don't need to be at LeBoeuf for several hours."

Clearly Nico led a charmed life. His SUV was where he'd left it, and there weren't any tickets flapping under his windshield wipers.

Deanna slid a peek at his profile as he pulled the huge vehicle into traffic. She'd have sworn from his behavior on the drive up from Alton that he was finished with her, but now he was going out of his way to be with her for a few more minutes. What had happened?

Had Nico's brother telephoned him about something other than LeBoeuf's dinner service? Maybe Marco had told him something about the financing of the new restaurant. Had the situation changed and Nico found out he still needed her for some reason?

Deanna slid her phone from her purse and checked to see if she'd missed a message from her boss. *Nope.* There had been no communication from Randolph since he'd acknowledged receiving her report. And in that email, he'd said that he wouldn't make his decision about Nico's financing until next week.

As Nico drove through the city's congested streets, he entertained her with stories about disasters in the kitchen, cranky diners, and crazy sous-chefs. His parking karma seemed to be holding up, and almost before Deanna realized that they'd arrived, Nico brought the SUV to a smooth stop and exited the vehicle.

Her office was in one of Chicago's older buildings. Randolph had purchased the property from the original owner's ninety-two-year-old grandniece. Considering her boss's usual taste ran to glitter and tackiness, she'd been surprised that he treated the structure with the respect it deserved. He'd upgraded only what was necessary and refurbished the rest, all the while retaining the vintage charm.

Because Randolph had preserved the integrity of the building, employees had offices instead of cubicles. And many of the offices even had windows. Deanna had lucked into one of those. It was smaller than many others, but the lack of space was a fair trade to be able to see the sky.

The old-fashioned elevator with inlaid walnut panels and brass framing was also amazing, as were the two massive chandeliers that hung in the three-story lobby.

But the best thing about the building was the kidney-shaped burled maple security desk. While the desk itself was gorgeous, it was the wonderful old guy who manned it who warmed Deanna's heart. Mr. Byron, as he preferred to be addressed, was in his late seventies or maybe early eighties, and his cheerful greeting and sincere interest was often the one bright spot in Deanna's life.

Today, when Nico escorted Deanna into the lobby, Mr. Byron stared at the chef as if trying to place him. Finally, he shrugged, caught Deanna's gaze, and held up both his thumbs. Nico had passed the old man's test.

The security desk was only a few feet from the entrance, but Deanna stopped before reaching it and held out her hand for her briefcase and laptop.

When Nico surrendered the items, she said, "Thanks again for the trip and for the ride."

His expression tightened at her banal words, and she knew she needed to say something more. Too bad that her mind was completely blank.

"My pleasure for both." Nico moved closer and whispered, "I like it a lot better when you wear your hair loose, but I'm glad none of the men you work with get to see you like that."

"Oh." Deanna blew out a surprised puff of air. "The chignon keeps it out of my way."

She felt her face flame, and she bent her head, studying her sensible beige pumps. Was he really implying he might be jealous?

Nico's lips grazed her nape as he murmured, "Will you take your hair down for me when we have lunch together tomorrow?"

"What?"

His mouth brushing against her earlobe was distracting, and fighting to focus on what he was saying, Deanna stepped back from him.

"From what you've said, even though tomorrow is Saturday, you'll be in your office, so I'll be here at one." Nico pressed a sweet kiss to her lips. "Don't worry. I'll bring something healthy for you to eat."

Deanna gazed into his eyes, and instead of the usual desire, there was a softness that made her heart stutter. Bemused by his expression, when she finally found her voice, Nico was already out of the door.

"But I don't take a lunch break," Deanna called through the glass to his retreating back.

She couldn't tell if he heard her or not since he didn't turn around.

CHAPTER FIFTEEN

That had gone better than Nico had expected. He had a date with Deanna for the next day, and she hadn't really objected. Of course, he hadn't given her a chance to say no. Which was exactly how he'd planned it.

Deanna liked being in control and didn't give it up easily. Except in the bedroom. He'd been surprised that when he'd restrained her wrists with his hands, instead of protesting, she'd relaxed and enjoyed his attentions. Maybe next time, he'd try using one of his ties to secure her.

However, right now, he had to deal with the real reason for Marco's call. Nico hadn't lied to Deanna when he'd said that his brother had reported LeBoeuf's kitchen was good to go. He just hadn't told her about the truly important part of the conversation. Mostly because he had no idea why his father was in town or what the hell the son of a bitch wanted with Nico and Marco.

Ian Thorne, legendary English chef, certainly wasn't in Chicago for a family visit. If he was in Illinois, demanding to see his sons, there was a damn good reason. And not one that Nico would appreciate.

The bastard wanted something from them. The only question was what.

Ian had made a nine p.m. reservation at LeBoeuf, and afterwards he expected to see his sons. While Nico was tempted to ignore his father's wishes, he knew his brother would insist on meeting their father. And allowing Marco to face the tyrant on his own was out of the question. Which meant Nico would have talk to the man he loathed. The man he hadn't spoken to since he turned eighteen.

Nico's birthday present to himself had been a ticket back to his mom's house in New York. As he'd stepped on the plane, he'd sworn an oath never to spend another minute in his father's company.

So far he'd kept that vow. However, as Nico shoved open the door of his apartment and found his brother waiting on his couch, he knew that was one promise to himself that was about to be broken.

Marco and Nico didn't live together, but Nico's apartment was only a couple floors above his brother's, and they had each other's keys. Nico rarely used the one to Marco's place, but his brother regularly wandered in and made himself at home in Nico's apartment.

Which was another reason Nico didn't bring dates to his place. He and his brother were close, but not that close. Nico was willing to share his food, his satellite, and his clothes, but not his women.

Looking away from the television screen, Marco said, "We need to talk about Dad, bro."

"Sure." Nico nodded. "Give me a minute to clean up and I'll be back."

Marco was the only person besides their mother that Nico loved. But even with him, discussing the situation with their father was rough.

As Nico strode into his bathroom, he shouted, "Any idea what the bastard wants?"

"He didn't say. Just he needed to see both of us," Marco yelled. "But we should—"

The rest of his words were cut off when Nico turned on the faucet and splashed cold water on his face. He didn't have to hear the rest to know what Marco wanted. Lately, his brother had been lobbying for them to establish some sort of relationship with their father.

Marco, being a couple years younger than his brother,

didn't remember the circumstances surrounding their parents' breakup as clearly as Nico. And because Marco hadn't shown any talent for cooking, he hadn't been forced to live with or train under Ian for twenty-three damn long months.

While Marco disapproved of how their father had treated their mother, he didn't hate the man. Until recently, Nico's hatred was strong enough for the both of them, but something had changed. And Nico didn't buy Marco's argument that life was too short to hold a grudge. Marco was an all-time champion grudge holder, second only to Nico.

Even after Nico had told his brother what their father's second wife, Clarissa, had said about Ian's motives for dumping their mother, Marco hadn't despised him. He'd maintained that it was more than possible that their former stepmother had been a lying bitch. While Nico agreed with his brother's evaluation of the vile woman's character, he still wasn't anywhere near ready to give dear old Dad the benefit of the doubt.

"Okay." Nico reentered the living room and took a seat across from his brother. "Start from the beginning and tell me everything."

"Dad called me this morning and asked to see us." Marco glared as Nico made a face. "Yes, I know you don't want to talk to him, but this time he wouldn't take no for an answer. And I tried."

"This time?" Nico raised a brow. "He's contacted you before?"

"He calls every few months to see how we are." Marco shrugged. "And I always put him off, but today he sounded more desperate."

"Which he must be, if he's in Chicago." Nico felt his blood pressure rocket. "The great Ian Thorne considers Illinois fly-over country."

"It really bugged you when he said that to the reporter." A

small smile appeared on Marco's lips. "You know he was just pissed that we refused to take a job in one of his restaurants in London or Los Angeles and accepted positions at LeBoeuf instead."

"Like us working for him would ever happen." Nico crossed his arms. "Back to his Lord Almighty's sudden visit. Any hint as to what's up with him?"

"All Dad said was that he needed to speak to us both, in person."

"He wants something." Nico leaned forward. "As far as I know, his restaurant empire is doing great, so it can't be money."

"If he needed cash, he'd go to Mom for it, not us." Marco stretched out his long legs, adjusting the sharp crease in his dress pants.

"And she'd probably give it to him." Nico ground his teeth in frustration.

"No doubt." Marco took a gulp from the water bottle at his side.

"He knows we'd never take a job from him." Nico shot his brother a worried glare. "You wouldn't, right?"

"Well, if he made me a really incredible offer," Marco needled.

"Asshole," Nico snapped, fighting the feeling of irritation this whole conversation was causing. "So what else could he want?"

"Maybe he's getting married again for the umpteenth time." Mischief sparkled in Marco's brown eyes. "And he wants us to be his best men."

"That must be it." Nico refused to rise to his brother's bait. "Because he'd certainly want sons, who to judge by his history are older than his next bride, to be at his wedding."

"I'm out of ideas." Marco crossed his arms behind his head. "Guess we'll have to wait until tonight after dinner service to find out."

"Well, if he needs one of my kidneys, he's out of luck." Nico scowled.

"We are his only offspring. At least the only offspring that he acknowledges." Marco slumped in his seat. "Maybe he just wants to get to know us."

"Hmm." Nico rubbed his jaw. It was odd that although Ian had had five or six wives, as far as Nico knew, he'd never fathered any more children. On the other hand, the guy had obviously never wanted the sons he did have, so maybe it really wasn't that strange.

"Ready to go to work?" Marco interrupted Nico's thoughts. "I'm sure you're itching to create a special to show the old man what he's missing."

"Definitely!" Nico forced enthusiasm into his voice. Marco was examining him closely, and the last thing Nico wanted was a long discussion about his feelings.

* * *

Deanna's stomach growled, and she glanced up from the papers in front of her, astonished to see darkness outside of her window. Where had the day gone?

According to her computer, it was a few minutes after eight. She and Nico had eaten an early lunch, so it was nine hours since her last meal.

There had been so much work piled up, she hadn't noticed how late it was. Except for one quick bathroom break, she hadn't left her desk since Nico dropped her off. And she really should finish a couple more reports before calling it a night and going home.

As she opened a file, her stomach growled again and Deanna frowned. She'd trained herself to go without food for long stretches of time, but evidently Nico's constant feeding had undone all her hard work.

It wouldn't be pleasant, but she had to nip her hunger in the bud again before it took over her life and she ballooned up to her high school weight. Nico claimed he liked curves, but she hadn't found one picture on the Internet that showed him with a woman above a size two.

Backsliding was not an option. She wouldn't give in to her craving. She'd never allow herself to become that chubby nobody again.

Muttering her mantra, "Money, looks, and power are the only things that matter," she continued to work.

The other twenty venture capitalist associates were long gone. Even Chad Jordan, her strongest competition, had left an hour ago. She could do this. Work harder. Eat less. Be perfect.

Her time with Nico was just a short detour on her path to success. She didn't like how she lost control of both her appetite and her arousal around him. Why had she been turned on when he'd restrained her wrists with his hands during sex? It was disturbing that she'd actually felt relaxed when he'd taken charge. She never felt comfortable if she wasn't the one making all the decisions.

She needed to stay away from him. She needed to stay in control or bad things would happen. She reminded herself that she was willing do whatever it took to get the life she'd always dreamed of living.

She'd had her moment of weakness. She'd taken a day off, cheated on her diet, and had amazing sex. But it was over. When Nico showed up for lunch tomorrow, she'd be unavailable. She'd just make sure Mr. Byron didn't let him upstairs, and that would be that.

Except, at the thought of not seeing Nico again, depression lodged in Deanna's chest. As she fought her irrational feelings, Franklin Randolph marched into her office and tossed a folder at her.

"You weaseled out good info from Thorne." Randolph grunted, gesturing to the file. "Looks like the investment is a go."

"Great!" Deanna kept a professional smile on her face, but she wanted to do a fist pump. "I wasn't expecting to see you until next week, sir."

"My plans changed." Randolph shot her an irritated glance and snapped, "I hope all your data is accurate." He ran his fingers through his hair, causing the thinning orange strands to stand at attention. "You didn't let him seduce you into a good evaluation, did you?"

"Absolutely not, sir." Deanna felt her cheeks redden as she thought of her time with Nico.

He had been charming, but he hadn't influenced her decision. She'd made up her mind and written her report before having sex with him. Still, probably better for everyone involved if Randolph had no idea how cozy she'd gotten with their newest investment partner.

"Does he know who you are?" Randolph's impatient voice brought her back to the present. When she nodded, he asked, "When did you tell him?"

"After emailing my report to you last night," Deanna answered.

"Good." Randolph laced his fingers over his paunch and nodded.

"So we're all set?" Deanna was too tired and hungry to deal with Randolph.

She needed to be sharp and rested for any interaction with her boss. He had a lot of unpleasant traits, but he was a shrewd man who ran a multibillion-dollar venture capitalist business that made money when others failed. And he didn't tolerate any screw-ups.

"Check the schedule with my admin and arrange a meeting for me with Thorne for early next week." Randolph turned to leave.

"Uh…" Deanna hesitated, then squared her shoulders—Randolph had told her to be more aggressive in her business negotiations. "Didn't you say I could run with this project if I did a good job?"

"I changed my mind." Randolph shrugged. "My gut tells me you're not ready."

"But…" How could she argue with his gut? "I am ready. Really."

"Next time." Randolph crossed his arms, scowling. "After your undercover work, you're too close to Thorne." He pasted an insincere smile on his face. "But you did a good job and I'll remember that."

"Thank you, sir." Deanna's voice was composed, but her mind raced. "I'd love to attend the meeting as a learning experience."

She hated missing the chance to handle her first client, but it was probably for the best. If Randolph allowed her to sit in on the discussion, she could at least see how a deal like this was finalized. And since she wouldn't be involved after that, she could avoid Nico, and her life would settle back into its pre-hot-chef routine.

Randolph pursed his lips, then leveled his index finger at her and said, "Okay. But you are strictly an observer. Questions directed at you are to be referred to me without any comment or suggestions."

"Yes, sir." Deanna rose to her feet, walked around her desk, and escorted Randolph to the door. "You'll barely know that I'm there."

After her boss left, Deanna saved what she'd been working on, packed up her briefcase and laptop, and turned off her office lights. Time to go home and eat her cup of Greek yogurt.

Yep. Things were back to normal, all right. But when had her routine turned into such a joyless rut?

CHAPTER SIXTEEN

Nico and his brother drove separately to LeBoeuf. While Nico readied his line cooks, Marco would be supervising the front-of-house setup. After his waitstaff had laid the tables, he would bring them to the breakroom for a pre-shift tasting and family dinner.

As Nico pushed through the kitchen door, it was as if a switch had been thrown. Mr. Easygoing disappeared and Mr. Perfectionist took his place. Stopping a few steps over the threshold, he scrutinized the prep work in progress. He had a good brigade, but with several newer members, he wasn't convinced they understood the importance of proper *mise en place*.

After satisfying himself that his sous-chef, Lorenzo, had everything under control and hadn't indulged in his favorite beverage—a speedball made up of espresso and Pabst Blue Ribbon beer—Nico put his things in his office, grabbed a clean set of whites, and shrugged into his jacket. He resisted the temptation to send a sappy text to Deanna and instead sent her a funny meme of a couple playing Monopoly, hoping she'd remember telling him how much she enjoyed playing board games with her sorority sisters.

Returning to the kitchen, Nico reviewed the evening's menu. Despite Marco's teasing, Nico had no intention of creating a special to impress their father. The dishes he had already planned would be the ones he served tonight. If they were good enough for the various restaurant critics who had tasted them, they would damn well be good enough for Ian Thorne's palate.

He was well aware that food was like fashion, and Nico had

fought to keep their selection up-to-date. However, LeBoeuf's owner insisted on maintaining the old standbys like quiche and chicken cordon bleu. Although the regulars might love the outdated entrees, they didn't create the buzz needed to draw new diners to the place.

Shoving aside his frustration with Ian and LeBoeuf's owner, Nico gathered the line cooks and prepared to demonstrate the correct preparation of the night's specials. The cold starter was a charcuterie plate featuring Nduja, a Calabrian spreadable cured meat, and the hot was a spicy chicken lettuce cup flavored with chili, brown sugar, and cider vinegar. The fish course was cod topped with tomato dressing, and the meat was a bison filet with date purée, sugar beans, and almond snow.

After his demonstration, Nico checked with his pastry chef. She had the Peruvian love cake in the oven and was readying the candied rose petals and saffron buttercream frosting. Nico's lips twitched. He was tempted to save a couple of slices of that for Deanna's lunch tomorrow. The cardamom in the batter was not only an explosion of flavor on the tongue but reputed to be an aphrodisiac. Too bad all Deanna would see was the calories.

An hour later, when he was assured that the kitchen staff was on track, Nico headed for the dining room. He paused to watch Marco instruct a new server on the proper placement of stemware, and chuckled when his brother whipped out a small ruler from the inside pocket of his jacket, silently handing it to the visibly trembling young woman. And Marco claimed that Nico was obsessive.

Deciding to save the poor girl, Nico walked over to his brother, clapped him on the shoulder, and said, "Pre-shift tasting in fifteen minutes."

"They'll be ready." Marco frowned at the young server and instructed, "Measure every table. I don't want to see any crooked settings."

As the brothers walked down the long, dark hall to Nico's office, Nico said, "You know you scared that girl shitless?"

"Like you don't terrify your staff?" Marco snorted as he flopped into a chair and stretched his legs. "When you're expediting and a cook gives you an unacceptable dish, I've seen you dynamite the whole plate. Hell! Last time there was halibut shrapnel everywhere."

"I've calmed down," Nico protested, sitting behind his desk to enjoy a last moment of peace before the craziness of dinner service. "I don't do that anymore."

"Right." Marco wasn't convinced. "Isn't your philosophy either make it nice or make it twice?"

"Oh, I still make them re-fire it." Nico kept his expression bland. "I just don't throw crockery anymore. That shit's expensive, and I'm getting into practice for my own restaurant."

"Speaking of that"—Marco narrowed his eyes—"how did the trip with the cute financial babe go? Did you charm her into a positive report?"

"I don't use people like that." Nico felt his ears turn red.

Maybe he had used women like that in the past. But Deanna was different.

"So you didn't get the money?" Marco tilted his head. "What happened?"

"I showed Deanna the property, shared my vision, and she agreed that the restaurant had a good chance to be profitable." Nico crossed his arms. "She informed her boss of her conclusion, and I'm waiting to hear from Randolph as to whether that's enough for him to invest in my place."

"Sounds promising." Marco frowned. "What aren't you telling me?"

Nico went rigid.

Forcing his body to relax, he said, "Nothing."

He wasn't ready to share his feelings about Deanna with his

brother. *Hell!* He didn't exactly know what they were himself.

"Dude, tell me you didn't sleep with her?" Marco leaned forward.

"I..." Nico clamped his mouth shut. He was not discussing her.

"You did." Marco's voice turned grim. "Fan-fucking-tastic. Will it screw up the deal when you don't call her again? Is she vindictive?"

"Deanna's not like that." Nico's jaw tightened. "And I'm not pulling my usual disappearing act."

"Don't bullshit me."

"I'm not."

"Seriously?" Marco's eyebrows vanished into his hairline. "You don't do relationships. Is something different about her, bro?"

What the hell! Nico shrugged. Maybe his brother would have some insight. Marco had at least attempted to have a long-term girlfriend. He never managed to make it past six months with a woman, but he'd tried. Nico never had.

"There's something about the way she carries herself. Her self-possession. Like she's a goddamn princess or something," Nico struggled to explain. "And she's strong. She doesn't want or need help from anyone. She's not fake and she doesn't try to hide what she feels. I can tell what she's thinking by the look in her eye."

"Like Mom," Marco murmured.

"Yeah." Nico slumped. "She isn't like the arm candy that I've been dating. She doesn't take away from me. She makes me better."

The brothers sat in silence for a while, until Marco looked at his watch and said, "Time to rock and roll."

* * *

It was nearly nine o'clock by the time Deanna trudged through her apartment door and kicked off her heels. She stood barefoot in her foyer and took a deep breath. She could swear she smelled Nico's aftershave lingering in the air.

Dinner service would be winding down at LeBoeuf. Would Nico be exhausted and go home? He'd sent Deanna a cute meme, but that didn't mean he wasn't going on a late date with one of the many models and socialites in his life. And it certainly didn't mean he wouldn't be sleeping with someone else tonight.

Stop it! Deanna mentally slapped herself. It wasn't as if they were in a relationship. There certainly hadn't been any mention of exclusivity. And she'd decided that even if he did show up for lunch tomorrow, she wouldn't see him. So why did she even care if he was with another woman? Or what he might be doing with her?

One thing that her trip to Alton with Nico had made clear, she needed to start reconnecting with her friends. She'd neglected them, and she had to make the time and effort to reestablish their bonds.

It was too late to text someone to go out for a drink or to grab a bite to eat, but she could certainly call Sage. Her BFF might be halfway across the country working at a big cat sanctuary in Nevada, but it wasn't as if they couldn't talk on the phone.

Deanna's neck and shoulders were stiff from hunching over her desk. She'd take her phone and relax in a warm bath while she caught up with Sage. Wouldn't her BFF be surprised to hear about Nico?

As the tub filled, Deanna took a carton of Greek yogurt and a bottle of water from the fridge, got her cell from her purse, and placed the items on a small table in the bathroom. She stripped off her suit and underwear, then eased into the soothing hot water.

Punching in her friend's number, Deanna put the phone on speaker and peeled back the foil lid from her dinner. After half a dozen rings, she was about to hang up when Sage finally answered.

"Hey," Deanna said. "What's going on? You sound out of breath."

"Charlie got loose again." Sage chuckled. "The old rascal has somehow learned to pick the lock on the ranch's gate, and I had to rescue a man he had trapped in his car on the side of the highway. Poor guy had pulled over near our driveway to change a tire, and Charlie was curious."

"Even if the ranch is fenced in, I still can't believe you let the animals wander around it." Deanna shivered at the thought of the five-hundred-pound lions and seven-hundred-pound tigers roaming free.

"All our babies are rescues, and we're not traumatizing them by sticking them in a cage." Sage's voice warmed. "We leash them when we have visitors, but they've all been used in movies or live acts, so they're socialized. As long as no one is stupid, everyone is safe."

"How are your boss and his wife?" Deanna asked. "Are the contributions rolling in?"

The sanctuary where Sage worked was a nonprofit established to take in lions, tigers, and ligers that had been trained for movie and live performance but, for various reasons, no longer worked in those settings. It was solely supported by donations from people who loved the big cats and wanted them to have a healthy and happy retirement.

"Ken and Kari are fine, but we need to figure out a way to get more money." Sage sighed. "You wouldn't believe what it costs to feed our babies, and we'd like to make improvements to the habitat soon."

"Any ideas how you'll raise the cash?" Deanna asked.

She wished she knew a way to help. Too bad a nonprofit wasn't a good investment or she'd try to get Franklin Randolph to cough up some funding.

"We've got feelers out about using our location for magazine and music video shoots." Sage sounded discouraged. "I wish we didn't have to do that to the animals. It feels like we're exploiting them the same damn way their original trainers did."

Deanna was silent for a few beats, then decided to try to cheer up her friend by changing the subject. "So besides the four-legged variety, have you been out with any of Las Vegas's other animals?"

"Nope. I stay away from the neon-lights crowd." Sage snickered. "And out here in the boonies, I don't exactly run across many eligible bachelors."

"So no one?"

"After that disastrous affair with the counterfeit cowboy at my last gig, I'm not exactly anxious to get back in the saddle again." Sage blew out a frustrated breath. "Since I moved to Nevada, it's just been me and BOB." She paused, then asked, "How about you?"

Until yesterday, Deanna had been making due with her own battery-operated boyfriend, and since she'd be back with BOB soon, she understood. But for once she had something exciting to share with her friend.

"Well..." Deanna drew out the word. "I did take a little ride last night."

"Oh. My. God!" Sage squealed. "I need details. Are you in a relationship?"

"No," Deanna said, ignoring the sudden ache in her chest. "It was a one-time thing."

"That's not like you." Sage's voice was concerned. "Who was this guy?"

"His name is Nico Thorne," Deanna said slowly. "He's a chef and Randolph Ventures is going to invest in his new restaurant. He and I went downstate to look at the property he's buying for it, and we spent the night in a hotel and..." She trailed off, then added, "We came home this morning, he drove me to work, and that's the end of it."

"Is he hot?"

"Sizzling."

"Was he good?"

"Amazing."

"So why won't you be seeing him again?" Sage demanded. "Was he an asshole afterwards?"

"No. He was very sweet." Deanna had to clear her throat. The lump lodged there was making it difficult to talk. "But his nickname is the Kitchen Casanova, which is why I know I won't be on his menu again."

"So he just dropped you off without saying anything?" Sage pressed.

"Actually..." Deanna started, then shrugged and continued, "He said he'd bring me lunch tomorrow, but I'm not going to see him."

"Are you out of your ever-loving fricking mind?" Sage screeched. "You meet a nice, handsome guy who rocks your world in the bedroom and wants to bring you lunch, and you're going to avoid him?"

"I'm not the type of woman he dates." Deanna's gaze flicked to her reflection in the mirror. "He's always photographed with gorgeous women who have perfect bodies. He'd never be satisfied with me."

"Please." Sage blew a raspberry. "I thought you were over your body issues."

"My stomach isn't completely flat; there's a little pooch under my belly button."

"Seriously?" Sage sighed. "You know I have my own insecurities about my appearance; every woman does. But if you're going to let this guy go without even trying just because you don't look like the airbrushed images you see in the magazines, you need to talk to a therapist." When Deanna snorted, Sage added, "I'm serious. If you don't promise me you'll have lunch with your hot chef tomorrow, I'm reaching out to Sydney."

Sydney was one of their sorority sisters. Deanna had lost touch with her when she'd moved her practice to one of the Chicago suburbs. After Deanna's conversation with Nico about friendships, Sydney was on the top of Deanna's reconnection list.

"Don't bother," Deanna sighed. "I plan to call Sydney myself to see if she'd like to get together for Sunday brunch. It's time for me to make my own intervention."

CHAPTER SEVENTEEN

"Blow it out, guys," Nico said, his voice hoarse from shouting.

He was relieved that service was over. They'd been in the weeds all night. The cook on the meat station hadn't been able to get his temps on the filet right, and there had always been orders dragging, which meant he'd had to kill more than one ticket.

Nico cringed at the amount of food they'd wasted. Maybe he should have let some of the plates go out even if they weren't perfect.

No! The brigade had to learn to maintain his standards. To ease his conscience, Nico made a mental note to give his neighborhood homeless shelter an amount of money equal to what had ended up tossed in the trash.

Nico trudged into his office and was chugging a bottle of water when Marco stuck his head around the partially closed door and said, "Ready to see Dad?"

Already in a sour mood, the thought of talking to his father nearly sent him over the edge. Picturing his father's favorite blown glass ornament, Nico crushed the empty bottle and tossed it in the recycle bin.

Wordlessly, he slammed the door wide open and marched into the hallway.

Before he made it into the dining room, Marco grabbed his shoulders and said, "If you go out there like this, you'll probably end up in jail for assault. Either get it together or let me handle the parental unit by myself."

Nico sucked in a lungful of air. The counselor he'd seen as a teenager had taught him to visualize a place or person who made him happy. Back then, he'd always pictured himself in his mom's kitchen cooking. Now when he closed his eyes, Deanna's pretty face popped into his head, and her calm, sweet expression soothed him enough that he was able to unclench his jaw.

After a few seconds, he said, "I'm good, bro. Let's get this fiasco over with."

Nico wasn't at all surprised to see that Ian had claimed a section of the restaurant's prime real estate. His father sat in the half-round rear booth with both his arms draped over the back, flirting with the female server busy pouring his coffee.

When the young woman backed away, her cheeks red, Nico's temper flared again, and he muttered, "That server is barely twenty-one. Ian's behavior is disgusting."

"He doesn't mean anything by it." Marco shrugged. "Dad flirts the same way most of us breathe. He's the charming Ian Thorne, celebrity chef. It's the persona he presents to the public."

Nico grunted.

"Sort of like your Kitchen Casanova rep." Marco raised a brow at Nico, then strode forward and said, "So what brings you to town, Dad?"

Shoving down the flash of cold fire that burned in his gut every time he thought about his father, Nico forced himself to walk across the room and stand next to his brother. He crossed his arms and stared at the man who had destroyed his mother's happiness.

Ian got to his feet, and Nico noted that his father moved with a certain stiffness. Maybe he really had come to ask for a kidney.

Snatching Marco in a bear hug, Ian said, "Do I need a reason to visit my sons?"

Ian turned to grab Nico, but his son's arctic sneer must have caused him to reconsider. Instead, he slapped Nico on the shoulder and resumed his seat.

Marco slid in next to Ian, but Nico remained standing and said, "Cut the crap and tell us what you want. Neither of us believes you're here because you've had a sudden paternal impulse."

"Not so sudden." Ian's voice was unruffled, but there was a flicker of pain in his eyes. "I've tried to visit you both on several occasions. You don't answer my calls, and whenever I'm in town, Marco claims to be too busy to meet with me."

"Most people would get the hint that we don't want to see them," Nico retorted.

"Oh. I got the hint." Ian's dark brows met across his nose. "But it's time for this nonsense to stop. You're both grown men who have been with more than your fair share of women. Surely you've realized by now that there are two sides to every breakup."

Nico's hands fisted and Marco quickly said, "Regardless of our own experiences, you hurt our mother. You've never told us any real reason for the divorce. Claiming that you'd grown apart isn't enough."

"But it was the truth." Ian shoved his fingers through his hair, making the white strands spike like icicles. "Mariella was contented with a little life in the Italian countryside. I wanted more."

"More women," Nico jeered.

"No!" Ian thumped the table. "More restaurants. More money. More fame."

"And you used Mom's social status and connections to get those things, then flung her aside like overcooked pasta," Nico scoffed.

"That isn't what happened." Ian sighed. "I asked her to go with me. She refused." He narrowed his eyes. "But for her career, she was willing to move to New York."

"Only because she needed the money to provide for us,"

Nico snarled.

"I sent her child support." Ian shook his head. "She never cashed the checks."

Marco and Nico shared a questioning look and Nico shook his head. No way was their father telling the truth. But he paused. Mariella had never given a reason for the divorce. Since she clearly still loved her ex-husband, Nico always assumed that she'd had no say in the matter. Was it possible Ian wasn't lying about the past?

It didn't matter. He'd still been a bastard the two years Nico had trained under him. And if he really loved his wife, he'd have stayed with her in Italy and been happy with a simpler life.

"Moving on." Nico used his hand to make a cut-to-the-chase motion.

His patience was about at an end. He wanted a shower and a beer. And if Deanna had texted him back, that might help erase this crappy night from his mind and help him sleep.

"Would you at least have a seat?" Ian asked in a put-upon tone.

"No." Nico's lips thinned. "I'm walking out of here in three seconds. So speak your piece or don't. I really don't give a flying fuck."

"Fine." Ian stood and said, "Your mother asked me to talk to you both."

Marco slid out of the booth, joined Nico, and said, "Why didn't Mom call us herself? Is she okay?"

"Mariella is well," Ian assured them. "She just thought this needed to come from me." He cleared his throat. "Your mother and I are getting remarried, and we'd like you to attend the ceremony."

"No," Nico said at the same time as his brother said, "Sure."

Marco turned to Nico and opened his mouth, but Nico stomped away.

Marco followed Nico out of the dining room and down the hallway to his office, but Nico blocked the door and said, "Leave me the hell alone." When Marco tried to push past him, Nico ground out between clenched teeth, "I need some space. We'll talk tomorrow."

* * *

Late Saturday morning, Deanna glanced at the lower left corner of her computer screen. She'd checked the clock repeatedly since arriving at her office, and she was halfway convinced that something had happened to the space-time continuum. Because she could swear there were now more than sixty seconds in a minute.

Could something like that even happen? She had no idea. Maybe instead of opting for Intro Geology for her college science requirement, she should have taken physics instead.

Thumping her head on the back of her chair, Deanna stifled a scream. If she could only figure out whether to have lunch with Nico and give the relationship a chance or stick to her original plan and avoid him, she could get some work done.

Yesterday, she'd made up her mind to tell Mr. Byron not to allow Nico upstairs. But talking to Sage made her reconsider her decision. Maybe she was crazy to let Nico go just because she was afraid he'd get tired of her, afraid he'd go back to his usual type of woman.

She and Sage had had a lengthy conversation, and the discussion had made Deanna reassess both her beliefs and her view of female beauty. Perhaps her opinion *had* been corrupted by the airbrushed pictures in the fashion magazines. And if that was truly the case, and she suspected it was, she might really need to talk to a therapist.

Straightening, Deanna took another peek at the time. It was 12:59. It was now or never. Her fingers grasped the telephone receiver, but she pulled her hands away. She'd take the risk. She'd have lunch with Nico and see where things went.

Ten minutes later, she stared at the phone. Why wasn't Mr. Byron calling to tell her Nico was there? In all her previous experience with him, he'd been exceedingly prompt.

Hell! Maybe he'd had second thoughts and wasn't coming today. But if that were true, surely Nico would have texted her to let her know he was breaking their date. He seemed too nice just to not show up.

Deanna buried her head in her hands. The irony wasn't lost on her that up until a few minutes ago, she wasn't even sure if she wanted to see him. Talk about karma.

Wait! Had she accidentally muted her cell? It wouldn't be the first time. Snatching the device from the desktop, she swiped the screen. *No.* The volume was turned on and there were no messages from Nico.

Resisting the impulse to call Sage for advice, Deanna got up and started to pace. It was silly to be so upset because the guy was a little late. It was entirely possible he was caught in traffic. Or couldn't find parking. Or had gotten delayed by a business call.

A nasty voice in her head whispered, "Or because he has another woman in his bed."

Stop it! Deanna silenced her doubts. If she was going to date someone like Nico Thorne, she couldn't turn into a jealous shrew over every little thing. She'd drive herself insane and him away.

Clutching her cell, she considered her options. She could text him, but she'd have to come up with something to say that didn't sound anxious or needy. It was a shame that she'd already sent him a smiley emoji after receiving his Monopoly meme. And that she was so damn efficient that first thing this morning she'd left him a message with the time and date of his meeting with Randolph.

How about asking him if he was bringing drinks with lunch? She could offer to grab a couple of sodas from the breakroom vending machine.

No! That was pathetic. There was no need to get the drinks before he arrived. It wasn't as if the breakroom was two miles away. Nico would see right through her subterfuge and know she was an insecure loser.

If only she'd made up her mind earlier, she could have sent him a flirty can't-wait-to-see-you text. If he'd responded in kind, she wouldn't feel as antsy. But she hadn't and now she had to suck it up.

Okay. She wasn't going to fall apart. Nico would show up and tell her a funny story about his adventures in getting to her.

She should use this time to fix herself up a little. Taking her brush and cosmetic bag out of her purse, she set to work unwinding her chignon and freshening her mascara and lipstick. While she was at it, she unfastened the top two buttons on her blouse.

Digging to the bottom of her makeup case, she found the vial of Fragonard Grain de Soleil and rolled the perfume onto her wrist and throat. It had a light, sweet fragrance that remained close to the skin rather than floating in the air, which made it perfect for work.

Once she was ready, she looked at the time again. Twenty after one. Had she misunderstood Nico? Was she supposed to meet him downstairs?

Deanna quietly opened her office door. No one in the hall. Could she make it to the elevator without being noticed, or should she refasten her collar? It wasn't as if she was about to flash anyone. You couldn't even see any cleavage, just a bit of her upper chest.

Still. Her colleagues weren't used to seeing her any way except fully buttoned up with her hair in a bun. They'd know exactly what she was planning if they caught sight of her.

Shrugging, she slipped her key into her pocket, checked that her door locked behind her, then made a dash for the elevator. As her grandmother used to say, in for a penny, in for a pound.

Emerging from the elevator car, Deanna scanned the lobby. It was empty.

Her courage rapidly dwindling, she walked to the security desk, pasted a smile on her face, and said, "Good afternoon, Mr. Byron."

The old security guard worked Monday through Saturday just like all the venture capitalist associates. Today, Deanna was especially happy to see his friendly face.

"Afternoon, Miss Sloan." Mr. Byron's wrinkled forehead became more creased as he scanned her unusual appearance. "What are you doing down here this time of day? Is there a problem upstairs?"

"No." Deanna pushed a curl behind her ear and drew her collar together with her other hand. "I was just wondering if anyone had left me a note or asked to see me. Maybe about twenty-five minutes ago?"

Mr. Byron shook his head, his expression sympathetic, but then he glanced over her shoulder and beamed. "Would that be the fella you're looking for?"

Deanna turned slowly and saw Nico impatiently pushing through the revolving door. His hair stood on end and his shirt was buttoned crookedly. He carried a large brown sack by its handles and cradled a huge bouquet of lavender roses in one arm.

When he spotted Deanna, his enormous smile warmed her heart. But then she frowned. He was nearly half an hour late. Did he think because she wasn't one of his bevy of beauties he could treat her like a convenience? Take her for granted?

CHAPTER EIGHTEEN

Son of a freaking bitch! Nico's damn head was already pounding from a monstrous hangover, but the pain increased tenfold when he saw the welcome light go out of Deanna's eyes and her mouth tighten.

She was pissed and he was screwed. Why in the hell had he allowed his father to get to him? He never got smashed, but last night after slamming into his apartment, he'd emptied every last beer in his fridge.

After that, he'd almost calmed down, but then Marco had shown up. Refusing to listen to his brother's arguments, Nico had thrown him out the door and started on the hard liquor.

The last thing he remembered was crunching down on the worm in the bottom of the Mezcal bottle. But if the mess in his living room was any indication, he wasn't a happy or peaceful drunk.

It was nearly noon when Nico had pried open his eyes, and the memory of the night before immediately slammed into his brain. When he'd tried to sit up, he'd realized that his legs were on the couch, but his cheek was pressed against the carpet.

He'd felt like shit, and his first inclination had been to call off his date with Deanna. But he had a sneaking suspicion that if he didn't show up, she wouldn't be open to rescheduling.

So instead of phoning her to cancel, he'd taken the fastest shower on record, then rushed to buy the food and a dozen roses. Both stops had taken a hell of a lot longer than they should have. He could understand why the deli was packed with people picking up lunch, but he had no idea why every dude in the city decided to buy his woman flowers at twelve forty-five on a Saturday afternoon.

When Nico realized he was going to be late, he'd tried to call Deanna. But last night in his drunken fury, he hadn't put his cell in its charger and the battery was dead. Looking at the angry expression on her face, he wished he would have tried harder to contact her.

Hell. He should have borrowed someone's phone. Hearing his story, any guy who'd ever kept his lady waiting would have volunteered his cell.

After missing his first chance to exit the revolving door and having to take an extra trip around, Nico finally managed to step into the lobby. Before he could get to Deanna, she shook her head, then, as if coming out of a trance, she said something under her breath, turned, and marched to the elevator.

For one terrifying moment, Nico was sure the old guy manning the security desk would stop him. But the guard informed him that Ms. Sloan's office was on the third floor and waved him through the turnstile.

Nico nodded his thanks and ran after Deanna. He made it just as the elevator door opened. When she walked inside the car, he was right behind her and quickly hit the close button.

When she reached around him and pressed three, he thrust the roses into her arms and said, "I'm sorry that I'm so late. I can explain."

"There's no need." Deanna tried to shove the flowers back at Nico, but he sidestepped her. "Since you appear to have just rolled out of bed, I think I have a good idea as to why you were delayed."

Nico wrinkled his brow. How could she possible know he'd drunk himself stupid last night? He must look worse than he thought.

Wait. Nico blinked. Deanna had scowled and spit out the word *bed* like it tasted bad.

Shit! Nico's head throbbed. Did she think he'd been with

another woman?

Of course she did. Behind the more obvious anger, hurt shimmered in her eyes. Deanna was so tough in all other aspects of her life, it was hard to remember that her confidence didn't extend to man-woman relationships. She'd brought up his Kitchen Casanova reputation quite a few times. Add that to the insecurity about her looks, and she'd definitely assume that he'd been screwing around.

The fragile thread of trust that they'd begun to weave had unraveled. Evidently, exclusivity was another issue they needed to clear up today.

Thankfully, the elevator was slow, but to increase his odds, Nico hit the red stop button. He'd been afraid that an alarm would sound, but he was willing to risk it, because one way or another, Deanna wasn't getting out of this car until she heard him out.

Placing the grocery sack on the floor, Nico took Deanna by the shoulders and said, "I did sleep in, but there was no one in my bed, not even me. I spent the night on the couch with a bottle of booze." When her only response was a lifted brow, he continued, "I'm not proud of myself, but I went on a bender last night and didn't wake up until noon."

"What stopped you from texting me?" Deanna tried to twist free of his grip.

"Let's go to your office, have lunch, and I'll tell you all about it."

Failing to break free from his hold on her shoulders, Deanna snapped, "Fine."

Nico knew it was anything but fine and said, "Please. Just hear me out."

Deanna's short, jerky nod made her unhappiness with the situation abundantly clear, but Nico counted his blessings. At least she was willing to listen to his explanation.

He pulled out the stop button, and when the elevator doors slid open on the third floor, Deanna silently led him the short distance to her office. Walking behind her, Nico noted that she'd done as he'd asked and left her hair loose. The cinnamon curls danced down her back as she strode down the hallway. They reminded him of how the silky strands felt like satin ribbons when they were entwined around his fingers.

Once they were behind her closed and relocked door, Deanna tossed the roses on her desk, then turned to Nico and said, "Really. There's no need to explain. I overreacted. In fact, I think it's best if we just forget lunch. You're the handsome upcoming chef, and I'm the frumpy numbers cruncher. It's pretty obvious this thing between us isn't going to work, so why prolong it?"

Fear dried Nico's mouth, and he couldn't recall what he'd planned to say. He knew her self-esteem was fragile; she reminded him of the first ceramic knife he'd ever owned. It was unbelievably sharp but painfully susceptible to being shattered.

For a nanosecond, Nico wondered why he was trying so hard with this woman. Why he didn't just let her end things and leave. That would have certainly been what he had always done in the past. He was never the pursuer. Never cared enough even to ask twice.

But his gut clenched at the idea of not seeing Deanna again. He'd been looking forward to being with her today. Talking to her. Hearing more of her suggestions for his restaurant.

Well, hell! He liked her. Liked being with her for something other than a superficial evening of dinner and sex. When had that happened?

His life was more real with her in it. The realization was eye-opening.

He didn't bare his soul to anyone, he even kept his brother at arm's length, but taking a deep breath, he wet his lips and said,

"My father showed up at LeBoeuf last night." Nico grimaced. "Although I don't have a very good relationship with him, he insisted on talking. What he had to say made me furious and I got plastered."

"What did he say?"

Deanna's voice was softly sympathetic, and when she took a hesitant step closer to him, Nico greedily inhaled her scent. She smelled edible, like his favorite vanilla and nutmeg sugar cookie.

"My father and mother are remarrying." Nico winced as the words came out of his mouth. "Ian deserted her when my brother and I were children. He used her to advance his career, then he treated her like day-old bread and threw her away. Now he believes that he can sweep back into her life and everything will be okay. He thinks that Marco and I will attend the wedding and welcome him back into the family."

"I take it your father is aware of your feelings about the past?" Deanna asked and when Nico nodded, she continued, "Then he sounds more than a bit delusional." Her forehead creased. "Sort of like my parents, who still think that I'll move back to my hometown, marry the boy next door, and start popping out babies."

Despite the disturbing conversation, Nico grinned at the idea of Deanna as a housewife. Although lots of women were happy in that role, he couldn't picture her content to stay home and raise kids.

"So you understand why I'm late for our date?" Nico asked cautiously.

Deanna was willingly standing closer to him, and her expression was no longer angry, but he wanted to make sure they were okay.

"I appreciate why you overindulged last night," she said slowly, then pinned him with a cold stare. "What I'm still fuzzy about is why you didn't just call me and tell me you were running behind schedule."

"I thought I could make it on time." Nico took both her hands and tugged her against his chest, wrapping his arms around her before she could move away. "Then when I realized I couldn't, the battery on my cell was dead."

"Really?" Although Deanna didn't try to leave his embrace, she didn't return his hug, either. The vulnerable look in her eyes nearly gutted him. Despite everything he'd done, she still didn't think he wanted to be with her.

"Guess I should have asked to borrow the florist's phone."

"So you knew you were running late, but instead of coming straight here, you stopped at the florist?"

Her brow wrinkled adorably as she tried to make sense of his illogical behavior, and he couldn't resist tightening his embrace. "I wanted to get you flowers. Since it'll be a few days until I can take you somewhere nice, I wanted you to know how much this lunch means to me." Nico stroked Deanna's back. "And my asshole father wasn't going to change my plans or ruin our date."

"Hmm." Deanna's breathing slowed and she laid her head on his chest. "He didn't, but your conduct and my overreaction almost did."

"I'll work on being more rational"—Nico smoothed her hair—"if you'll try to relax and believe that I really want to be with you."

Nico could feel the warm spot on his T-shirt from Deanna's breath. The sensation thawed the iciness that had held his heart hostage since she'd said they should end things. How in the world had she grown so important to him in such a short amount of time?

Bending down, he lifted her chin and kissed her softly. When she leaned into him, he teased her lips with his tongue. Having screwed up once already today, he proceeded slowly, waiting until she made a tiny noise that sounded like unadulterated welcome to him. Then he swept inside and deepened the kiss.

She tasted of coffee and something sweeter than sugar. When they came up for air, he saw that her cheeks were a pretty pink, matching her swollen lips. And her eyes were glazed with pure desire.

Watching her reaction closely, he slid the buttons on her blouse from their holes and lightly ran his fingertips across the top of her bra. When she quivered, he released the clasp. With an urgent moan, she pushed her breasts into his hands.

They were soft and silky, and Nico fondled them as he nibbled down her throat, nipping at the sensitive cord that connected her neck to her shoulder. The sounds of her arousal were like an aphrodisiac, and he brushed her nipples with his thumbs. When they immediately came to attention, he plucked at them, rolling the stiff points until they lengthened, and Deanna moaned her enjoyment.

Even though he was well aware that they had to stop—because once Deanna had a chance to think, she wouldn't be happy if they had sex in her office—he wanted her to know how much she turned him on. Pressing her hand down the front of his jeans and around his hardness, he gritted his teeth as her soft fingers stroked his erection.

A hundred years later, or so it seemed, when he finally got himself under control, he forced himself to remove her hands from his shaft, refasten her bra, and button up her blouse. Sighing, Nico put a few inches between their bodies but kept her in his arms.

Deanna blinked, her eyes slowly refocusing, then in a husky voice that reminded him of raw sex, she asked, "Why did you stop?"

"Because I knew you'd regret it if we made love in your

office."

"But you wanted to?" Deanna's expression was thoughtful.

"More than I wanted my next breath."

"So you stopped for me?" Deanna gazed at him as if he'd fought a dragon to rescue her. Her eyes simmered with admiration and something more important, trust.

He nodded, and she wrapped her arms around his waist, snuggling against his chest. Holding her like that, Nico knew that there was no going back for either of them.

CHAPTER NINETEEN

Deanna sighed in utter contentment. When she was wrapped in Nico's arms, all her worries and insecurities seemed to fade. They didn't completely go away, but the hamster wheel in her mind slowed down enough that she could shove them aside for a while and take a breath. What was there about him that helped her relax?

She'd been so mad when he hadn't arrived on time for lunch. But the anger had been only a defense to cover the hurt. Then when he'd shown up, looking as if he'd just rolled out of another woman's bed, the pain had slammed into her like being sucker-punched in the boxing ring.

Rubbing her cheek against his chest, Deanna was thankful Nico had made her listen to reason. When he'd opened up about his father, it felt as if the vault where she kept her heart had unlocked.

Then when he'd cared enough about her sensibilities to realize that she would be uncomfortable afterwards if they had sex in her office, the door had swung wide open. And she knew at that moment that she had enough faith in them as a couple to go forward with a relationship. God help her if she was making a mistake, because she wasn't sure she'd survive if he walked away.

Glancing up at Nico, she took a shaky breath and asked, "Ready for lunch?"

"Sure thing." He kissed the top of her head, then released her and said, "Let's clear off your desk and pull up some seats."

"Okay."

Deanna tenderly retrieved the roses from where she'd so callously tossed them and put the flowers in the water carafe sitting on top of the filing cabinet. Then, while Nico moved the two visitors' chairs, she pushed everything else on the desktop to the side.

"I tried to get you something light." Nico emptied the brown bag, handing Deanna plastic flatware and paper napkins. "There's chicken and barley soup, vegetable salad with balsamic dressing on the side, and a fruit plate."

"That's so sweet of you." Deanna's voice cracked. "Thank you."

"You're welcome." Before sitting down, Nico brushed his lips against her cheek, then handed her a can of La Croix. "I noticed that you drink unsweetened sparking water. I hope you like mango."

"I do." Deanna popped the tab and took a sip. "That was very thoughtful of you."

"That's me." Nico clinked cans with her. "Mr. Sweet and Thoughtful."

Deanna giggled, then slapped her hand against her mouth. She never giggled. What was getting into her? Time to get serious.

"Did you hear my message regarding the meeting Mr. Randolph has requested Tuesday at one?"

"Yes. I played it just before my cell died." Nico grinned, his excitement obvious. "Should I wear a suit?"

"Definitely." Deanna smiled to herself as she pictured him all dressed up.

"What should I expect?" Nico paused, a spoonful of soup at his lips. "Will you present your report, then the three of us discuss it?"

"My report was for Mr. Randolph, so he could make a decision regarding your restaurant." Deanna's cheeks flushed. "My part is finished. I'll only be at the meeting as an observer. I've never been involved in finalizing an agreement, and my boss doesn't think I'm ready to do that yet. From now on, you'll go back to dealing with him directly."

"I understand he's the head honcho and is in charge, but you've been in on things from nearly the beginning." Nico scowled. "Did you get in trouble because of me?"

"Not at all. Mr. Randolph even gave me a 'that a girl,'" Deanna assured him. "Anyway, as it appears we're starting a relationship, it's probably best I'm not involved. This way there's no conflict of interest."

Deanna hid her frown. She'd asked to see Nico's contract, but Randolph had snapped at her. He'd made her feel as if she'd overstepped her bounds, and she hadn't pressed him. Still, she'd like to get a peek, if for no other reason than to see what went into this type of arrangement.

"I suppose it is better for you not to be put in a bad position if the negotiations get rough," Nico agreed. "But I'm glad you'll be there for moral support."

"Me, too." Deanna smiled, then cautioned, "But I won't be able to say anything."

"That seems odd." Nico paused, then shrugged. "But hey, what do I know?"

As they continued with their lunch, they chatted about their trip to Alton, gossiped about what was going on with mutual acquaintances from Rocco's gym, and discussed various ideas for Nico's restaurant.

"I've been thinking about how you like to eat light," Nico said.

"Oh." Deanna hoped they weren't about to get into it about her diet again.

"Maybe I should have an entire section of my menu with entrees under five hundred calories." Nico glanced at her as if to gauge her reaction.

"I've seen fast casual restaurants with that type of offering,

167

but not fancier places." Deanna finished her soup and threw the empty container in the trash. "I think it would be a wonderful addition to fine dining." She tilted her head. "It allows folks to feel like at least they're *trying* to adhere to a healthy eating plan."

"My thoughts exactly." Nico poured the entire little cup of dressing on his salad and picked up his fork.

"Actually, it's very clever." Deanna pushed her untouched container of vinaigrette toward him. As she took a bite of her plain lettuce, he dumped her dressing on his salad. "Since most people will feel virtuous if they order from the light options, they'll persuade themselves that it's okay to have dessert."

"Which is one of the highest markup items." Nico winked. "Only booze is better."

After they'd finished their salads and were nibbling on the fruit plate, Deanna glanced at Nico and asked, "Have you figured out how you're going to handle the situation with your father yet?"

"Ignore him," Nico grunted. "Hell, I'll change my phone number if I have to."

"It's my impression you are extremely close to your mother." Deanna raised a questioning brow and Nico nodded. "So won't it hurt her more than your father if you don't go to their wedding?"

Nico stopped popping grapes into his mouth and froze. After a few seconds of scowling, he said, "You're right. I hadn't thought that far ahead. Mom will be devastated if Marco and I aren't there."

"Then you'll attend the ceremony?" Deanna asked. "For your mother?"

"That's not going to happen." Nico's expression was mutinous. "What I'm going to do is to talk some sense into Mom." He folded his arms. "After I'm finished, there won't be a wedding."

"I see," Deanna murmured. "Well, I need to get back to earning my salary."

Once Deanna and Nico were finished cleaning up their lunch debris, they walked to the door and Nico asked, "We're on for Monday night dinner, right?" When she nodded, he put his arms around her and said, "What are you doing tomorrow?"

"Church in the morning, then work from home for a while, and in the early afternoon I'm meeting with some women I haven't seen in a long, long time for a late brunch." Deanna smiled, happy she'd texted her friends and they were willing to go out. "How about you?"

"Sleeping in, then hitting the gym and giving Mom a call before I go to the restaurant."

"You're going to talk her out of marrying your father over the phone?"

"She lives in New York." Nico wrinkled his brow. "And this can't wait."

"One thing to think about before talking to her," Deanna said softly. "How would you feel if she called you out of the blue and told you not to open up your restaurant? That it was a bad decision? Too risky?"

"I..." Nico trailed off. "That's different. That's business, not personal."

"Everything is personal between a mother and son." Although Deanna knew she'd said as much as she could, she couldn't stop herself from adding, "Just think about it some more before you call her."

* * *

Nico glared at the poor female sitting next to him on the plane. She'd been trying to engage him in conversation, but he wasn't in the mood for her simpering efforts to gain his attention, and she hadn't taken the hint that he wasn't interested.

It appeared that his desire to flirt with other women had vanished at his first sight of Deanna. And didn't that just suck?

Squirming in the uncomfortable airline seat, Nico tried to ease his long legs into the aisle to stretch them, but an attendant pushing a beverage cart shoved them back into the cramped space in front of him. His knee hit the lowered tray table, and a full cup of coffee sloshed in his lap. Good thing it was lukewarm or he might have lost some of the skin covering the family jewels.

Instead of enjoying his Monday off of work and catching up on his sleep, he was on a red-eye flight to New York to talk to his mom in person. All weekend, Deanna's warning about how his mother might react to a phone call had ricocheted through his mind like a bullet in a handball court. And when he'd mentioned his plans to telephone Mariella to Marco, his brother had echoed Deanna's words.

This was all her fault. His lips quirked upwards. But he'd get even with her tonight. His flight back to Chicago arrived at four forty-five, and he'd told her to meet him at LeBoeuf at eight. With the restaurant dark, they'd have the kitchen to themselves, and he would feed his little venture capitalist a meal she'd never forget—with her as dessert.

Nico tilted his seat back and daydreamed about Deanna and a big bowl of whipped cream. An hour later, when the flight touched down in New York, he mentally redressed Deanna and turned his thoughts to what he would say to his mom.

At first he'd been going to surprise Mariella at her apartment, but then he decided it was better if she knew he was coming. He figured she'd be less likely to cause a scene in public, so he texted her to meet him at Edwards, her favorite spot for a late breakfast.

He was a few minutes early to the restaurant and asked for a quiet booth. He'd just been seated when his mom walked through the door. She was a beautiful woman, and every man in the place watched her as she made her way toward Nico.

Her black hair was carefully wound into an intricate style on top of her head, her smooth olive complexion was flawless, and she wore her own designs better than any of her models.

She hugged Nico and asked, "To what do I owe the pleasure, *figlio mio*?"

"Uh." He'd texted her rather than called her to avoid that very question.

As he debated claiming that he was in town for business, his mother tapped his chin and said, "Let me guess. Your father finally told you that we're getting remarried?"

"Yeah," Nico grunted. "He came to LeBoeuf Friday night to drop the bomb."

Before he could continue, the server approached to take their order.

Mariella asked for the smoked salmon, bagel, and cream cheese plate with an espresso, and Nico told the guy to make it two.

Once they were alone, Mariella took Nico's hand and said, "I know you don't approve, but your father and I have been seeing each other for the past year. We've both matured and Ian has changed."

Nico had never told his mother what his father's second wife had said about Ian using her. Although he hadn't wanted to hurt her, he'd do it if it was the only way to stop her from making a terrible mistake. But first he'd try something else.

"Doubtful. Men like Ian don't change." Nico crossed his arms. "Since you've been dating Ian for a year, why not just keep doing that?"

Mariella shook her head, paused while the server brought their espresso, then said, "Everyone changes. Some for the better, some for the worse. Don't let the hatred you have for your father make you a bitter man. You need to open yourself up to people more."

"I'm not bitter." Nico grabbed his cup and sipped, needing the caffeine. "I'm charming. I have lots of friends. People like me."

"You pour on the charisma, but it doesn't come from the heart. You have a lot of superficial relationships with men and women." Mariella shook her finger at Nico. "But you don't let anyone see the real you. Maybe your brother, but I doubt you even let him that close."

"I—"

"When's the last time you dated anyone for more than two weeks?"

"Now," Nico snapped, then grimaced.

Hell! He hadn't wanted to say anything about Deanna until he was more certain about where their relationship was going. He knew he wanted to be with her, but he wasn't entirely sure she was on board with the plan. He was making headway with her, but she was still guarded.

"Who is this woman and how long have you been seeing her?" Mariella's voice sparkled. "How did you meet her? Is she a chef, too?"

"Her name is Deanna Sloan and she's a venture capitalist." Nico knew resistance was futile when his mother's romantic radar had been alerted. "She works for the company that I contacted about investing in my restaurant." He tried for a diversionary tactic. "Did I tell you that it looks like Randolph is going to give me the money? I'm meeting with him tomorrow."

"Is that why you've been dating Ms. Sloan?" Mariella's warm brown eyes grew as frosty as a root beer float, and she frowned. "Have you been using her?"

"No!" Nico was hurt that his mother would think that. "We

didn't..." His cheeks flushed. "I mean, until she wrote her report, we never..."

"So you didn't seduce her to get the money?" Mariella's eyes twinkled. "When do I get to meet her?"

"I'm not sure." Nico felt himself getting redder. "She's a little skittish."

"Because of your reputation as the Kitchen Casanova." Mariella's knowing little smile was the same one that women have had since Eve, and Nico realized that he was in trouble. "Don't you think meeting your mom would help ease her concerns about your intentions?"

"Maybe," Nico admitted. "Why don't you come visit me next week and I'll introduce you." He grinned. "You can tell her I'm a good guy."

"Wonderful." Mariella clapped her hands. "I can't wait to meet the girl who has put a happy expression on the face of my son."

"And we can talk more about why you shouldn't remarry my father."

Mariella stuck out her tongue, then refocused the subject on Deanna. Nico was back on the plane heading toward Chicago before he realized his mother hadn't promised anything regarding her relationship with Ian.

CHAPTER TWENTY

Monday crawled by. Deanna kept her cell on her desk, hoping that Nico would call to tell her what happened when he talked to his mother. Strangely, his willingness to take her advice regarding his mom made her feel more like a real girlfriend than anything else he'd done. The flowers, picnic lunch at her desk, and the best sex of her life had been wonderful, but sharing his family concerns with her had been what convinced her that he might truly want a real relationship with her, rather than just a few weeks of hot hookups.

However, as morning turned into afternoon with no word from Nico, Deanna was concerned that the visit with his mother had gone badly. That he and Mariella had had a horrible fight and he blamed Deanna for sticking her nose where it didn't belong.

Anxiety gnawed at her concentration, and she finally closed her laptop, admitting that she wouldn't get any work done. When she left her office at five, instead of the usual seven or eight, she felt like a slacker, and guilt tickled her spine as she walked down the hall toward the elevator. She fought the urge to look over her shoulder to see if anyone noticed her early departure.

Throughout her commute home, Deanna worried about Nico's radio silence. Was their dinner still on? Surely, if he was canceling their plans, he'd have let her know. He wasn't callous enough to let her show up and not be there. Her breath snagged in her lungs. That would be too humiliating.

As she entered the lobby of her building, the doorman handed her a giftwrapped box, and her spirits soared when she saw Nico's handwriting on the envelope under the ribbon. She made herself wait until she got inside her apartment to read the card.

The message was only a few words: THESE ARE FOR TONIGHT. And it was signed with a large N.

Opening the package, she folded back the white tissue paper and gasped. She'd never had a man send her sexy lingerie. She fingered the pink ribbon ties of the delicate black lace thong, then held up the matching demi bra. Both pieces were gorgeous and a lot more daring than her usual selections.

She frowned. How had Nico known her size? Had he checked the tags on her clothing that night in the Alton hotel? Or was he so experienced with women that he could gauge their measurements at a single glance?

Deciding not to fixate on how he gained his knowledge and just enjoy his gifts, Deanna lifted out the last items—a pair of sheer lace-topped thigh highs with seams down the back. Guess she was wearing a dress tonight.

With a good idea of how their date was going to end, Deanna took a long shower, carefully shaving until she was perfectly smooth everywhere. When she was finished and dry, she applied her favorite vanilla-scented lotion, then slipped on her new underwear.

As she curled her hair and applied makeup, she admired how the demi bra showcased her breasts, but she wished the panties had more fabric. She never wore thongs because they didn't cover her stomach pooch.

Finally, she put on her dress. She didn't have a lot of choices. She hadn't had time to go shopping again, and Nico had already seen two of her limited non-work outfits. However, she'd bought the black-and-white dress on a business trip to San Diego when she had to attend an unexpected cocktail party, and had only had it on that one evening.

Although, at its shortest, the hem hit mid-thigh, the handkerchief style gave the illusion of more coverage. And while the V-neck was relatively modest, the dress was a hell of a lot sexier than her professional wardrobe.

During the short taxi ride between her apartment and LeBoeuf, the butterflies in Deanna's stomach danced to a different tune than they'd tangoed to on her previous visit to the restaurant. This time, instead of being nervous about her job performance, she was excited to see what Nico had planned. Especially considering the sexy undies that he'd sent her to wear.

The stockings had been wrapped around a note containing an access code and instructions to use the door marked private in the rear of the building. Her hands were shaking so badly it took her two tries to enter the numbers correctly on the keypad, and as she crossed the threshold into a dark hallway, her pulse accelerated into overdrive.

This was a little too much like those horror movies she and her sorority sisters had loved to watch. She and Sage had often scared themselves silly and ended up having to keep the lights on in their bedroom in order to fall asleep.

A tiny sigh of relief escaped Deanna's lips when she heard music and saw a glow at the end of the corridor. She followed the lively sounds and found Nico engrossed in whatever he was doing at the stove.

For a few seconds, Deanna just stared. Was it really possible this dazzling man wanted someone like her? She didn't have a model's face or figure. She wasn't the life of the party. And she worked mostly with numbers rather than people. What did he see in her?

Before her insecurities could make her turn and run, Nico spotted her. His sizzling look and brilliant smile drove away her doubts. Or at least forced them into hiding for a while.

Nico crooked his finger, and she moved toward him. As soon as she was close enough, he wrapped her in his arms and kissed her. His tongue teased her lips with feathery touches until she sighed and he swept inside.

When they came up for air, Nico said, "I missed you yesterday."

"I missed you, too," Deanna murmured, her head on his chest. "But I'm glad I got to see my friends."

"Was it hard reconnecting after losing touch?" Nico tucked a curl behind her ear. "Or were you able to pick up where you left off?"

"At first, it was a little awkward," Deanna confessed. "Sort of like I'd come into the middle of a movie. But once I caught up, it was great."

"Good." Nico kept a firm arm around her waist but turned to stir something heavenly smelling in a big metal pot. "From what you've told me about your work schedule, you need more fun in your life."

"I've been thinking that, too." Deanna leaned against his side and asked, "How did it go with your mother?"

"Hell if I know." Nico's dark brows drew together. "But you were right about talking to her in person. Thanks for making me listen."

"You're welcome." Deanna inhaled the spicy odor wafting from the stove, and her mouth watered. "How did you leave things with your mom?"

"She's coming here next week to meet you, and we'll discuss her wedding plans then." Nico held a small spoon to Deanna's lips and said, "Try this."

"Hmm." Creamy sauce with a peppery bite flooded her taste buds. "Delicious." She fidgeted. "So you told your mother about me?"

"Yep." Nico tapped Deanna's nose with the spoon she'd licked clean, then tossed it in a metal bin holding dirty utensils. "She said she can't wait to meet the girl who put the happy expression on my face."

"Really?" Deanna's heart fluttered. "That's such a sweet thing for her to say."

"Mom is brutally honest." Nico lowered the fire under a couple of pans, then said, "If she didn't really believe it, she wouldn't say it."

She glanced sideways at Nico and asked, "What did you tell her about me?"

"Only that we'd met because of your job and had been seeing each other a few weeks." Nico grinned. "And that you're beautiful."

"You shouldn't have said that." Deanna's forehead wrinkled. "As a fashion designer, she works with the most stunning females in the world. She'll be expecting me to look as amazing as those women."

"No. She won't." Nico took Deanna by the shoulders and stared into her eyes. "You're perfect the way you are and Mom will see that." He chuckled. "Plus, I'm sure she's had one of her assistants Google you by now."

"Terrific," Deanna groused. "My online presence makes me look like a total nerd."

"We can fix that." Nico seated Deanna on a stool next to a stainless steel prep station, took his phone from his back pocket, and before she could protest, snapped a couple of pictures. "There, now you have better photos to post.

"Let me see." Deanna reached for his cell, but he stepped back.

"Later." Nico tucked his phone away. "You can get rid of the pictures you don't like, and then I'm putting the ones you approve on my Facebook page so everyone can see my hot girlfriend."

"That's probably not a good idea." There were too many sensations swirling inside of her to sort out exactly what she felt about Nico's declaration. Fear that people would wonder what he saw in her. Delight that he wanted to declare publicly that they were together. And something else. Something warm and sweet and wonderful that she refused to identify.

"I'm going to do it, so pick a few snapshots or I will." Nico turned back to the stove.

"Okay. But don't forget that I get to delete the others." Deanna leaned against the metal counter and watched Nico return to his cooking. As he worked, she asked, "What's for dinner?"

"See if you can guess." Nico switched off the oven, then pulled a red silk scarf from the pocket of his chef's coat and walked behind her. "Let me blindfold you and feed you the first course."

"I'm not fond of having my eyes covered." Deanna tensed. "I'm a little claustrophobic and I don't like the feeling of being helpless."

"Give it a try." Nico nibbled her ear. "It's not as if your hands are tied. At least not yet. So if you hate it, you can always take it off."

Shivering from both his suggestive words and the touch of his lips, Deanna nodded. Nico's eyes lit up, clearly pleased at this sign of her trust, and he quickly fastened the scarf around her head. But instead of the darkness she was expecting, a pink glimmer seeped through the fine silk.

Nico's voice soothed her as he said, "You're doing great." He kissed her and ran his knuckle down her cheek. There was a few seconds' pause, then he tapped her bottom lip with his finger and said, "Open up."

Buttery dough melted in her mouth, followed by creamy artichoke and fennel. Deanna chewed and swallowed, then moaned, "Yum."

It felt so decadent to be pampered like this. With every bite of food that Nico had made just for her, Deanna believed more and more that it was not just sexual attraction between them. Not just a mutual craving for sensual satisfaction. Not just erotic need.

His breath tickled her ear when he whispered, "Any idea what you're eating?"

"Not a clue," Deanna admitted, then smiled. "But it's delicious."

Nico untied the scarf, and Deanna saw the plate of scrumptious little pockets of goodness. The golden pastry was beautiful.

"Empanadas," Deanna laughed. "I would have never guessed correctly."

Nico poured a glass of sauvignon blanc for each of them, then made himself comfortable on the empty stool next to her. As they enjoyed the rest of the warm appetizer, Nico described his flight to New York.

"That's precisely why I hate flying." Deanna made a face. "The cabins are designed for skinny pygmies, not someone with my derrière or your long legs."

"There aren't too many people who find airline seating comfortable. And the bus and subway weren't any better," Nico complained. "If I wanted to share my personal space with hot, smelly people, I'd rather do it at the gym."

"Me, too. Give me Rocco's any day." Deanna licked a crumb from the corner of her mouth, then caught her breath when the blue in Nico's eyes changed to the exact color of the hottest part of a flame. Swallowing, she asked, "What's our second course?"

"Mussels ménage à trois." Nico got up and fetched three tiny plates.

"Sounds naughty," Deanna teased. "I hope no one is joining us."

"I'd never share you." Nico's voice deepened and he

scowled.

"Good to know." Deanna watched him closely as she added, "I don't want to share you, either."

"I wouldn't dream of being with anyone else."

Nico had just confirmed that they were exclusive, and Deanna felt something in her chest ease. She cradled the idea to her heart, even happier that he'd announced his intentions so casually, as if he'd never considered any other options.

She grinned and said, "So what *are* we eating?"

"The first of the trio is mussels in wine and herb sauce."

He picked up a shell in one hand and a fork in the other and speared the meat. Gently pulling it loose, he slid it between Deanna's lips, then ate one himself.

"Oh. My. Gosh." Deanna groaned at the flavor. "That was exquisite."

"Now try the tomato and saffron." Nico fed her a taste from the second plate and took one for himself. "It's completely different."

The mixture of bitter with a tiny bit of sweet slipped over Deanna's tongue like Nico's callused fingers over her sensitive skin.

She swallowed and said, "Now I can't decide which is better."

"This is my favorite." Nico offered her a bite from the final dish. "Green curry."

After they finished the mussels, Deanna sighed, "I can't choose. All three are amazing. Will these be on your menu?"

"Some of the time." Nico grinned, then tempted, "Wait until you try the entree. You said you like spicy food, so I made you fiery vanilla-scented sea bass." He winked. "Hope you can take the heat."

"I've never heard of anything like that." Deanna realized that she was having fun. Nico was so sweet. The portions were small, and she wasn't panicking about all the calories. "You're going to spoil me for my usual dinner of grilled chicken and steamed broccoli."

"Good." Nico kissed her fingertips, nipping at the sensitive flesh. "How about if I promise to lighten my cooking for you and you promise to eat foods that are enjoyable rather than just sustenance?"

"We'll see," Deanna said lightly.

Her chest tightened. Could she change for him without reverting back to her bad habits and gross body? She'd have to be extra careful of what she consumed when she wasn't with Nico.

After they finished the scrumptious fish, Nico cleared the plates and wiped down the stainless steel counter. Once the surface was spotless, he disappeared around a corner, returning with a tray containing a glass bowl of sour cream, a small saucer of brown sugar, and a plate holding fresh figs cut into quarters.

Placing the platter between them, Nico sat on his stool, twisting it and hers until they faced each other. He dipped the fig in the sour cream and rolled it in the sugar. Cradling her nape, he held the sweet treat to her lips.

"I'm really full." She shook her head. "And I try to avoid sugar."

"This is about the sensuality of food. It heightens the moment. It can be suggestive, playful, sexy." Nico rubbed the fig against her closed mouth until she opened. "It's about tongues against skin."

Giving in to his enticing words, Deanna allowed him to feed her the fruit. Then, looking into Nico's dark blue eyes, she sucked his finger into her mouth and licked the sugar from the tip. Gliding her lips up and down, she flicked her tongue against his skin.

Nico groaned, then rasped, "That's exactly what I want you

to do to my cock." He reached behind her and unzipped her dress. "Only on your knees."

Heat and shock collided inside of her at his crude words. She should be outraged. None of the men she'd dated had ever spoken to her like that. They'd never tried to take over. They'd never bluntly told her what they wanted.

But Nico's demand made her sex clench. And suddenly wicked images filled her imagination. Images of her lips wrapped around him, tasting him, bringing him pleasure.

Her bones might not be melting, but they were definitely feeling squishy. She frowned at the loss of control.

CHAPTER TWENTY-ONE

Nico smiled. What had brought on that endearingly grumpy look? He stood, moved between Deanna's legs, and kissed the crease between her brows. Time to unsettle her before her brain could muster all the reasons she shouldn't follow her body's wishes.

"We're wearing too many clothes for our last course." Nico shrugged off his chef's jacket and T-shirt, then stepped back, pulled Deanna to her feet, and slid her dress down her shoulders.

"What?" Deanna's eyes widened and her mouth dropped open in surprise. "Not here." She attempted to shift away from him.

"You can't always be in charge," Nico said. He ran his fingers down her spine, enjoying the way she shivered at his touch. "During our lovemaking, I'll be taking the reins and controlling our pleasure."

Although the frown returned, she didn't voice another protest. Acting quickly before she could summon up her resistance, Nico slid the silky knit material down her hips, allowing the fabric to pool around her sexy high-heeled sandals. Stepping back, he admired the perfection that he'd revealed. She was wearing the lingerie set that he'd sent to her, and she looked perfectly edible.

He immediately hardened. From the gorgeous cinnamon ringlets cascading down her back to her pretty pink toenails, and everywhere in between, she was perfect. He'd let her keep the bra and panties on for a bit while he enjoyed the view.

"Up you go." Nico put his hands on her waist and boosted her onto the counter.

"It's cold." Deanna hissed, trying to lift her naked butt

cheeks off the metal.

He hid a smile. The thong he'd sent didn't provide much insulation.

"Don't move," Nico warned with a stern look. "I'll be right back."

He walked around a corner and grabbed the supplies he'd prepared before Deanna's arrival. When he returned a few seconds later, he was happily surprised that she'd followed his order to stay put.

Nico rewarded her, and himself, with a searing kiss. Reluctantly lifting his mouth, he took her hands and placed them palms down on the counter behind her. Then he tugged her arms until she was leaning backwards.

"So I'm the next course?" Deanna asked with a hint of both apprehension and eagerness in her voice.

Pleased to hear that anticipation, Nico placed a kiss on her forehead and murmured, "I always save the most delicious morsel for last."

A rosy blush colored her cheeks, and Nico was happy that she was now enjoying his surprises instead of trying to regain control of the evening. Would she continue to permit him to take charge of their lovemaking?

Her need to be in command of every situation would make her try to take over, and he had to stop that from happening. Quickly, he twisted off the top of the Frangelico bottle and poured a splash of it into her bellybutton, topping it with a dollop of whipped cream.

Spreading her thighs apart, he moved between them and sipped the liqueur. After lapping the last of the Frangelico from her navel, he took her mouth in a deep kiss, allowing her to taste the hazelnut flavor. When they were both gasping for air, he raised his lips.

Deanna's beautiful green eyes were glazed, and he caressed

her jaw with his thumb before straightening. Grasping her curvy hips, he pulled her toward the edge of the counter, and easing his fingers under the wide lace band of her stockings, he pushed her thighs wider apart.

Standing back, he admired the picture she made. She was a feast spread out for his enjoyment, and he intended to savor every taste.

When Deanna started to squirm under his scrutiny, Nico gave himself a mental smack on the forehead. He needed to keep things moving. He had to flood her senses, force her to stay in the moment, otherwise she'd be overwhelmed by her insecurities.

Untying the ribbons that held her thong together, he removed the scrap of damp lace, delighted at the evidence of her arousal. Next he dispensed with the bra, stroking her creamy breasts. They were exquisitely plump and unbelievably soft.

Nico couldn't resist taking a taste, and the feel of Deanna's hard nipple against the roof of his mouth made him hungry for more of her. Her shallow breath and urgent moans were an aphrodisiac, and he unzipped his jeans to ease the discomfort of his growing erection.

As he rolled one nipple and sucked the other, the sight of Deanna writhing on the counter made him even harder. Her tiny gasps of pleasure were satisfying, but he was determined that the noises he would soon coax from her would be even better.

After another long, sensuous kiss, Nico nibbled his way slowly down her body. He wanted to know her more intimately than he'd ever known another woman. He leisurely explored every inch of her enticingly soft skin. When he reached the apex of her thighs, he trailed his fingers through the small tuft of cinnamon curls between her ivory thighs. Thighs he could hardly wait to have wrapped around his hips.

Damn! He wanted her. She was sensuous, beautiful, smart,

and spirited. Everything he'd been searching for without ever realizing it.

Moving his hand lower, he spread her silky folds until she was fully exposed. And when he lowered his mouth to her moist center, Nico sighed in pure delight. He'd finally found the sweetest flavor of them all.

Deanna's hips jerked and she made a mewling sound. Nico grinned, then used his tongue and fingers to drive her need even higher. He wanted her to make those little whimpers in the back of her throat. The ones where she couldn't hide her arousal. Couldn't hide how much she wanted him inside of her. Couldn't hide their connection.

As he continued to lick and nibble, demanding cries filled his ears. Then she tensed and screamed her satisfaction.

Nico stroked her until he'd wrung the last ounce of pleasure from her body. Deanna was exactly how he wanted her. Satiated and oblivious to anything except him and the moment they were sharing.

He studied her face as she floated up to full consciousness. Her eyes were heavy-lidded, reflecting emotions from delight to a flicker of uncertainty. But she immediately shook off her insecurity and smiled at him.

"That was..." Deanna started. "I've never been able to... not with oral sex..." She smiled and shook her head. "But with you, wow!"

Nico's chest expanded with pride, and he gathered her into his arms, stroking from her head down her back to her bottom. He was touched at how she fought her self-consciousness to share her feelings with him. She didn't say much, but that she'd said anything at all magnified her words a hundred times over.

Reluctantly releasing her, Nico stepped over to the rear of the kitchen, where a small desk was pushed against the wall. Above it was the bulletin board where he pinned the menus and recipes for his line cooks. Opening the top desk drawer, he pulled out a box of condoms and walked back to Deanna.

Although he was beyond aroused and wanted her more than he wanted a Michelin star for his new restaurant, he didn't miss the unhappiness in her eyes. She'd sat up and was now huddled on the edge of the counter. There was a tiny line between her brows and she was biting her lip. Dismay was etched on her face.

With a forced smile, she said, "I see you're always prepared, Chef."

He followed her gaze to the box of Trojans in his hand, and her meaning became clear. She thought she was one of many. That he regularly brought women to his kitchen, prepared them a special dinner, and then had sex with them.

Although her tone had been light, Nico heard the self-doubt in her voice, and he needed to fix that before it ruined everything.

He hurried to where she sat, moved between her legs, and gathered her in his arms, then whispered in her hair, "I bought the condoms on my way here to cook. I swear to you that I've never invited another woman into my kitchen."

"Oh." She hid her face in his chest. "Good." She blinked. "I mean, not that I don't know that you've been with… Or that I expect…"

Deanna trailed off, and after a long moment of silence, she straightened and took the box from his hand. Flipping open the lid, she grabbed a foil packet and tossed the carton aside. She shoved off his jeans and boxer briefs, sheathed him, and guided him inside of her.

She was hot and wet and so tight he was afraid he'd hurt her. But she wrapped her legs around him and refused to permit him to go slow or to be gentle.

She felt like heaven, and Nico clenched his jaw to make it last. But Deanna gripped his hips and thrust against him. Her movements were relentless and didn't allow him to show any tenderness. Understanding her urgency and her need for him, he let her set the pace.

All too soon, she tensed and clenched around him. A half second later, she screamed his name, and he followed her over the cliff.

When he was certain his legs would hold them, he carried Deanna into his office. Sitting on his chair, he cradled her on his lap. Although the room was warm, she was trembling, and he pulled a tablecloth from a stack of clean linens near his desk. Drawing it around her, he snuggled her to his chest and rested his chin on the top of her head.

Nico had known from their initial encounter that Deanna was attracted to him. That she desired him. But tonight had opened the lock she kept on her heart. The trust she'd shown had destroyed the wall around his soul and changed everything between them.

He held her close, caressing her hair and willing her to see how much she meant to him. When they'd first met, he'd desired her, but in the last few weeks, he'd also grown to like her. To enjoy being with her outside the bedroom. To depend on her.

Nico was ready to admit that he wanted her in his life not as a casual girlfriend but as more. Much more.

Did he love her? *No!* Loving made you vulnerable. Look at his mother. He wasn't willing to go down that road.

A voice in his head laughed and sneered, "You already took that turn. It's too late for a detour now."

Evidently, Deanna felt his restlessness, and she tried to sit up, but Nico kept her against his chest.

She tilted her head and, in a soft, sated voice, asked, "Aren't we done?"

"We've hardly begun." He hugged her tighter. "Think of this as a seven-course meal." At her confused expression, he grinned. "And we're still on the appetizers."

CHAPTER TWENTY-TWO

Deanna refused to dwell on the fact that she'd just been utterly naked with Nico buried inside of her on a counter in the kitchen of LeBoeuf. Instead she concentrated on remembering the sensation of his tongue licking and sucking that oh-so-sensitive spot between her thighs. And later, how amazing it had felt when they'd both tumbled over the edge together.

With a happy sigh, Deanna snuggled in Nico's caring embrace. It was so good to be held, to have the warmth of his breath on her cheek and soothing stroke of his hand down her back. His tender touch reached far past her skin and wormed its way into her soul.

Deanna's eyes drifted shut. Nico was filling her with experiences she'd treasure forever, whether or not he was there to share that lifetime with her. She frowned at that thought but pushed it away. Tonight, she'd enjoy him while she could.

The moment embraced her with a sweet warmth and satisfaction that she'd never felt in achieving her personal goals or in her professional accomplishments. Reaching a single-digit size and adding that extra zero to her bank account hadn't made her happy. She'd shrunk her whole world to the numbers on a scale and on an investment statement. Even with all she'd achieved, she still felt an indescribable emptiness. But in Nico's arms, that was no longer true.

Deanna must have dozed off for a second, because suddenly the lip of a plastic bottle was nudging her mouth. She parted her lips and took a sip. Although room temperature, the water was refreshing, and she realized she'd been thirsty. Apparently incredible sex was dehydrating. She took the Dasani from Nico and drank deeply.

After she was finished, Nico said, "Let's head to my place for the second course."

She'd been satiated, but the huskiness of his voice and brush of his thumb against her nipple shot her back into immediate arousal.

"Okay." Deanna nodded against his chest, pressing tiny kisses to his hot skin.

Grinning, Nico carried her into the kitchen, and as she slipped on her clothes, he pulled on his jeans and T-shirt. Once they were dressed, he led her out the rear door and tucked her into his SUV. He hurried around the vehicle and slid behind the wheel.

As he drove, he held her hand. Deanna stared at his tanned fingers entwined with hers and half expected to feel embarrassment. They'd just had sex, and Nico was clearly intending to do it again as soon as they reached his apartment, but all she felt was turned on and eager to experience whatever he had planned. Actually, if her pulse raced any faster, the police would pull them over for speeding.

Evidently there had been a sensual woman hidden inside of her that she had never allowed to emerge. But Nico had gradually lured that woman to the surface, and there was no way Deanna was reburying her.

Nico's building had an underground garage, and after pulling into his reserved space, he helped Deanna out of the SUV and hustled her into the nearby elevator. As the car rose to the seventh floor, he flicked his tongue along her neck, and pleasure hummed through her blood.

Tugging her by the hand, Nico hurried her through the hallway. He used his key, then pulled her over the threshold and slammed the door behind them.

"I can't wait another second. I'm going to take you right here, right now," Nico rasped.

He looked at her with such hunger Deanna could only force out one syllable, "Yes."

He pushed her against the wall, lifted her skirt, and tore away her thong. After taking a condom from his pocket, he unzipped his jeans and sheathed himself.

Drawing her arms over her head, he shackled them with one large hand and said, "It's going to be hard and rough." His voice was harsh and commanding, the tone sending a shock of excitement between her legs. "All day tomorrow when you're at your desk, you'll remember that you're mine every time you move or take a breath."

The words *you're mine* echoed in the silent foyer, and Deanna shuddered at the image he was painting. The pressure of his fingers around her wrist and his dark, sexy voice short-circuited her mind, and she gave herself up to his control.

He rubbed his erection through her folds, and she knew that he had to feel how wet, how ready she was for him. A second later, he slid inside of her with a single thrust. Slow, thick heat spread through her, and her hips bucked, needing even more.

Nico grunted and used the fingers of his free hand to gather her moisture and spread it against her swollen bud. He pressed the heel of his hand to that sensitive bundle of nerves, and Deanna gasped at the intimacy of the act.

Shivering, Deanna tried to force him to apply more force. But while he pounded into her harder and harder, the pressure from his palm remained too light for her to come, and her needy wail shocked her.

His unrelenting thrusts drowned her in waves of desire. It was too much. Every part of her was throbbing. From her tight nipples to the engorged nub pressed against his hand, she ached for release.

Nico let go of her wrists, dragging down the neckline of her dress and the tops of her bra cups. Once her breasts were exposed, he bent his head and sucked.

Deanna moaned, loving the intense draw of his lips and the sharp nips of his teeth. With her hands finally free, she grabbed his hips and tried to change the rhythm of his thrust to get that little bit of something more she needed to take her over the cliff. A cliff that Nico seemed determined that she'd only reach when he allowed it.

She whimpered, but Nico continued at his own pace. Finally, his thrusts sped up, and he slid his fingers between their sweat-slicked bodies, gliding them downward until he reached her distended bud. He stroked harder and harder until her need built up to the point of no return and she ground herself against him, frantic for the pleasure she desperately sought.

Then, without any warning, Nico pinched her aroused flesh between his thumb and index finger. The sensation was just past pleasure, into the edge of pain, and it sparked something dark inside of her.

Deanna tunneled her fingers into his hair and gripped the soft strands, sealing her mouth to his. Nico was pounding into her so hard a picture next to her head fell, but she barely noticed the sound as it crashed to the floor.

His tongue mated with hers. Neither of them held anything back, and as she cried out her need, he let go of her aching nub.

When the blood flowed back into it, her body stiffened. Then every muscle shook as she broke apart.

The white-hot explosion was so powerful that she screamed Nico's name. For a split second, she was overwhelmed. She was afraid that she wouldn't survive the scorching pleasure. That she would burst into flames.

But before she could panic, Nico's merciless thrusts pushed her into another climax. And as the bright white stars flashed beneath her eyelids, he followed her over the precipice into paradise.

Deanna was still slumped against the wall with Nico draped over her when she heard a noise. Before she could react, the door swung open and the maître d' from LeBoeuf strolled into the foyer. As she peered over Nico's shoulder, the intruder stopped and stared into her eyes.

The guy smirked and asked, "Am I too late to join in the fun?"

Nico shielded her nudity as he yanked down her skirt and pulled up her bodice. Then, keeping her behind him, he turned toward the intruder and roared, "What the hell are you doing? Get out!"

When the maître d' didn't budge, Nico grabbed Deanna's hand and tugged her down a hallway into a tiny powder room. While he disposed of the condom and jerked up the zipper of his jeans, Deanna straightened her dress and ran her fingers through her hair.

Ignoring Nico's order to stay put, Deanna trailed behind him when he left the bathroom. The intruder was waiting in the corridor.

He stepped around Nico, held out his hand to her, and said, "I'm Marco Thorne. The handsome brother. You must be Deanna."

"I...uh...yes." Deanna's face was burning, but she automatically put her fingers into his and said, "Pleased to meet you."

"You, too, sweet pea." Marco brought her knuckles to his mouth.

"Asshole." Nico wrenched Deanna's hand from his brother's grip and shoved Marco back from her. "Don't call her sweet pea." His jaw clenched. "She's Ms. Sloan to you."

"Nah. She's definitely sweet pea." Marcus tilted his head appraisingly. "Her skin is the same color pink of Mom's prized flowers."

Nico gritted his teeth, then took a deep breath and demanded, "Why would you barge in like this?"

"Hey. Chill, bro." Marco shrugged, a smug grin on his face. "You never bring women here. How was I supposed to know you had company?"

"Just get out." Nico seized his brother's arm and yanked him toward the foyer.

"Sure." Marco held up his hands in surrender. "How about I come over for breakfast tomorrow so Deanna and I can get to know each other."

"Don't even think about it!" With a snarl, Nico wrenched open the front door, pushed his brother over the threshold, and slammed the slab of steel in his face.

"I should probably get going," Deanna said, upset at Nico's angry expression.

Was he mad at his brother or her? Or maybe at himself for bringing a woman into his home when he clearly had a policy against that sort of intimacy?

"No!" Nico barked, then inhaled and said, "What I mean is please stay. Don't let my idiot brother ruin this. How about a drink?"

"A glass of wine would be good." Deanna truly didn't want the evening to end. "But first, would you mind if I took a shower?"

"Not at all." Nico took her hand and led her into what was plainly his bedroom. "The bath is through there. Help yourself to anything you need." He paused. "Or I could join you?"

"I need a few minutes by myself," Deanna said gently. "Okay?"

"Sure." Nico showed her the cabinet that contained towels, soap, and shampoo, then, closing the door behind him, left her alone.

His parting smile reassured her that he really did want her in his home. But her emotions were a wreck, and she wanted to sort things out in her mind.

As she cleaned up, Deanna thought about how Nico had made love to her against the wall in the foyer. She wasn't sure why she'd been turned on when he'd taken over. She certainly wouldn't have allowed that in any other type of situation. But during sex, there was something about giving up control to him that made her lose both her breath and her panties. Something that certainly had never happened with any other man she'd dated.

Deanna heard the door open and close while she was showering, and when she finished, she found a T-shirt and a pair of boxers lying on the counter. Since Nico had torn the ribbon fastenings from her thong, she had no choice but to put on his briefs. It felt strangely personal, but at the same time, she was oddly comfortable wearing his clothes.

Stepping out of the bathroom, Deanna found Nico sitting on the bed with his back against the headboard. The lights were dimmed and soft music was playing. He held up a wineglass, flipped open the covers, and patted the mattress.

She slid in next to him and accepted the merlot. He put an arm around her, nestled her to his side, and they sipped in comfortable silence.

The next thing Deanna remembered was Nico taking the glass from her fingers and pulling a sheet over them. As he cuddled her, she fell into a contented sleep.

* * *

Deanna blinked at the faint rays of sunshine peeping through the sheer curtains of Nico's bedroom. Although it was wonderful to wake up beside him, it had been even better sleeping in his arms.

Everything about Nico just seemed right. He was so big that

for once Deanna didn't feel too fat or too tall or too anything. Instead she felt pretty and feminine and cherished. Words that, before meeting Nico, she never would have associated with herself.

Sometime during the night, the T-shirt and boxers she'd been wearing had come off, and the warmth of his chest pressed against her back radiated a sensual heat. His callused fingers cupped her breast, sending tiny jolts of pleasure through her body. And his breath stimulating the sensitive spot below her ear gave her a delightful shiver.

But it was the stirring inside her heart that overruled her head when her brain tried to convince her that what she had with Nico wasn't significant. She traced the curve of his biceps with her fingertips. There was no way that she could deny that there was a special connection joining them together. This morning was different from the one in Alton. This time there was no going back.

Deanna panicked. Facing what she and Nico had between them popped the cork out of her bottled-up emotions, and she was swamped by the feelings she'd always rejected. Affection, desire, and love overwhelmed her.

Finally, pushing away her fear, Deanna squirmed until her bottom was nestled against Nico's groin. Immediately, his fingers moved from her breast to stroke the curve of her hip. He trailed his thumb over the bare skin, then slipped his hand between her legs.

Deanna gasped, the air escaping from her lungs in a soft whisper of longing. The utter pleasure of Nico's touch brought back every decadently wicked and wonderful moment of the last twelve hours.

Glancing over her shoulder, Deanna saw that despite his caresses, Nico was still asleep. A wisp of relief settled over her.

She needed time to adjust. She couldn't magically change

the way she was wired. But he, no, they were worth the effort to at least try.

Until Nico entered her life, Deanna hadn't allowed herself to recognize what she'd been missing. He'd made her open up to all the colors, all the flavors, all the sensations that she denied wanting or needing.

The recognition of everything she'd been sacrificing made her feel a little raw. Almost as if a cloth had been ripped from her eyes and the unaccustomed light was blinding her. What if, like Icarus, she was flying too close to the sun? When Nico grew tired of her, would she be able to stop herself from a painful plummet into reality?

No! Deanna banished her negative thoughts. She wouldn't allow her insecurities to intrude on this perfect moment. Closing her eyes, she snuggled against Nico and drifted back to sleep.

CHAPTER TWENTY-THREE

Nico woke with his groin pressed against Deanna's lush ass and his hand wedged between her legs. *Seriously?* Could there be a better way to start the day? He brushed his fingers through the soft curls at the apex of her thighs, and she made an adorable sound that reminded him of his mother's cats purring in their sleep.

His throat tightened. Deanna was so fucking sweet. Being with her made him feel invincible. As if he could do anything. Handle anything. She even made his crazy family situation seem almost bearable.

Nico smiled, remembering the moment that her defenses had finally crumbled. When he'd breached those walls, what had happened between them had been beyond perfect. She'd let him make love to her in ways that she'd obviously never before experienced with another man.

He grinned. He'd never be able to look at the prep station counter the same way again. Could he arrange to buy it for his new restaurant? He'd definitely like an encore of last night's dessert.

Nico sobered. It wasn't just the physical part of the act. Deanna had allowed him past her emotional barricades, as well. Now, in the cold light of day, would she try to rebuild her fortifications?

Not if he could help it. He'd had sex with a lot of other women, but in his heart, he knew that he'd never made love to anyone but her.

"Nico?" Deanna's sleep-clogged voice broke into his thoughts.

"Yes, sweetheart?" He rolled her toward him so he could

look into her eyes. "Is everything okay?" She nodded and he brushed a strand of hair from her cheek. "Thank you for agreeing to stay the night with me so we could wake up together. I was really worried when you kept saying you should go back to your place."

"I just thought since your brother said you don't bring women here, you might have wanted me to leave." Deanna's expression held a glimmer of hope. "But when you said you didn't, I was glad."

"Marco is an idiot." Punctuating his words, Nico kissed her forehead, her cheek, and her jaw. He wanted to bury his nose in her neck and breathe her in. "There's a difference between bringing a casual date home and having someone you really have feelings for share your bed."

Nico didn't care if every other woman on the planet ceased to exist, as long as Deanna kept looking at him as if he was everything she'd ever wanted.

Pressing his mouth to hers, he licked and nibbled until she opened her lips. As their tongues slid and sucked, he stroked her breasts.

Suddenly Deanna pushed him away, scrambled off the mattress, and stared at the alarm clock on the nightstand. "Shit! Shit! Shit! It's almost nine o'clock. I'm late for work."

"Call in sick," Nico suggested. "I bet you have a ton of accumulated sick days."

"Are you crazy?" Deanna rushed into the foyer to gather her discarded garments, and Nico followed her. "Associates do not take sick leave. Ever! Amanda had them induce labor so she could have the baby on Friday and be back at her desk on Monday morning." Deanna carried her bra and dress into the bathroom. "And Jon scheduled his gallbladder surgery for Christmas Eve so he could be at work when the firm opened up after the holidays."

"Hell!" Nico yanked on jeans and a T-shirt. "Your hours are worse than mine."

"At least I showered last night. Call me a cab while I subdue my hair," Deanna ordered, dragging a brush through her snarled curls. "And please, please, please find my stupid sandals."

"I'll drive you." Nico stuffed his feet into sneakers.

Deanna frowned at herself in the mirror. "Thank goodness I keep a set of clothes in the office. With luck I can change before anyone sees me. Wearing your boxers for underwear all day would make me feel like a slut."

"Sorry about tearing your thong," Nico apologized, then said, "Meet me by the door."

Nico jogged into the kitchen, put a pod in the Keurig, and then rummaged in the freezer until he found the leftover muffins from the batch that he'd made for their Alton trip. Damn if he'd send her to work without coffee and something to eat.

As he popped the frozen goodie in the microwave, he noticed the red light blinking on his kitchen phone. He hesitated but couldn't resist.

After punching in the code for his voice mail, he heard, "Chef Thorne, I'm calling for Mr. Bristle. He has been rushed to the hospital and won't be able to attend your meeting this afternoon. We will inform you when he is recovered and able to reschedule."

Nico hoped his attorney was okay, but shit, now what was he going to do? He quickly dialed Randolph Ventures and was surprised to reach Franklin Randolph rather than an answering machine. Nico explained the situation and asked to postpone the meeting until he hired a new lawyer.

"Absolutely not." Randolph clipped the words as if he grudged the breath they took to utter.

Nico scowled. Randolph's oily voice had oozed impatience,

but there was also something else—could it be satisfaction? He shook his head. Why would the guy be happy that their deal might fall through?

"But—"

Randolph interrupted, "I'm a busy man. Either we meet today as scheduled or I'm no longer interested in investing in your restaurant."

Nico counted to ten. The man had him by the short hairs. He didn't have much choice. If he didn't get the money by the end of the week, Walker couldn't pay for the rehab materials, and the renovations would grind to a halt. If the remodeling wasn't completed, the restaurant couldn't open. If it didn't open, he'd lose the building.

He wouldn't miss this chance. Although his lawyer hadn't been happy that he'd only been given a draft of the contract and wouldn't see the final document until their meeting, Bristle had admitted that the agreement was fairly standard.

"Hell!" Nico swore under his breath. He wasn't a fucking moron. How hard could the contract be to understand? He would just have to read the agreement very carefully before signing it.

After assuring Randolph the meeting was still on, Nico went in search of Deanna's missing shoes. As he hunted for the elusive footwear, he decided not to tell Deanna about his lack of legal representation.

He'd already made his decision. She had enough on her mind, and it wasn't as if she could do anything about the situation. Plus, he didn't want her caught in the middle between him and her boss.

Yep. Nico nodded to himself. It was better to keep her out of it.

A few minutes later, Nico juggled a to-go cup, a muffin, and Deanna's sandals when he met her in the foyer. She put on her shoes, grabbed the coffee, but stuffed the muffin in her purse.

Nico narrowed his eyes, pretty damn sure she didn't intend to eat the breakfast pastry. Choosing not to start an argument— he'd bring her some food after he saw Randolph—Nico permitted her to hustle them into his SUV. Once they were buckled in, he turned the car toward her office.

Deanna was glued to her phone for the entire drive and only gave him a distracted kiss when he stopped the vehicle in front of her building.

She jumped out, then leaned back in and said, "Don't forget your meeting at one."

"I won't." Nico took her hand and kissed her fingers. "See you then."

She waved and Nico watched her disappear into the building. As he drove home, he racked his brain trying to remember if he knew any other attorneys.

* * *

Deanna lucked out. Except for Mr. Byron, there was no one in the lobby. And because the associates were crowded into the tiny offices of the third floor and the receptionist's desk was on the fourth, Deanna didn't have to pass through the firm's reception area.

Instead she was able to take the elevator directly to her floor. She sent up a prayer of gratitude when the hallway was empty and another silent thank you once she was behind the locked door of her office. Although she didn't have her laptop and would have to make do with her desktop computer, at least the overnight bag she kept in the corner for emergency business trips was there to provide her with toiletries, clean underwear, a tan suit and ivory blouse, and a pair of beige pumps.

Once she transformed herself from Nico's lover back to serious businesswoman, Deanna blew out a relieved sigh. She stuffed her sexy dress, lacy lingerie, and high-heeled sandals into the suitcase and put it against the wall.

Catching a glance of herself in the window's reflection, she touched her skirt and made a face. Now she looked as boring and professional as usual.

Wait! When had she started equating professional with boring? She grimaced. Evidently being with Nico had changed her entire outlook.

Her chest tightened, then she let out a breath. Truth be told, she wasn't sure that was such a bad thing. She had to admit that she felt happier now. But how about the possible impact on her career, not to mention her waistline? There was a good chance both of those would suffer if she continued on this new path.

When Deanna sank into her chair, rather than booting up her computer and getting to work, she thought about last night. Why had she been so turned on when Nico had taken over? Was it *just* because it felt so good to be desired? Or was there something else?

She'd never been the kind of woman who was willing or able to use beauty to get ahead. It had been her brain, not her face or her body, that had gotten her where she was today. She'd earned every A, every opportunity, and every professional advancement by sheer hard work. But the complete concentration and perfection required for that type of achievement was exhausting.

Deanna had spent the years since high school hyperfocused on achieving her goals. She expended all her energy to climb the corporate ladder and was too drained to use her limited time off even to think about personal satisfaction. Certainly not her sexuality.

Her few bedroom encounters had been so uninspiring that she hadn't been motivated to look any further. Until Nico, BOB had taken care of her needs better than any of the men she'd ever dated. All she required was fresh batteries and a sexy book to satisfy her.

Maybe what had been missing in her previous encounters with men had been the power and control that oozed from Nico's every pore. Turning over the reins to him during sex had been unbelievably liberating. She trusted him to take care of her needs. To push her out of her comfort zone but still keep her safe.

Lovemaking with Nico had been heart-pounding, body-shattering, and emotionally trailblazing. He respected her, listened to her, and told her again and again that she was beautiful.

The dynamic between them was unique. He treated her as an equal out of bed, carefully considering all her suggestions—even when it came to his family. However, during sex, the dynamic switched.

The sensation was heady. It was okay to expose her vulnerabilities when she was with Nico. He didn't see them as weaknesses, only proof she was human. He wasn't stealing something from her when he took charge in the bedroom, he was giving her everything.

Shocked that she was okay with not being in control, Deanna leaned back in her chair and stared at the ceiling. She'd never been willing to relinquish the power before, but at the end of the work day, it felt wonderful to let Nico call the shots.

After a luxuriously sensual stretch, Deanna buckled down to work. Having come in late, she continued through the morning without a break, and when her desk phone rang at twelve forty-five, she rubbed her neck before answering.

Randolph's admin was on the line. "Mr. Randolph wants you in his office right away."

"For the one o'clock meeting?" Deanna asked. "Does he need something from me?"

"All Mr. Randolph said was get your butt up here," the admin answered, then hung up.

Deanna hurriedly smoothed the stray strands of hair into her bun and, as she walked down the hall, applied a coat of lipstick. Using the mirror in the elevator, she checked her appearance.

When the doors swooshed open on the fourth floor, Deanna quickly exited and hastily headed toward Mr. Randolph's suite. His admin waved her in without a word, and when she entered the inner office, Randolph was on the phone. He gestured to a chair and she sat.

Seconds ticked by, and the longer her boss ignored her, the more Deanna worried. Had she done something wrong? Was she about to be fired?

Randolph finally finished his call, turned to her, and said, "Don't open your mouth during the meeting." He pointed his finger at Deanna. "If Thorne asks you a question, let me answer it."

"But—"

"Just keep quiet," Randolph cut off her question, and before she could protest, she heard the door swing open. As Nico came around the Japanese black lacquer screen that separated the entrance from the rest of the office, Randolph hissed at her under his breath, "Don't screw this up."

* * *

Nico straightened his tie as he walked across the huge office's thick carpet. He shot Deanna a smile and she nodded but didn't smile back. He widened his eyes in question, and she gave an infinitesimal shake of her head, clearly not wanting her boss to see them communicate. What was up with that?

Despite the drab suit and low-heeled shoes, Nico's blood heated when he looked at her. Now that he knew what was under her clothes and beneath the shell of cold calculation she showed the world, even dressed like a nun, he found her totally hot.

Nico shook hands with Randolph, then took the chair next to Deanna. As Randolph pushed a file toward him across the shiny desktop, Nico caught a glimpse of a tiny muscle throbbing in Deanna's jaw. A sure sign of tension. What was she so stressed about?

"It's good to see you again," Randolph's hearty voice interrupted Nico's thoughts. "I'm happy Ms. Sloan was able to recommend we invest in your restaurant. She's a tough one to impress."

A tiny smile flitted across Deanna's lips but was gone before Nico was certain he'd even seen it. It had held gratification and something else. Could it be a glimmer of uneasiness?

"Thank you, sir." Nico opened the file and saw the thick sheaf of papers. "Wow. It looks like I'm going to need quite a while to read through all this. Since I don't want to waste your time, how about I take it with me and drop it back here tomorrow?"

"Sorry, Chef. As I said on the phone, it's now or never." Randolph raised a brow and his dark eyes were cold. "I'm leaving for London tonight and won't be back for a couple of weeks or so."

"But I need the funds by Friday in order to keep the renovation on track and open on schedule," Nico protested. "Once you told me that you'd approved the investment and guaranteed that the money would be in my account by Wednesday, I proceeded under that assurance."

"And it will be." Randolph's smile had too many teeth. "As long as you sign the contract before I leave for the airport at five."

"I—"

Randolph interrupted, "That gives you nearly four hours to

read thirty pages." He gestured to the file in Nico's lap. "I can have my admin set you up in a conference room. When you're done, if you sign, the money can be available for your use tomorrow."

Nico's brain started firing on all burners. Every competitive and ambitious cell in his body jumped to attention. He could do this. He'd take his time, read every word, and fulfill his dream. Nothing would stop him from owning his own restaurant.

"Do you want to do that?" Randolph leaned back in his big leather chair, clearly indicating he didn't care what Nico decided. "Or perhaps you'd be more comfortable looking for another source for the financing you need. If so, tell me now. I'm a busy man."

"No." Nico gritted his teeth to stop himself from shouting.

"That's acceptable." He nodded at Deanna. "Perhaps Ms. Sloan could assist me."

"Sorry, Chef." Randolph stared down his nose, his expression unsmiling. "I need Ms. Sloan to finish up the paperwork on the London project. But you and I went over the terms when you first applied, and I'm certain she'll assure you that our standard contract is more than fair." He turned to Deanna. "Right, Ms. Sloan?"

A shadow crossed her face, but it disappeared so swiftly Nico wasn't sure if he'd imagined it.

"Yes." Deanna cleared her throat. "The standard contract is fair to both sides."

She hesitated, glanced at her boss, then back at Nico, and closed her mouth as if to stop herself from adding something more.

Nico wondered what she hadn't said.

CHAPTER TWENTY-FOUR

Deanna stared at Nico as he stood up. The jacket of his charcoal-gray suit stretched across his strong shoulders, and although nicely tailored, the pants couldn't conceal his muscular thighs. A crisp white shirt emphasized his broad chest, and his beautiful black hair had been trimmed to just above the collar.

She'd never seen him freshly shaven before, and she wasn't sure she liked it. She loved the feel of his rough cheek rasping against her skin as he kissed his way down her body. Oh, well. His sexy stubble would be back by this afternoon, and she'd just have to make sure he didn't remove it again.

Suddenly, all of Deanna's playful thoughts disappeared, and a sense of unease settled over her as she watched him move toward the door. Her gut told her that signing that contract in haste was a mistake. Where was his attorney? She put up a hand to stop him and was startled to see that her fingers were trembling.

As if Nico had heard her concerns, he stopped halfway over the threshold, turned to look at her, and asked, "Is something wrong?"

Deanna chewed her lip as she considered an acceptable response. Something that warned Nico but didn't anger Randolph. Concluding there was no way to protect both Nico and herself; she attempted to weigh the pros and cons. But in her heart, she knew there was only one answer.

Knowing that her next words might torpedo her career, she sucked in a deep breath. But before she could force the warning from her mouth, Randolph loomed over her chair and clamped his hand on her shoulder.

"Chef Thorne, the clock is ticking." As he gestured for Nico to leave, Randolph said, "Every second you stand here takes you further away from owning your restaurant."

Nico hesitated, staring at her. Should she caution him to have a lawyer look at the contract? What if he lost his funding because of her? While Deanna was frantically weighing possible scenarios, Randolph dug his fingers into her deltoid, and she flinched.

Hearing a snarl, she glanced at Nico. He was staring at Randolph's painful grip on her arm. The glimpse of Nico's raw male protectiveness thudded into her chest, and she gasped.

Nico narrowed his eyes and ordered, "Take your hands off of her."

Everything inside of her turned to mush at his possessive command, but she couldn't let him sacrifice himself for her. She had to convince him she was okay. He needed to concentrate on the contract.

As soon as Randolph released her, she got up and hurried to where Nico stood next to the lacquered screen. Smiling reassuringly, she said, "I'm fine. Go do what you need to do to get your restaurant."

Nico hesitated, but Deanna put a hand on his back, pushed him out the door, and closed it behind him. After wiping all expression from her face, she walked back and stood in front of her boss.

Irritation radiated from Randolph, but in a calm voice, Deanna said, "You have some work you need me to do on the London project?"

"I do. That is, if, after that touching scene between you and Thorne, you're ready to concentrate on business," Randolph sneered. He didn't wait for an answer, instead returning to his desk. He yanked open a drawer and pulled out half a dozen thick folders. "I need these by five."

"Yes, sir." Deanna clutched the files to her chest. She

pushed down her anger and resentment. Once they were buried deep enough that they couldn't escape, she said, "I apologize if I was unprofessional."

Randolph rolled his eyes and waved her away. Fearing that if she lingered she'd end up saying something that would get her into more trouble, Deanna hurried out of the office. As she dashed down the hall toward the reception area elevators, she was surprised to find Nico waiting for her by of one of the small conference rooms. He took her hand, tugged her inside, and closed the door.

Nico snaked an arm around her waist and brushed her lips with his. Deanna's first instinct was to pull away—there was no lock, and anyone could walk in on them. But Nico was looking down at her as if she was the reason for his existence, and she couldn't bring herself to give up his warm embrace.

No man had ever looked at her like that before. Or made her feel so protected and treasured. The moment was too sweet to end.

After a lingering kiss, Nico said, "Did Randolph give you hell after I left?"

"Not much." Deanna couldn't meet Nico's eyes, so she toyed with his tie. "Just shoved some paperwork at me and told me to leave."

"So you're not in trouble?" Nico tilted her chin up. "Is he always like that?"

"Like what?" She stalled. "Driven? Impatient? Demanding?"

"That, too." Nico scowled. "But I meant has he ever grabbed you and hurt you before?"

"Never." Deanna sighed. "Of course, I've never acted like that before."

"Like what?" Nico's brows rose. "Human?"

"Mr. Randolph believes that his associates are part of his

army," Deanna explained. "Our only loyalty is supposed to be to the company."

"Bullshit!" Nico snapped. "Everyone is allowed to have a personal life."

"To him, they aren't." Deanna sighed again, then changed the subject. "What are you going to do about the contract? You should have a lawyer—"

Deanna was interrupted by the door slamming open and her boss glaring from the threshold. "Ms. Sloan," he snapped. "Have you already finished the files that I gave you?"

"Uh." Deanna stole a peek at Nico, who nodded his understanding. "No, sir. Sorry. I'll get to work on them right away."

Randolph waited, not giving Deanna a chance to say anything more to Nico.

As she walked out of the conference room, her boss tapped her shoulder and said, "Come back to my office. I've decided it will be easier and more productive if we work on the files together."

"Yes, sir." Deanna glanced back at Nico.

He mouthed five thirty, pointed downward, and she nodded her understanding. They'd meet in the lobby after Randolph left for the airport.

* * *

Nico hated that in the past six days he hadn't seen Deanna, except for a couple of quick lunches. Since signing the contract with Randolph Ventures, time had whizzed by like an out-of-control Tilt-A-Whirl. Wednesday through Sunday, Nico had been tied up with his duties at LeBoeuf, and on Monday, he'd had to drive down to Alton to finalize some interior choices for his new restaurant.

Adding to his frustration, even his calls to Deanna were

rushed, their conversations consisting of nothing more than hi, everything's okay. Randolph had dumped a shitload of work on her before leaving for London, and he emailed more to her every afternoon.

When Nico had texted Deanna with the time and place for dinner with his mother, she'd tried to wiggle out of the invitation, and he'd been afraid that she was pulling away from him. That she was rebuilding the walls around her emotions. That she was once again becoming that aloof woman she'd been when they first met.

However, after some poking and prodding, she had admitted that she was worried about what to wear to meet a famous designer like Mariella Borghese. Nico had assured Deanna that he would take care of her wardrobe issues. And after consulting with his mom, he'd sent her one of Mariella's creations. A flirty black skirt and peach silk T-shirt that would be perfect for a casual dining spot like South Water Kitchen.

He grinned. He was beginning to enjoy picking out Deanna's clothes. Maybe next he'd send her a sexier business suit. *No!* On second thought, it was best all around if she looked a little less gorgeous at the office.

Seeing Randolph touch Deanna had made Nico's blood boil, and when he'd grabbed her shoulder so hard, it had taken all his self-control not to tear the asshole off of her. Especially since, when Deanna flinched in pain, the douchebag's expression and sudden boner had revealed a sadistic pleasure. It was pretty damn clear how that piece of shit got his jollies in the bedroom.

Gritting his teeth at the memory, Nico shook his head. He certainly didn't want to encourage Deanna's boss or any of her other male colleagues to think of her as anything but a co-worker. *Hell!* Maybe he should buy her some uglier outfits and get some orthopedic shoes for her to wear to the office.

Nico frowned. He'd never been jealous about any of his

previous girlfriends. But then again, those relationships had been casual, rarely lasting even a couple of weeks. What he had with Deanna was special. She was special. And as his mother could testify, he'd never been big on sharing.

Which was why tonight's dinner would be so hard. Mariella would notice his feelings and be arranging a double wedding. *Hell!* Nico wasn't even certain that Deanna wanted a future with him. She certainly wasn't ready to pick out a white dress and bridal bouquet. *Shit!* Now, not only would he have to talk his mom out of remarrying his father, he'd have to keep her from including him and Deanna in her matrimonial plans.

Nico's thoughts were interrupted when he noticed the time. He hurriedly tucked his shirt into his jeans and put on his belt, then shoved his feet into a pair of loafers. They were meeting his mother for dinner at eight, and he needed to pick up Deanna within the next fifteen minutes or they'd be late.

As promised, Mariella had arrived yesterday and checked into a suite at the Hotel Monaco. She never went anywhere without her cats, Sergei and Nadia, and the Monaco was among her favorite pet-friendly hotels.

Sighing, Nico resigned himself to an evening of his mother's gentle interrogation. How bad a son would he be if he cancelled on his mother? He could text her that Deanna had a headache. Then they could order takeout to eat in bed. And if they didn't get around to the eggrolls and moo shu pork right away, hey, Chinese food reheated really well in the microwave.

All he really wanted to do was be alone with Deanna, but he couldn't disappoint his mom. With no other choice, Nico scooped up his wallet and keys and walked out the door. But even as he drove to Deanna's, picked her up, and headed to the restaurant, he continued to toy with the idea of calling off the dinner.

He was still fantasizing about it when they entered South

Water Kitchen. And as soon as he spotted his mother's table companions, he knew he should have bailed when he had the chance.

When Nico involuntarily tightened his grip on Deanna's hand, she looked up at him and asked, "Is something wrong?"

"Mom didn't mention she was inviting anyone else." Nico jerked his chin in the direction of his family, then rubbed his knuckles against Deanna's cheek, hoping the sensation of her soft skin would help him relax. "I thought it was just the three of us."

Nico felt Deanna stiffen. "I recognize your brother from the other night, but is the older guy your father?" When Nico nodded, she said, "The four of you should talk about things alone. I can catch a cab and you can come over to my place afterwards."

"No!" Nico shouted, then added in a softer tone, "The only way I'll get through this meal without punching out someone's lights is if you're with me."

"Me?" Deanna squeaked. "How will me being here help you stay calm?"

Her beautiful green eyes had widened in surprise, and Nico pressed a kiss to her forehead before he explained, "I had a pretty bad temper when I was a teenager. I learned to control my anger by visualizing a place or person who makes me happy. You make me happy."

"Oh." Deanna curved an arm around his waist and laid her head on his chest. "That might be the sweetest thing anyone has ever said to me."

Nico tucked her closer to his side and rubbed his cheek against hers. He was in awe of her ability to soothe his soul with nothing more than a look and a touch.

Taking a cleansing breath, he asked, "So are you ready to meet my parents or shall we leave?"

"If I've learned anything working in the venture capital business, it's to never back away." Deanna straightened her shoulders. "It gives the opposition too much of an advantage."

"Then let's do this." Nico wiped his sweaty palms on his jeans, took her hand, and squeezed her fingers. With one last glance at the exit, he led Deanna toward his family.

Marco and Ian stood when they reached the table, but Nico steered Deanna to where his mother sat. Mariella tilted her face for his kiss.

"Mom." Nico leaned down and pressed his lips to her cheek. "This is Deanna Sloan."

"Sweetheart"—Nico stroked Deanna's shoulder—"this is my mother, Mariella Borghese."

"Pleased to meet you," Deanna and Mariella said simultaneously.

Nico watched carefully as the two of them exchanged pleasantries. His gut clenched in fear that the two most important women in his life wouldn't like each other.

He was relieved when his mother's eyes warmed and she murmured, "*Perfecti.*"

"Ms. Borghese"—Deanna smoothed her hand down her skirt—"thank you so much for the beautiful outfit. I've never had clothes that fit me so well."

"You are very welcome, my dear." Mariella reached out and fingered the dart on Deanna's shirt. "I design for real woman, not undernourished waifs, and you have nearly the ideal figure for my garments."

"Well, that's..." Deanna's voice faltered. "I mean, I'm working on shedding those last few pounds."

As Deanna's cheeks turned red in embarrassment, Nico frowned at his mother. He was just getting Deanna over her body image issues, and he'd be furious if Mariella wiped out all his hard work.

"No! No! No! You mustn't lose any weight." Mariella shook her head. "You are already a little too thin." She pointed to the seam on Deanna's skirt. "See, it should hug your hip just a bit more."

"I..." Deanna blinked and seemed to be searching for words, then smiled and said, "Or I could try to get into a size smaller."

"Definitely not." Ian ran an appraising gaze over Deanna's figure and added, "Listen to my wife. She knows what makes a woman look her best."

"She's not your wife," Nico snapped, then calmed himself by running his hand up and down Deanna's arm. After a deep breath, he said, "Sweetheart, this is my father, Ian Thorne. Ian, this is my girlfriend, Deanna Sloan."

As Nico watched his father flirt with Deanna, he realized he'd never introduced a woman as his girlfriend before. He waited for the panic to sweep through him, but instead, he felt contentment.

Ian pulled out the chair next to him for Deanna, and as she sat, she glanced at Nico as if to gauge his mood. He nodded that he was doing fine, and surprisingly he was okay. His anger toward his father seemed to have faded a bit. He still didn't want his parents to remarry, but he no longer wished his father would book a ticket on the next rocket to Mars.

Thumping Marco on the back, Nico said, "Change seats with me."

"Sorry, bro." Marco crossed his arms. "No can do. Mom wants you to sit next to her."

Nico glanced at his mother, who pointed to the chair by her side.

Sighing, Nico smiled weakly at his mom and nodded, but before moving around the table to take his seat, he growled in his brother's ear, "You touch Deanna or upset her in any way and I break every bone in your body."

The teasing expression on Marco's face vanished, and his dark brows nearly disappeared into his hairline. "That serious, huh?"

Nico didn't answer. He wasn't about to bare his emotions and expose his heart to his brother. Although that didn't stop him from keeping a close eye on both Marco and Ian as he listened to his mother talk about her latest collection.

When a server appeared to take their drink orders, Nico asked for a beer, but he noticed that Deanna requested mineral water. *Smart.* Although she might not realize that she was sitting between two wolves, she was still keeping her wits about her.

"I like your girl," Mariella said. "But she needs more self-assurance."

"She's confident about everything except her looks," Nico defended Deanna.

"And what do you think of her appearance?" Mariella asked softly.

"She's so gorgeous she takes my breath away," Nico admitted.

"Then you must persuade her she is beautiful." Mariella tilted her head. "Convince her that it isn't important what she sees in the mirror. What's important is what she sees in your eyes."

"I've tried." Nico ground his teeth. "But she drives me insane with her obsession about calories."

"Ah." Mariella nodded. "She makes you crazier than anyone else. Yes?"

"Uh-huh."

"It's because she makes you feel so unbelievably good that she can also make you feel so exceedingly bad." Mariella glanced at Ian. "You just have to decide if the highs are worth the lows."

"And you've decided they are?" Nico nodded his head

toward his father, resigned that he probably wouldn't change his mother's mind about remarrying the jerk.

"Yes." Mariella patted his hand. "And so have you. I can see how special Deanna is to you."

"Mom," Nico leaned closer and whispered in her ear, "I think she might be the one."

CHAPTER TWENTY-FIVE

Deanna got up from behind her desk and stretched. Checking the time, she was surprised that it was already noon. In order to make up for leaving early—well, early for her—yesterday, she'd gotten to the office before six a.m. And except for a couple of trips to the break room for a dose of caffeine and the bathroom to get rid of that coffee, she hadn't taken a breather since then.

Fighting a yawn, Deanna rubbed her burning eyes. She hadn't gotten home until well after midnight, and when her alarm had woken her at five, it'd seemed like she'd just crawled into bed a few minutes earlier. Now she was pooped.

The dinner with Nico's family had been the longest meal she'd ever sat through. With their drinks, they'd shared a variety of small plates—including the yummiest smoked goose charcuterie she'd ever tasted.

An hour later, they'd had starters—she'd selected a salad of carrots, pea tendrils, and cucumber with apple cider vinaigrette. For her entrée, she'd chosen red cornmeal-dusted scallops with sweet peppers, Swiss chard, cayenne cream, and shaved Tasso ham. It had been so good that even though she'd planned to eat only half, she polished off every last bite.

Deanna had been astounded when, after all that food, everyone had ordered dessert and coffee. Declining the tempting offerings, she had sipped her decaf while the others devoured the bourbon bread pudding with butterscotch sauce and butter pecan ice cream.

Although it had been tough to resist when every single person kept offering her tidbits to taste, she'd held firm. Maybe her feelings of deprivation were why she'd snapped at Nico and pushed him out the door when he tried to talk her into letting him spend the night.

But it was exhaustion that had caused her to ignore Nico's pleas to meet him for lunch. She was beat and there were just so many applications to wade through. More landed on her desk every day. It almost seemed as if Randolph was trying to keep her so busy she wouldn't have time to do anything but work and sleep.

Great! Now she was getting paranoid. Why would her boss care about her social life?

Deanna shook her head. She needed to let her mind rest before tackling the next project. Maybe she'd call Nico and surprise him. He was coming over to her apartment at nine for a late dinner, but a little phone foreplay might whet his appetite.

She locked her office door, turned off the overhead light, and took off her jacket. Settling into her chair, she dialed his cell.

When he answered on the first ring, she asked, "Are you home and alone?"

"Yes. I'm leaving to take Mom to the airport in about ten minutes," Nico answered.

"Then we'd better make this quick." Deanna chuckled. "What are you wearing?"

"Shorts and a T-shirt."

"You're overdressed," Deanna cooed, then fibbed, "All I've got on is your favorite lingerie."

"The black bra and stockings?"

"Uh-huh," Deanna purred. "I know it's naughty to wear them at work, but I couldn't resist. And since you destroyed the thong, I don't have on any panties."

"I'll have to punish you for that tonight." Nico's rasping voice caressed her.

"How?" Deanna gasped as she immediately dampened.

"First, I'll order you to strip."

"What if I disobey?" Deanna nearly drowned in the flood of desire sweeping over her body.

"Then I'll rip off your clothes myself."

"Oh." Deanna swallowed, trying to get a little moisture back in her mouth. Evidently, the blood rushing to other parts of her body dried out her throat.

"Once you're naked and at my mercy, I'll pull you across my lap," Nico rumbled. "Then I'll turn your little bottom a pretty shade of pink."

"That doesn't sound like fun," Deanna protested, even as her nipples pushed against the lace of her bra.

"Punishment isn't supposed to be fun." Nico's tone was difficult to read.

"And why would I let you do that to me?" Deanna asked, relishing the slick heat radiating through her body.

"To show that you trust me," Nico said. Then he chuckled.

"And you might be surprised at the sensations my hand on your ass creates."

"And what do I get to do to you?" Deanna asked, allowing herself to ride the wave of desire she had created.

"Anything you want to," Nico answered without hesitation.

"Are you hard?" Deanna lowered her voice.

"Since I answered the phone."

"Are you stroking yourself?" she asked.

"Yep."

"Are you close?" Deanna felt as if all the air in her lungs had been sucked out.

He made a low guttural sound of confirmation.

"Too bad," Deanna snickered. "I want you to save that orgasm for me tonight. And if you do, I might let you spank me. If you don't, I'll spank you."

"You're evil," Nico groaned. "I don't even have time for a cold shower. How am I supposed to meet my mother in this condition?"

Giggling, Deanna hung up. Although her body thrummed with arousal, the sexy conversation with Nico had energized her, and she was able to get back to work. The pleasant hum of anticipation helped her power through the piles of folders on her desk.

Several hours later, she heard a stampede of footsteps in the hallway indicating her colleagues were leaving for the day. Looking up from her computer, she rolled her neck. It was six o'clock.

Deanna had planned to stay until eight. But if she quit now, she could stop by the gym for a workout and still have time to shower, do her hair, and put on some makeup before her nine-o'clock date with Nico.

She considered the small stack of documents remaining in her inbox. Could she finish those tomorrow before Randolph's deadline? *No problem.*

Before she could change her mind, she shut down her laptop and jumped to her feet. As she rounded the corner of her desk, she brushed against a file, and it fell to the floor, scattering its contents across the carpet.

Shit! Deanna squatted down to gather up the stray papers. As she shoved them into the folder, she glanced at the first few lines. How odd. It was the final paperwork for another downstate restaurant.

Her boss had never mentioned a similar investment when she was assessing Nico's application. Why hadn't he had her compare the two?

Her chest tightened. Had Randolph deliberately kept her in the dark? At the time, she'd thought it odd that he hadn't allowed her to see Nico's contract, but she'd let it go as another one of her boss's eccentricities. Now she wondered if there was more to it than that.

The past week, every time she'd been in Randolph's office to get a file or to return one, she'd meant to sneak a look at Nico's agreement. But she'd been so overwhelmed with all the work her boss kept dumping on her that she'd always forgotten until she was back behind her own desk.

The hair on the back of Deanna's neck stood up. Was this some kind of sign from the universe that she needed to read that document? She'd never been a big believer in heavenly portents, but she was getting the feeling that the cosmos was screaming at her to pay attention.

Gathering her laptop and purse, Deanna picked up a stack of folders as camouflage and headed to the fourth floor. When the elevator opened, the reception area was dark.

It appeared that the employees who worked on this floor were long gone, but to be safe, as Deanna walked toward her boss's suite, she called out, "Marcy, I've got some more completed files for Mr. Randolph. I'll just put them on his desk."

There was no response, and as Deanna entered the area, she saw that the admin assistant's desk was empty. Glancing behind her, she hurried to her boss's office and ran her fingers over the painting that hung next to the door.

Once, when Randolph's admin couldn't find her key, she'd used the one hidden on top of the picture frame to let Deanna into the office. Marcy had had her turn around, but Deanna could see what the admin was doing in the mirror on the opposite wall.

Grasping the tiny piece of metal, Deanna inserted it into the slot. She quickly slipped inside and immediately shut the door behind her.

Rushing toward the antique wooden cabinet where Randolph kept all the pending projects, Deanna was relieved her boss had chosen form over function. The vintage cabinet had no lock, and she swiftly yanked open the drawer labeled S-Z.

Flipping through the files, she located the one marked

THORNE, NICO and pulled it out. Her report was attached to one side, and the contract was stapled to the other. She pried out the tiny metal fastener and freed the agreement.

As she waited for the Xerox machine to warm up, she scanned the pages. The contract looked like all the others that she'd seen in the past. Maybe she was just being paranoid and Randolph wasn't really hiding anything.

After making a copy of the document, Deanna carefully lined up the holes and made sure the staple she used to fasten it back into the folder went into those previous perforations. When everything was as she'd found it, Deanna slipped out of the office, returned the key to the top of the painting, and headed home.

Once she was in her apartment, she changed into a robe, grabbed a bottle of water, and settled on her couch with the contract and a legal pad. She'd read the thing line by line, and she hoped by the time she was finished, she could laugh at her suspicions.

An hour later, Deanna's finger stopped midsentence. *Holy shit!* The taste of bile flooded her mouth.

The clause stated that if Nico didn't follow an extremely complex financial payback formula to the letter—which would be nearly impossible for him to do—Randolph Ventures gained full ownership of the business, and for the next five years, Nico would be forced to work for a very modest salary as the restaurant's chef. Not only would Nico lose all the money he'd put into the deal, he'd be unable to start over elsewhere anytime in the near future.

There was no way on God's green earth that Nico had seen this section of the contract or he never would have signed it. This was why Randolph had been so pleased that Nico's lawyer wasn't present. And it was also why he'd pushed Nico to sign it right away instead of giving him a chance to consult with his attorney.

After thinking it over, Deanna had a good idea how Randolph had managed to screw Nico. She'd read an article about this in a professional journal. The page hadn't been a part of the contract that Nico read. Her boss had slipped it in after it was signed. No one, except maybe an attorney, would notice that the page numbers skipped from twenty-eight to thirty.

Stunned, Deanna sagged against the sofa cushions. At that moment, so much of what she considered strange about Randolph's business practices clicked into place. In her head, she heard all the conversations that she should have had with her boss but chose to avoid because she was afraid to question him or what he was doing.

In the past, Deanna had assured herself that she wasn't turning a blind eye to unethical dealings. It was just that she didn't fully comprehend Randolph's strategies. Her inexperience caused her to misunderstand his actions. Now she realized that she lied to herself a lot, especially when it came to the authority figures in her life.

She'd made excuses for her parents' lack of support, for the professor who had sexually harassed her, and for her bosses. But no more.

Like a binder clip clamping down on an unwary finger, Deanna snapped back to the present. Needles of dismay and self-loathing pierced her soul, and tears leaked out of her eyes as she realized what she'd done.

Digging into the pocket of her robe, she grabbed her cell and sent a text to Nico cancelling their date. She was in no condition to see him, and before she told him about the awful clause, she needed to find a way for him to get out of the contract.

CHAPTER TWENTY-SIX

As Nico walked out of LeBoeuf and into the restaurant's employee parking lot, his cell vibrated. Checking the phone, he saw that he had a text from Deanna cancelling their date. Disappointment was a stab in the gut. Ever since her naughty lunchtime call, he'd been looking forward to getting her naked and across his knees.

Nico shoved the phone into his pocket and snarled, "Damn it all to hell!"

"What's wrong, bro?" Marco asked, standing between his BMW and Nico's SUV. "Did your pretty little financial genius dump you?"

"I sure as hell hope not," Nico growled. "Though she did break our date with no explanation."

"Maybe she's on the rag and didn't want to broadcast it," Marco suggested, bumping his shoulder against Nico's. "Some girls are shy about shit like that."

"Yeah." Nico scrubbed his face with his fist. "But even if she didn't feel like messing around, we could have still had dinner."

"You are so whipped, man." Marco snickered, then said, "Hey, how about we order pizza and play some Xbox at your place? We need some bro time. You never did let me go over that investment contract you signed."

"I only got it this afternoon," Nico protested. "For some reason, they needed to keep all three of the original copies, but they said they'd send me mine the next day. When it never came, I called to ask what was going on, and they finally messengered it to me just before I left for work."

Marco had always been the one who handled the business

end of things. But he hadn't wanted to open a restaurant in, as he put it, Butt Crack, Illinois, so for the first time in their careers, he and Nico were going their separate ways. When the brothers' employment agreements with LeBoeuf ended in a couple of months, Marco was off to Nevada to manage a club in Las Vegas.

"Okay then." Hooking his arm around Nico's neck, Marco thumped his brother's head. "Let's pop open a brew, and while we wait for the pizza, I'll give your contract a look-see."

"Deal." Nico smiled for the first time since reading Deanna's text.

He'd miss seeing her, but it would be good to chill with his brother. Until Nico had met Deanna, he and Marco had hung out two or three nights a week.

"I'll change out of my suit and meet you at your place." Marco climbed into his car and said, "See you in a few."

Three hours later, Marco was sprawled on the couch with a beer in his hand and the contract spread over the cushions. As Nico demolished the last slice of pizza, he watched his brother's expression.

Just as Nico crammed a huge bite into his mouth, Marco jumped up and yelled, "You've got to be shitting me!"

Nico choked, then wheezed, "What?"

"Did you read this thing?" Marco demanded.

"Yeah." Nico stood to peer over his brother's shoulder.

"And you still signed it?" Marco poked Nico's chest.

"Fuck!" Nico's pulse pounded in his head. "What did I miss?"

"If you don't make every single payment, and each one multiplies from the previous one in a freakily complex financial reimbursement formula"—Marco handed Nico the page and pointed to the paragraph—"you agreed to be this Randolph dude's indentured servant."

Nico squinted, read it twice, then shook his head. "No way in hell was that piece of paper a part of the contract I read."

Marco flipped through the document and said, "That page is numbered twenty-nine and that number isn't duplicated on either the preceding or following page. It would be hard to prove it wasn't there when you and Randolph signed the contract."

Nico sank into a chair and buried his face in his hands. "What the hell did I get myself into?"

"Good question." Marco thumped Nico's back supportively. "But the better one is did Deanna know about this? And now that you have the contract, is that why she's suddenly not seeing you tonight?"

Nico leaped to his feet, drew his fist back to punch his brother in the nose, then stopped. What if Marco was right? What if the whole relationship with her had been a setup to get him to sign away his life?

The thought of her betrayal slammed into his chest like a rolling pin. And along with the pain came a realization that had been tucked away inside of his heart. He was in love with her. And there was a very real possibility that all he was to Deanna was a steppingstone on her way to the top of Randolph Ventures. What if she had used him the same way his father had used his mother?

"Bro!" Marco gripped his biceps and shook him. "Don't zone out on me here. We have to come up with a plan. Find a way out of this contract."

"I need to talk to Deanna." Nico shrugged off his brother's hands. "I'm going over to her place and having this out right now."

"Dude, it's after midnight." Marco blocked the door. "If she's innocent, barging into her apartment in the middle of the night when you're out of control will ruin whatever you have with her."

"Get out of my way!" Nico thundered.

"No." Marco squared off. "I'm not letting you do this while you're having a temper tantrum."

Nico's patience wasn't plentiful on the best of days. Throw in that he'd just discovered he'd been scammed, possibly by the woman he loved, and Marco was a hairsbreadth from having the shit beaten out of him.

"Let. Me. By." Nico gritted out each word between clenched teeth.

"Uh-uh." Marco shook his head.

A red film was starting to seep across Nico's vision. He hadn't been this enraged since he was a teenager. He didn't want to hurt his brother, but he couldn't handle one more minute without knowing if Deanna had deceived him the way his father had betrayed his mother.

Forcing his features into a calm expression, Nico relaxed his posture and said, "You're right." He walked back into the living room and flopped on a chair. "I'll catch her in the morning."

"Good man." Marco narrowed his eyes but followed Nico and sat on the couch. "First thing tomorrow, I'll call my friend Steele. He's a corporate attorney, and if anyone knows how to get out of a contract, he does."

"Great." Nico pasted on a smile. "Thanks."

Nico waited until Marco picked up his beer and leaned back, then he leaped up, rushed to the door, and slammed out of the apartment.

As he pounded down the stairs, he muttered, "Sorry, bro. This can't wait."

* * *

Deanna paced her living room. It had taken quite a while for her mind to come back online after discovering that her boss had pulled a fast one on Nico. And it had taken her even longer to remember that her sorority sister Savannah was one of the top corporate attorneys on the West Coast.

Savannah suggested a couple of ways to prove the contract had been modified after signatures were affixed. She said that if Deanna could locate the electronic file, the document might have been saved in its original version. Or failing that, perhaps there was an email or fax that could confirm the true text of the contract. If Deanna could obtain those versions of the contract, they would be admissible to authenticate it. Unfortunately, she didn't have the security clearance to access any top-level files at work.

Which meant the only way out of the agreement was to pay off the investment in full. Including a five percent penalty. Deanna knew that Nico had already spent a good portion of the check he'd received last week. And from his comments, she suspected there wouldn't be any way for him to produce the amount of cash he'd need to free himself from the contract.

Was there anything she could offer her boss to make him tear up the agreement? Would he take a part of her salary against the penalty until Nico was able to repay the whole investment?

Deanna was jerked from her thoughts by a loud thumping on her door. She hurried into her foyer and looked out the peephole. What was Nico doing here at quarter to one in the morning?

Her first instinct was to ignore his pounding. She didn't want to see him until after she'd figured out a solution to his problem. But as the banging grew louder, she was afraid he'd wake her neighbors.

Leaving the chain on, she opened the door a sliver and said, "Go away."

"No." Nico wedged his shoulder in the opening. "We need to talk right now."

"You woke me up," she lied. "Meet me at my office for

lunch and we'll talk then."

"Let me in." Nico's voice cracked. "This can't wait until tomorrow. Please, Deanna. I'm begging you."

Shit! Deanna blew out a frustrated breath. Something was seriously wrong. Either he'd seen the clause or someone in his family had died. Clearly, she couldn't turn him away.

"Just a second." Deanna flew to her room and pulled on a bra, a pair of yoga pants, and a T-shirt. She had a feeling this was not a conversation she wanted to have wearing nothing but a robe.

* * *

Nico focused on quieting the rage echoing through his mind. But when she finally let him inside, he had too much adrenaline pumping through his veins to sit.

Deanna had taken a seat in her living room, and once he was calm, Nico squatted in front of her. He stared at her as he asked, "Do you know about the 'gotcha' clause in my contract?"

Before she even opened her mouth, he read the answer in her eyes.

The agony of her betrayal shattered his control, and he snarled, "What did Randolph promise you? Did he tell you to f—?" Nico clamped his lips together. *Shit!* No matter how angry he was, he couldn't say that to her.

"No!" All color drained from Deanna's cheeks and she stuttered, "I didn't... I'd never..."

"I don't believe you." A combination of nausea and rage fueled his words.

"You need to let me explain," Deanna pleaded. "I had no idea—"

"No idea that I'd find out so soon?" Disappointment and regret mixed with the anger churning in his gut. "Or no idea that I'd blame you?"

233

"You've got it all wrong," Deanna whispered.

"The only thing wrong here," Nico snarled, "is that I was too stupid to see who you really are."

"You have no concept of what I've risked for you." Deanna leaped to her feet, her voice vibrating with anger.

"I don't want to hear any more of your half-truths." An unpleasant smile on his face, Nico forced out a punishing lie, "I guess I got what I deserved since I only slept with you to get the money."

Deanna shuddered and her face lost all expression. Nico couldn't tell whether she was about to cry or just plain infuriated.

Several long seconds later, she sucked in a gigantic breath, then exhaled and said, "I would never have done anything to hurt you or your dreams." Her voice trembled, "Can you say the same about me?"

Nico felt a flicker of doubt. Had he misjudged the situation? *No!* How could he believe her when it was clear she was fully aware that Randolph had manipulated him into a corner with no way out?

Raising a brow, Nico said, "Your dreams should have been bigger than conning people for your boss."

"Funny you should say that." Deanna's harsh laugh startled him. "When you burst into my apartment, I was considering conning my boss to save *you*."

Nico's conscience squirmed and he almost asked her to explain. But then he remembered how many times his father had managed to convince his mother that he wasn't a lying, cheating bastard, and Nico remained quiet.

Ignoring the ache in his chest, he turned and walked away from Deanna. He couldn't bear to look at her for one more second.

As he slammed out of her apartment, he shouted, "Tell Randolph this isn't the end of it by a long shot. You two picked the wrong guy to screw over!"

As Nico drove home, a pulse pounded behind his eyes, and his lips twisted with the sour flavor of Deanna's treachery. When they'd made love, it hadn't been just a few fun hours to him. She'd touched him deep in his heart, and her betrayal felt like a knife through his soul.

* * *

Deanna wasn't sure how long she stood staring at the closed door, and even though she knew Nico was long gone, when she could finally find the breath to speak, she yelled, "Tell Randolph yourself!"

Her voice was spiked with fury, but the words came out a lot shakier than she thought they would. And at that moment, the reality of what had just happened thumped into her chest. The pain pushed her to her knees. She pressed her fingers to her eyes and refused to allow the tears gathering behind her lids to fall.

Nico had joined the rest of the men in her past who had let her down. Not her father, her professors, or her boyfriends had ever put her before their own aspirations. And certainly no one had made her feel like the most important thing in their life.

An eternity later, Deanna struggled to her feet, shuffled into the bedroom, and threw herself across her mattress. How had things gone so wrong so fast?

Her throat hurt from holding back the sobs that were still trying to escape. Nico's lack of trust echoed through her soul. It felt as if he'd taken a whip and sliced her flesh from her bones.

Why hadn't Nico given her a chance to explain? He'd decided she was guilty before he'd arrived and refused to hear anything that might prove that conclusion wrong.

She should have never let him break down the walls around her heart. Feeling nothing at all had been better than this pain. She'd exposed her vulnerabilities and he'd gone for the jugular.

She'd allowed him to see who she was behind the professional mask, and he'd ripped her apart.

Her mouth flooded with the bitter taste of heartbreak, and at last wetness seeped down her cheeks. She'd opened herself up to love and it had destroyed her.

*   *   *

Shards of light stabbed into Deanna's eyeballs, and she blinked awake. The last thing she remembered was polishing off the bottle of champagne that Randolph had given her last Christmas. She'd been saving it for a special occasion, but there wouldn't be anything in her life to celebrate for a long, long time.

Deanna winced as she sat up. Did booze go bad? She felt too awful for this to be just a hangover. Maybe what she really had was food poisoning.

As she reached out for her phone, the memory of last night slammed into her stomach, and her hand dropped to her side. A band of pain tightened around her chest, and she sank back down on the mattress.

The idea of going into the office set off another wave of nausea. And the thought of never seeing Nico again brought on a tsunami of grief.

After a few minutes, she forced both the queasiness and the misery down deep inside of her, then headed to the shower. Nico might not deserve it, but Randolph was due back from London today, and she would figure out a way to get her ex-lover out of that contract.

She might not have known about the "gotcha" clause, but she still felt responsible for Nico's situation. During their meeting with her boss, she should never have allowed Randolph to stop her from following her gut feeling. She'd kept silent when her instincts had told her that Nico signing that contract in haste would be a mistake. She couldn't let him suffer the consequences of her cowardice.

Once she was dressed in her severest black suit, she used makeup to disguise the anguish in her eyes and coiled her hair at the base of her neck. Looking like the emotionless businesswoman she'd been before Nico had peeled away her façade and made her love him, she headed to the office.

CHAPTER TWENTY-SEVEN

Thursday morning Nico peeled rubber out of his apartment building's garage. When he'd spoken to Randolph's assistant, she'd told him that the douchebag's flight from London had arrived at O'Hare a couple of hours ago and the asshole was due at the office any minute.

Pressing the accelerator to the floor, Nico wove in and out of traffic. He had quite a welcome back party planned for the prick and couldn't wait to yell surprise.

Marco had already faxed the contract to his friend Steele, who was trying to find an escape clause, but Nico wasn't in the mood to wait around for the lawyer's response. Besides, the contract was no longer his first priority. What he really wanted to know was whether Deanna had been a part of her boss's scheme.

During the endless night, while Nico thought over and over about what he'd said to Deanna, he'd come to the miserable realization that he'd been a colossal jerk. Her shadowed eyes had haunted him, and he knew he'd fucked up royally.

Why hadn't he listened to Marco? If he'd waited until he calmed down and thought things through, he would have never said what he had to Deanna.

Instead, he'd lost control of his temper and hadn't listened to a word she tried to say before finding her guilty. She might have known about the clause, but the real question was, when had she found out about it?

As he'd paced from one end of his bedroom to the other, noting every carpet stain, every chip in the paint, every dust bunny, Nico had remembered how Deanna had tried to say something to him at the end of his meeting with Randolph. Had she wanted to tell him about the clause?

Maybe.

And afterwards in the conference room, before her boss yanked her away, she'd cautioned him that he should have an attorney. Either she knew about the "gotcha" or her instincts had warned her that something wasn't right.

When she'd told him that Randolph would be the person finalizing Nico's contract, she'd mentioned that she'd never been involved in that part of a transaction before and had hoped that his would be her first one. Which meant that if all she'd ever seen was the same preliminary contract that had been sent to Nico's lawyer, it was entirely possible that she had no idea that her boss was such a devious bastard.

Jolting him back from his thoughts, a loud horn warned Nico that he'd nearly rear-ended a limo. *Hell!* He hit his forehead with his palm. Why hadn't he had an actual conversation with Deanna last night instead of acting like such a dickwad?

He needed to stop letting his father's treatment of his mother influence his own behavior. Although Deanna might still be guilty, he should have stuck with innocent until proven otherwise. He should have at least heard what she had to say about the situation before leaping to conclusions.

Yanking the steering wheel of his SUV to the right, Nico pulled into a parking spot in front of Randolph's Ventures. He shut off the engine and fisted his hands. Self-protection might have been a smart move in the past, but failing to give the woman he loved the benefit of the doubt was a damned stupid one.

It was time to get his head out of his ass. What had happened might still be unclear, but more than anything, even more than opening his own restaurant, Nico wanted to figure out where he stood with Deanna.

If she was innocent, and with every minute that passed, he

believed more and more that she was, could she forgive him for what he had said to her last night? He'd all but accused her of the most demeaning of acts and then told her he'd only had sex with her to get the money for his restaurant. Was there any way to repair the damage he'd done to their relationship?

Snatching his cell from the cup holder beside him, Nico called his favorite florist. After ordering a bouquet of pink roses and white calla lilies, he dictated an apology for his hurtful words, adding an assurance that she meant more to him than his restaurant. When he was finished, he asked for the arrangement to be delivered as soon as possible to Deanna's office.

After hanging up, Nico grabbed a carton from the passenger seat, got out of his SUV, and entered the building. As he exited the revolving door, his heart clenched with the idea that Deanna might not forgive him and this might be the last time he ever saw her. Forcing himself to appear relaxed, he greeted Mr. Byron. The old man gestured for him to go through the turnstile, and once he was past the security desk, the elevator arrived within seconds.

When Nico entered the car, he was tempted to push the button for Deanna's floor but tapped four instead. First, he'd confront Randolph, then he'd straighten out things with Deanna. He hoped by the time he was done with the bastard upstairs, the flowers he'd ordered would have arrived and she might be in a more forgiving mood.

Thankful that his dessert chef had come through for him, Nico pasted a grin on his face and breezed past the receptionist with a wave. He strolled toward the head honcho's suite, noting that Randolph's assistant was on the phone. Approaching her, he held the open pastry box out to her. The woman beamed and selected a cupcake.

"Can I pop into your boss's office for a minute?" Nico whispered. "I just want to give him these as a thank you gift."

The assistant hung up the receiver and said, "Ms. Sloan just went in a second ago."

"Good." Nico edged toward his goal. "I can give her one, too."

The assistant took a big bite of the chocolate peanut butter cupcake and mumbled, "Okay."

Nico smiled grimly. So Deanna was with Randolph. It might be enlightening to eavesdrop on that conversation.

Unable to hear anything through the heavy wooden door, Nico eased it opened just enough for him to slide through. He recalled that a large lacquer screen shielded the entrance from the rest of the office, and as he stepped behind it, he spotted Deanna standing in front of her boss's desk. Nico squinted between two of the hinged panels and saw that the bastard was laughing at her.

"Deanna. Deanna. Deanna." Randolph's voice was full of disdain. "I had high hopes for you. I thought you were smarter than the rest of them. But to allow your libido to get in the way of your career is beyond stupid."

"Mr. Randolph, this has nothing to do with my personal feelings for Chef Thorne." Despite her smooth tone, there was a thread of fire underlining her words. "The simple fact of the matter is that slipping in that page containing the 'gotcha' clause after Nico signed the contract is ethically reprehensible, not to mention illegal."

"Only if you can prove it." Randolph chuckled meanly. "And you can't, because speaking hypothetically, if I had done what you're accusing me of doing, I'd also have erased the electronic footprints that you'd need to file a lawsuit."

"You're destroying a person's dream," Deanna gasped. "How can live with yourself?"

"You, my dear, are a softhearted fool." Randolph stood and walked around his desk until he was facing Deanna. "Did you think that I was unaware of your relationship with Chef Thorne?"

"That has nothing to do with this," Deanna protested. "I would be upset if you did this to any client."

"Bullshit," Randolph sneered. "Although I've never allowed you to participate in finalizing one of my deals, you had to suspect from working on them that there was some reason I end up possessing so many of the companies in which I invest."

"How would I know that?" Deanna asked. "I just figured the owners couldn't make a go of them."

"There's this type of clause in all my small business contracts. Guess you never went back and read the final documents after they were signed. You really should be more thorough," Randolph tsked and moved closer. "But I'll give you one more chance. Dump the chef, become my mistress, and you can keep your job."

"Never!" Deanna snapped, stepping away from him. Then, smoothing out her voice, she said, "Just deduct Nico's penalty from my stock options, cancel his contract, and I'll turn in my resignation without exposing your duplicitous business practices."

"You have no proof. If you try to contact the authorities, you'll just look like a disgruntled employee." Randolph grabbed Deanna's upper arms and jerked her against him. "And for your impertinence, I'll destroy Thorne, which will be entirely your fault."

A surge of rage so fierce Nico could hardly breathe pushed him forward, and he stormed around the screen. As he emerged, he saw Randolph's mouth plastered against Deanna's and his fingers were around her throat.

Nico roared and charged toward the pair. He was going to tear that bastard apart for touching her. And for hurting her, he was going to make the asshole disappear.

When Nico hauled Randolph off of Deanna, her joy-filled gaze warmed Nico's heart. Then her eyes shuttered and all the delight in them drained away. Her smile vanished and unhappy lines bracketed her lips.

Shoving Randolph into a chair, he gave him a hard look that warned the douche not to move. Then Nico faced Deanna and reached out a hesitant hand. She shook her head, turned, and walked away.

Nico felt like a shaken can of soda right before the tab is popped. One tiny opening and all his pent up emotions would spew out of control.

* * *

After the scene in Randolph's office, Deanna went home, packed a bag, and headed to the airport. Too much had happened for her brain to process, and she needed to get away. She wanted to see her best friend and have Sage tell her that everything would be okay.

Deanna would have sworn Randolph was asexual. His demand that she become his mistress had been a surprise. Losing her job—whether she'd quit or been fired was up in the air—had been a shock. And Nico's sudden appearance had been staggering. Maybe her friend could help her make some sense out of the chaos.

While waiting for the plane to take off, Deanna took out her cell. She needed to text Sage that she was coming to visit and to let her know approximately when she'd arrive. When she glanced at the screen, there were half a dozen voice mails and twice that number of messages from Nico. She deleted them all, turned off her phone, and closed her eyes.

During the four-hour trip, Deanna alternately dozed and stared out of the window. She refused to think of the mess she'd left behind in Chicago and instead focused on how wonderful it would be to see her best friend again. Maybe she'd hunt for a job in Nevada.

When Deanna arrived in Las Vegas, directions to Sage's place were waiting for Deanna on her cell. There were also more texts from Nico, which she again deleted. She'd deal with him and their situation later. Much later.

Once she secured a rental car, it was an easy drive to her friend's place, and when Deanna turned into the driveway, Sage was sitting on the porch. She met Deanna at the car and wrapped her in a welcoming hug.

Sage was a curvy woman with butterscotch-blonde hair and big brown eyes. They'd met at a sorority rush party their freshman year of college and ended up pledging Alpha Sigma Alpha together. They'd been BFFs ever since.

Guiding Deanna inside, Sage took a seat on a sofa and tilted her head. "Your text said that you were out of a job and a boyfriend. Tell me everything."

A bottle of wine later, Deanna finished explaining and said, "So what do you think?"

"About what?" Sage raised her brows. "Your asshole boss or your asshole boyfriend?"

"Let's start with the easy one. While Randolph's demand for sex was a surprise, I have to say his illegal business practices weren't as much of a shock as they should have been." Deanna shoved her hair out of her eyes. "I knew he was ruthless, but I guess I refused to admit to myself how crooked his deals could be."

"Sweetie, give yourself a break. How could you know if all you ever saw were the preliminary files?" Sage patted Deanna's knee. "Are you going to turn him in?"

Deanna nodded. "I made the calls while I waited to board the plane." She shrugged. "The authorities told me that they've had their eye on him for a while and will add my information to their files."

"Then, eventually, he'll get caught and karma will take care of him." Sage popped up from the couch and walked into the kitchen. When she reappeared with another bottle of Merlot, she asked, "What will you do about a job?"

"Do you remember me saying that I wanted to be a millionaire by the time I was thirty-five?" Deanna asked. When Sage nodded, she said, "I've been saving and investing since finishing grad school, and I'm well on my way to that goal." She stuffed a handful of potato chips into her mouth and mumbled around them, "I have plenty to live on even if it takes me ten years to find another position."

"Nice." Sage refilled both their glasses and sat down. "I guess I should have gotten my MBA instead of my DVM." She took a sip of wine. "I couldn't live a week without a paycheck. And don't get me started about my student loans."

"You should let me help you invest." Deanna noticed that her words were beginning to slur. "I could make you tons of money."

"Good to know." Sage smiled wryly. "So Randolph is permanently out of your life. Does the same go for Nico?"

"Yes." Deanna nodded, then a tear slipped down her cheek. "I mean, he might not have come out and said it, but it was pretty damn clear he thought I had sex with him to secure the deal. Even if he now realizes that I had nothing to do with my boss's scheme to grab his restaurant, how do I forgive him for something like that?"

"I guess that depends on if you love him enough to try." Sage hugged Deanna. "Knowing you, if you didn't really care for him, you would have never allowed him to get between you and your ambitions."

"Yeah." Deanna chugged her wine. "I let him past my dreams and what do I have to show for it?"

"It seems to me Nico helped you peel away the layers of protection you'd been accumulating around your emotions throughout your whole life," Sage said thoughtfully. "Now that your shell is cracked wide-open, that part of you is exposed for the first time in years. And, although I know it hurts, isn't it better to feel something instead of just existing in the state of numbness you were in before?"

"Maybe." Deanna blew out a long sigh. "Do you think I should talk to Nico? He's been calling and texting, but I haven't picked up."

"I think you should at least hear him out before you make a decision."

"What if what he said to me is true?" Deanna's voice hitched and she whispered, "What if he only slept with me to get Randolph Ventures to invest in his restaurant?"

"That whole scene at your apartment sounds like a man who was in so much pain he was hitting out at the person closest to him," Sage said. "Besides, you told me that he knew you had already sent in a positive report before you two slept together."

"That's true." Deanna chewed her thumbnail. She fought the doubt and fear weaving together inside of her like macramé around a flower pot. "It's time I took a chance. Up until this happened, Nico has been wonderful. He's helped me get over my insecurities, told me over and over that I'm beautiful, and up until now, he hasn't done anything to make me distrust him."

"He sounds terrific." Sage licked her lips and grinned. "And if his pictures on the Internet are to be believed, he's sizzling hot."

"Yep." Deanna smiled, then wrinkled her brow. "You know, from what Nico's told me, I think the reason he was so unreasonably furious with me was because his father used his mother to advance his career. I'll bet in Nico's mind, it seemed as if I had done the same thing."

246

"So you're going to talk to him?" Sage emptied what remained of the second bottle of Merlot into Deanna's glass.

"I haven't decided." Deanna gulped the wine, yawned, and said, "I'll think about it in the morning."

* * *

"Deanna?" Nico asked, his voice a hoarse rasp.

He'd been trying to reach her for hours and had been relieved when she'd finally answered, but this didn't sound like her.

"No. This is her friend Sage."

"Why do you have her cell?" Nico's pulse raced. "Is Deanna okay?"

"She's passed out in my guest room, and except for the horrible hangover she's going to have tomorrow, she's physically fine."

"Give me your address," Nico demanded. He needed to see Deanna. Make things right between them.

"I'll consider your request." Sage paused, then asked, "Are you a good guy or a bad guy?"

"I promise you I'm not usually a bad guy," Nico said slowly, cringing at his recent behavior. "But lately, I haven't been a good guy."

"Why?"

"Because I lost my temper." Nico's voice cracked.

"Go on."

"Look. I'm not talking about this with someone I've never met."

"Then I guess I'm not telling you where Deanna is." Sage's tone was implacable. "And I'll 'lose' her phone so you won't be able to reach her."

"You win." Nico gritted his teeth to stop from punching a hole in his apartment wall. If he had to open a vein to some stranger in order to find Deanna, he'd do it. "There's never been a woman who meant as much to me as Deanna. That's why it hurt so much when I thought she'd betrayed me."

"You know Deanna would never do that, right?" When he grunted his agreement, Sage said, "Then if I were you, I'd catch the next flight to Las Vegas. What you two have to discuss shouldn't be done on the phone."

"Just tell me where you live, and I'll be there first thing in the morning."

Nico grabbed a pen and paper. There was nothing he wanted more than to see Deanna and hold her in his arms again. And he was willing to crawl through the Mojave Desert if that was what it took.

* * *

"What time is it?" Deanna whined, squinting as Sage opened the guest room blinds.

Waking up for the second day in a row with a hangover was ridiculous. If this kept up, she'd have to join AA.

"It's eight thirty." Sage handed Deanna a bottle of water and two aspirin. "You need to get dressed."

"Why?" Deanna downed the pills. "Are you kicking me out of your house?"

"Don't be stupid." Sage whipped off Deanna's covers. "I'm leaving for work, and I don't want you to miss any important visitors." Her smile dimmed. "If I ever am as lucky as you, I'd want you to do the same for me."

"Lucky?" Deanna narrowed her eyes. "What kind of important visitors?"

"You'll find out," Sage teased. Then, as she bopped out of the room, she yelled, "But if I were you, I'd get my butt in the shower right now."

What was Sage up to now? Deanna hoped her friend hadn't done something crazy like arrange a blind date. The last thing she wanted to do was go out with some guy Sage had roped into entertaining her.

As Deanna drank the rest of the water, she fumbled on the nightstand for her cell. Where was it? Had she left it by the couch?

Padding barefoot into the living room, Deanna spotted her phone on the end table. She scooped it up and peered at the screen.

There were no more missed calls or messages from Nico. Her heart sank. He must have given up on her. Had he decided whatever they had between them wasn't enough to pursue? Or maybe he couldn't get over her association with Randolph, the man who had trapped him into an untenable situation that could very well end up costing Nico his restaurant and five years of his life. It could be that Nico had figured it was easier to let fallen soufflés lie rather than to try to rebuild his relationship with her.

The doorbell rang just as a tear leaked down Deanna's cheek. Before going to see who was there, she wiped the wetness away with the back of her hand and wrapped herself in a throw from the back of the couch. She'd forgotten to pack a robe.

As she headed to the foyer, she glanced at the mirror hanging on the wall. Her hair was smooshed on one side and a mass of curls on the other. She had mascara smeared under her eyes. And there was a crease running down her cheek from the pillow. Whoever Sage had sent to take her out was in for a shock.

The bell chimed again, and a voice yelled, "Deanna, I know you're in there! We need to talk."

Shit! How had Nico found her? And more importantly, why hadn't she listened to Sage and made herself presentable?

CHAPTER TWENTY-EIGHT

Deanna heard a distinctive click and stared in horror as the doorknob turned. A second later, Nico stepped over the threshold carrying an overnight bag.

"How did you..." Deanna stuttered. "Where did... I mean, I'm not ready to speak to you yet."

"Your friend answered your phone, gave me this address, and told me the key would be under the mat." Nico answered all the questions Deanna couldn't quite form. "And ready or not, we're talking."

Deanna wrapped the blanket more tightly around her and shook her head. "Come back later. I'm not dressed."

"You look great to me." Nico's voice deepened, and he stared at her with enough steam to clean an entire hotel full of Persian carpets.

When he reached for her, she moved toward him, then stopped. *Yes.* As always, the sexual attraction between them was off the charts, but first they had to clear the air.

"I'm not having this conversation dressed in a Hello Kitty nightshirt." Deanna held firm.

"Whatever you say." Nico grinned. "I'll make us some breakfast while you change."

"Just coffee for me," Deanna yelled over her shoulder as she ran into her room and locked the door behind her. "You and your food are both too tempting," she muttered as she turned on the shower and stepped beneath the cold water.

Thirty minutes later, dressed in shorts and a T-shirt, her hair pulled into a ponytail, and concealer camouflaging the dark shadows under her eyes, Deanna emerged to the enticing aroma of bacon and cinnamon.

Nico stood at the stove, flipping over slices of golden-brown French toast. When he turned and saw her, his eyes lit up.

He opened his arms, plainly hoping she'd walk into them, but she shook her head and stood her ground. They had a lot of issues to resolve before she was ready for him to touch her. His smile faded and his shoulders slumped.

Pressing his lips together, he motioned her to the table and turned back to the stove. A couple of seconds later, he placed breakfast and a mug of steaming coffee in front of her.

Putting his own plate and cup down opposite her, Nico took a seat, picked up his fork, and said, "Eat."

"Why are you here?" Deanna ignored her growling stomach and reached for the coffee. It was exactly as she liked it with two fake sugars.

"To apologize for being an asshole." He gazed at her. "Please, please forgive me for the awful things that I said to you." He cleared his throat. "There's no excuse, but I promise that I'll work every day to make it up to you. To make everything up to you."

Well. He certainly didn't beat around the bush. Deanna had never met anyone who so readily owned up to their mistakes.

"I take it you heard my conversation with Randolph." She raised an eyebrow. "And know I wasn't aware that after you signed the contract, he slipped in an extra page containing that awful clause?"

She took a careful drink of the hot coffee, hoping it would help her concentrate. It was too tempting to fall into his arms and forget how he'd hurt her.

"Yes." Nico stopped eating. "But even before hearing the asshole's confession, I realized that I had been a jerk and should have talked it over with you rather than losing my temper."

"How convenient." Deanna gave in and took a bite of the perfectly crisp bacon on her plate.

"It's true," Nico protested, then smiled. "And I can prove it."

"Oh?" She tilted her head.

"I sent flowers to you with an apology before I set foot in Randolph's office." Nico took his cell from his pocket, swiped the screen with his thumb, and handed it to her. "Call the florist at this number and ask him what time I placed the order."

"Later." Her heart warming at Nico's statement, Deanna waved away the phone. "I accept your apology." Still, she wasn't convinced that he'd ever completely trust her or anyone. "But maybe we both have too much baggage for a relationship to work between us."

"Never." Nico jumped up, knelt at her feet, and took both her hands. "We're like the perfect knife. You need a sharp blade *and* a sturdy handle for the knife to work. Neither one is good without the other."

Deanna felt herself wavering but stiffened her spine and asked, "How can I forget that you thought I had seduced you for a business deal?" When he opened his mouth to answer, she shook her head and continued. "You might not have said it, but it obviously crossed your mind."

"I'm sorry that I doubted you." Nico's lips thinned. "I know why I'm like that, and I promise you that I'm going to work on it."

"That's good." Deanna nodded. "But you told me that you only slept with me to ensure Randolph Ventures would invest in your restaurant. How can you expect me to believe you weren't telling the truth about that?"

"Because of this." Nico got up and walked into the living room.

Deanna followed him and watched as he took a sheaf of papers from the outside pocket of his suitcase.

He handed the pages to her and said, "After you left,

Randolph offered to replace my contract with this one that doesn't contain the 'gotcha' clause."

"But there was a catch?" Deanna flipped through the document. As far as she could tell, it looked like Randolph Ventures' standard agreement.

"Yes." Nico nodded to the contract in Deanna's hand. "Check out the last page."

She quickly scanned the handwritten text. It stated that the agreement would be null and void if Nico ever saw Deanna again. Randolph had scribbled his name underneath. How had she not realized that her boss was so obsessed with her?

Deanna gazed at Nico and whispered, "You turned down the chance to open up your restaurant without that horrible clause hanging over your head?"

"In a heartbeat." Nico pulled her against his chest. "I love you, and you're more important to me than a million restaurants. If I can't fulfill the original contract, I'll just have to work for the asshole for a few years and try again."

"You'd do that for me?" Deanna couldn't believe anyone could love her that much.

"For us." Nico tightened his arms around her. "Tell me you forgive me and feel the same way."

* * *

Nico's heart stopped when Deanna remained silent. What if she didn't love him?

Then, she drew in a ragged breath and sobbed, "I do. I love you enough to forget about all of my superficial ambitions. Money, looks, power mean nothing without happiness." She snuggled against him. "I know you're sorry for what you said to me. I know you'll never doubt me in the future. And now I know that unlike anyone else in my life, you'll always put me first."

Nico took the first easy breath he'd drawn in the past forty-eight hours. Deanna's words were coming so fast he could barely understand what she was saying. But what he did understand was that she wasn't a woman who gave her trust to many people, and she was giving it to him.

The vise that had squeezed his chest since he'd been so fucking cruel to her snapped open. And the sweet scent of vanilla and nutmeg, her own unique fragrance, filled all the empty places inside of him.

Finally she wound down and asked, "How did your father use your mother to further his career?"

Pressing Deanna's head to his shoulder so he wouldn't have to see the sympathy in her beautiful eyes, he said, "When I moved in with my father as an apprentice, his new wife told me that Ian had exploited Mariella's social status to wine and dine the people who could make him the next hot celebrity chef." Nico kissed Deanna's temple. "My loving stepmother said that she and Ian had planned the whole thing and that once he didn't need Mariella's influence any longer, he couldn't wait to divorce my mom."

"Did you ever ask your dad or mom about that?" Deanna rubbed her hand up and down his back, and the warmth eased the tension from his muscles.

"No," Nico admitted. "I figured Ian would lie. And in case Mom didn't know, I didn't want to hurt her by being the one to tell her."

"I can understand that." Deanna nodded. "But I think you need to discuss it with them both so you can get rid of your anger once and for all."

"You could be right." Nico took a kiss from her parted lips, desperate to feel her soft body under his hands and mouth. Desperate to reestablish that bond with her. Desperate to reaffirm their love.

"So you'll sit down with your parents and find out the

truth?"

"I'll ask them to meet us in Chicago." Nico slid his hands beneath Deanna's top and unhooked her bra. "But right now, I need to know when Sage is getting home."

"Around five thirty." Deanna grabbed the bottom of his shirt, pulled it over his head, and tossed it to the floor.

"How about you show me your room?" Nico skimmed his fingers down the front of Deanna's shorts and under the elastic of her panties. As he caressed the sensitive flesh and explored her slick folds, he walked them into the guest room and backed her against the bed.

Her moan nearly sent him over the edge, and he quickly stripped them both of their remaining clothes. He needed to fill her with proof of his love.

* * *

Deanna's heart and body came alive again. Since the night Nico had banged into her apartment, hurt blazing from his eyes, she'd been numb. Afraid that if she allowed herself to feel all the pain, her emotions would destroy her.

She'd needed the words. Needed him to apologize and say that he loved her. To her, Nico's willingness to admit he'd been wrong, to tell her how much he cared for her was the crucial piece in making everything okay again.

When he'd said that he was sorry and acknowledged how cruel he'd been, the weight that had been pressing down on her chest for the past two days lifted. Deanna had never felt as alive as she did right now with his warm, smooth skin sliding against hers. Every cell in her body pulsed with desire for him.

Nico's lips traveled along her jaw and down her throat. As he tasted her, she made a tiny incoherent sound. And when his mouth reached her breasts, all she could do was moan.

Deanna had completely opened up to him. Every fence was

torn down and every barrier lowered. There was no going back. Now as he slowly slid into her, he filled all the hollow spaces in her soul.

The throbbing force that fused them together gave Deanna an incredible sense of completeness. A staggering sense of rightness. An overwhelming sense of finally finding the loving shelter that she'd missed all her life.

Then, the hot ache inside of her grew and took away what little breath she still possessed. And with an explosion of sparks, the landslide struck. Unrelenting, it freed the brilliant pleasure rushing through her and shattered into dazzling bliss.

Nico gave one final thrust, then stiffened, pouring his soul into her. And as he collapsed on top of Deanna, he whispered in her ear, "*Amore mio.*"

Deanna stroked his back and vowed, "Always and forever."

EPILOGUE

One Year Later

Deanna smiled at the handsome fifty-something man approaching the hostess stand and asked, "Do you have a reservation?"

"Yes. David, party of two." The man curled his arm around the curvy woman at his side. "We're celebrating our anniversary." He brushed a kiss on his wife's cheek and said, "What better place than a restaurant called Amore Mio?"

"Absolutely. Right this way." Deanna led the couple to a secluded booth, then headed into the kitchen.

Her handsome husband was standing next to one of his line cooks frowning. He leaned over the woman's shoulder and said, "Roll as much pasta as you can. Tonight's special is flying out of here."

Deanna snuck up on him and said, "Behind you, Chef."

Nico whirled around, a grin creasing his cheek, and pulled her into his embrace. After pressing his lips to her forehead, he asked, "What brings you into my lair, sugar?"

"There's a sweet couple celebrating their anniversary." Deanna smiled. Although Nico always welcomed her into his kitchen, she didn't often venture there during service. She preferred to stay out of his way when he was engrossed in creating his masterpieces. "I wondered if you'd do your fruit flambé for them."

"Of course." Nico ran his thumb down her cheek. "If my business partner wants a special tableside dessert for her new friends, who am I to say no?"

"Funny, you aren't as obliging when I tell you an ingredient is too costly and won't have an adequate return on investment,"

Deanna teased.

After the conversation about her financial situation with Sage, Deanna had realized that even without cashing in her hefty 401(k), she had enough assets in savings and stocks to pay off Nico's contract with Randolph. It had taken a few days to convince Nico to take her money. He hadn't wanted to risk her capital, but once she presented him with an agreement that clearly outlined a payoff schedule, she was finally able to persuade him to accept.

When Randolph had found out that Deanna had reported his illegal practices to the authorities, he had spread vicious rumors about her in the venture capital community. And the gossip surrounding her had only gotten worse when her ex-boss had been arrested a few weeks later.

After a long discussion with Nico, Deanna had decided that instead of trying to find a job in the financial field, she would take over as Amore Mio's manager. She'd run the front of the house and Nico would rule over the back.

While the restaurant's renovation was being completed, Deanna had taken a course on restaurant management and had shadowed Nico's brother during his remaining stint at LeBoeuf. Between Marco and the class, she'd learned about public relations, inventory, dealing with staff, and customer service. Her MBA gave her a leg up on interpreting sales trends, handling payroll costs, customer counts, and predicting future sales.

At first, Marco had been doubtful that Deanna could integrate all she needed to know quickly enough to run Amore Mio. But she'd eventually won him over, and the two had worked well together. Almost too well. Any time Nico was around, Marco would deliberately flirt with Deanna until his brother lost his cool.

Deanna knew Marco was needling Nico, but it was almost a relief when it was time for Marco to pack up and move to his

new job in Nevada. She'd been tempted to try to fix Sage up
with Nico's brother, and she still might, but that could wait until
she and Nico were able to enjoy the honeymoon trip to Las
Vegas that had been Marco's wedding gift to them.

Sage was still a little miffed that Deanna hadn't waited for
her to fly to Chicago before getting married. But with money
tight and Deanna's parents' refusal to leave their small town, she
and Nico had been married by a judge at the courthouse.

Although Mariella had wanted to host a reception for them,
they'd declined but assured her that she could throw them a party
for their one-year anniversary. They only had a couple of months
to figure a way out of that promise.

A voice calling her name brought Deanna's thoughts back
to the present. A server was trying to get her attention. Nico still
had one arm around her as he supervised his brigade, so she
kissed his cheek and wiggled free of his embrace.

Deanna walked over to the young woman and said, "What's
up, Roxy?"

"There's a party of six without a reservation."

"Do we have any free tables?" Deanna asked. If her
memory was correct, they were fully booked.

"No. But when I told them that, they insisted on speaking to
you."

"Okay. I'll take care of it." Deanna followed the server to
the entrance area but stopped a few feet away from the hostess
stand when she saw the people gathered around it.

Shit! Deanna pasted a smile on her face and whispered to
Roxy, "Tell Chef that his parents, as well as the judge of
Restaurant Clashes, are waiting for him."

"Deanna!" Mariella rushed up to her and hugged her. "You
must squeeze us in somewhere. Gina De Luca called me out of
the blue. She saw an article about Nico and thinks he'd be
perfect for her show."

Ian had joined them and added, "Gina persuaded the producer, head writer, and director to fly down with us to taste Nico's food and to talk to him." He winked. "She's dying to meet him."

Deanna glanced at the beautiful chef and fought down the nibble of jealousy. Gina had the body that Deanna had always wanted—a tiny waist, nonexistent hips, and big boobs. Since marrying Nico, she'd relaxed her rigid diet. He'd convinced her that she didn't have to be a size two to be beautiful, and she now fit into Mariella's fashions the way her mother-in-law envisioned the clothes to be worn.

Before she let her old insecurities overwhelm her, she kissed Mariella's and Ian's cheeks and said, "I'll put you all at the family table. Give me one minute to fix it up."

She'd just gotten everyone settled when Nico appeared. He kissed his mother's temple and nodded to his dad. He still wasn't entirely convinced that Ian hadn't used his mother's social status to further his career, but both of his parents had denied it.

Deanna waited until Nico had finished greeting his mom and dad, then opened her mouth to introduce him to Gina De Luca. But before she could speak, the TV chef popped out of her chair and grasped Nico's hand in both of hers.

Gina leaned close and said, "We finally meet. How is it that two great chefs such as us have never gotten together before?"

"Because you live in New York and I live in Illinois?" Amusement sparkled in Nico's blue eyes. "But it is an honor to cook for you and your friends."

Deanna saw that Nico tried to free his hand, but Gina's claws dug in and she refused to let go.

"After we eat, we'd like to talk to you about appearing on *Restaurant Clashes*." Gina pressed her breasts against Nico's arm. "My show is the hottest new cooking competition on television, and you are exactly the type of handsome, sexy chef that our female viewers tune in to watch."

"I see." Nico arched a brow at Deanna, then once again attempted to step away from Gina, but the woman clung to him like Saran wrap. Chuckling, he asked, "What do the male viewers tune in to watch?"

"Me, of course." Gina pouted her collagen-filled lips. "Have you not watched my show?"

"I saw one episode," Nico admitted. "Between the time the dessert left the kitchen and was served, the raspberries on the losing chef's dish mysteriously developed mold."

"Ah, yes. It was a shame that he didn't turn out to be as good as I'd hoped." Gina reached up and brushed a strand of hair from Nico's forehead. "Now, you must promise to come with me to New York and audition."

"I really can't." Nico finally succeeded in liberating his hand from the clinging woman and put his arm around Deanna. "I can't be away from Amore Mio for more than a week, and my wife and I have plans for that time."

"Your wife? No one mentioned that you had a wife." Gina scowled, then turned to Mariella and snapped, "You did not tell me your son was married."

"You didn't ask." Mariella frowned. "Besides, what does that have to do with Nico's talent or his wonderful new restaurant?"

"My viewers want to fall in love with the chef. If he were married to a beautiful woman, that would be different." Gina's gaze flicked up and down Deanna. "But someone who looks like her will make my fans question whether Nico is as hot and trendy as he seems." Gina tilted her head and pointed at Deanna. "Perhaps, if she remained here, and we said he was getting a divorce, we could work something out." She nodded. "Yes. The two chefs always stay in my penthouse, and the show encourages rumors of them vying to win both the competition and my attention."

Deanna's cheeks burned, but before she could order the witch out of Amore Mio, Nico tucked Deanna closer to his side and said, "I'm sorry you flew all this way for nothing, but I have no interest in hiding my marriage or being away from my wife for even a few hours, let alone long enough to tape your show."

Gina plastered herself against Nico's other side, and although she whispered, Deanna heard every word.

Gina's voice dropped and she said, "Don't be a fool. Come to New York. Not only will your restaurant get amazing television exposure, I'll make sure you never miss your dreary little wife."

"Why you—"

Nico interrupted Deanna, "Sweetheart, didn't we agree that you'd let me handle the trash?"

"Yes, darling, we did." Deanna beamed at her wonderful husband. "After you."

Nico stared down at the petite chef, who must have finally realized she'd gone too far and retreated to stand behind her producer and director.

"Ms. DeLuca, I'm going to have to ask you to leave. Anyone who doesn't believe that my wife is beautiful and amazing isn't welcome in my restaurant."

"You're kicking me out?" Gina shrieked. "I'll... I'll ruin you in the culinary world."

Deanna bit her lip. Was she going to be the reason Amore Mio failed?

"Oh, I seriously doubt that." Nico chuckled. "Maybe if my restaurant were in New York or LA, but not in the Midwest. If you try anything, I'll have my publicist set up an interview for me with the tabloids, and I'll reveal everything you said tonight. Folks here in the heartland won't be happy that you not only rig your reality TV show but that you tried to break up a marriage.

Midwesterners can see right through someone like you."

"You can't prove anything," Gina sputtered. "I'll sue you for slander or libel or whatever the hell it is."

"You want proof?" Nico gestured around. "I'm pretty sure half the diners in here have video of us on their cell phones. You better hope the entire thing isn't already posted on every social media platform in existence."

Gina's mouth snapped shut, and she jerked her head at her entourage. As they marched out the door, Nico took Deanna in his arms and sealed his lips to hers.

Deanna's pulse pounded as her husband took the kiss deeper and she only faintly heard the room full of diners applauding.

THE END

Thank you for reading Sinfully Delicious. I'm thrilled you chose to spend your time with my characters and I hope you enjoyed their story.

Reviews help other readers find the books they want to read. So before you go, please leave a review [link to Amazon or Nook], tweet, share or recommend it to your friends.

Join me on Facebook [http://www.facebook.com/DeniseSwansonAuthor] or visit my website [http://www.DeniseSwanson.com] or follow me on Twitter [DeniseSwansonAu].

Subscribe to the Denise Swanson e-newsletter for quarterly or semi-annual updates about her books and events, plus occasional recipes and other news!

Write to Denise at **ScumbleRiver@aol.com** with **Subscribe** in the Subject line and your own **E-Mail Address, First Name** and **Last Name** in the Body:

Send To: ScumbleRiver@aol.com

Subject: Subscribe

E-Mail Address:
First Name:
Last Name:

ABOUT THE AUTHOR

New York Times Bestseller author Denise Swanson was a practicing school psychologist for twenty-two years. Sinfully Delicious is her first romance in the Delicious contemporary romance series, which continues with Dangerously Delicious. She also writes the Change of Heart contemporary romance series, and the Scumble River and Devereaux's Dime Store mysteries.

Denise's books have been finalists for the Agatha, Mary Higgins Clark, RT Magazine's Career Achievement, and Daphne du Maurier Awards. She has won the Reviewers Choice Award and was a BookSense 76 Top Pick.

Denise Swanson lives in Illinois with her husband, classical composer David Stybr, and their cool black cat Boomerang.

For more information, please check her website http://www.DeniseSwanson.com or find Denise on Facebook at http://www.facebook.com/DeniseSwansonAuthor or follow her on Twitter at DeniseSwansonAu

Made in the USA
Middletown, DE
21 December 2016